PRAISE FOR *GOODBYE LEMON*

"A family drama that makes Oedi[...] [...]a-
tive and emotionally true. *High[...]* [...]ill
devour it as quickly as a three-m[...] [...]*y*

"Heartrending...A droll delight. [...]   —*Harper's Bazaar*

"Smart and vicious and cutting."   —*New York Post*

"Davies does an excellent job of showing how childhood events can
become distorted through time and memory."   —*Elle*

"A story that soars on the same jet stream of inspired wordplay and
literary tics that made *The Frog King* a dazzling read. Bitter, smart,
and soaked in dark humor, Jack and his narrative harbor enormous
heart."   —*Publishers Weekly* (starred review)

PRAISE FOR *THE FROG KING*

"Probably the funniest young-guy-in-New-York novel since *Bright
Lights, Big City*."   —*Bret Easton Ellis*

"The literary invention, metaphorical pizzazz, and sheer cleverness
of the prose and wordplay in *The Frog King* is astonishing."
            —*The Wall Street Journal*

"Truly hilarious and so much more—*totally* original and yet classic,
romantic, and real. With his first book, Davies has become one of
my all-time favorite authors. And since I can't kiss Harry—hard to
believe he's just a character in a book—I'll kiss the book instead."
            —*Jennifer Belle*

"In his sly, slippery way, Davies picks apart language and puts it back
together, offering us a tell-all exposé of the publishing industry....
Davies's story is as touching and hilarious as Nick Hornby's *High
Fidelity*, as heartfelt and ironic as Dave Eggers's *A Heartbreaking
Work of Staggering Genius*. [And] unlike Eggers, Davies delivers right
to the last page."   —*The Baltimore Sun*

continues...

"One of the more appealing literary narrators to surface recently... Davies has created a clever tale that delivers moments of simple beauty." —*Chicago Tribune*

"A frisky coming-of-age novel sure to have reviewers reaching for *Bright Lights, Big City* analogies and *High Fidelity* comparisons." —*Entertainment Weekly*

"Adam Davies has a delicious command of the English language. He coins so many phrases in *The Frog King* he should probably start his own currency.... Kiss this frog. You won't be sorry." —*St. Petersburg Times*

"Wildly funny and original, Adam Davies perfectly recalls the crazy days of being young and daring and clueless about love and life and work. *The Frog King* is a captivating joy ride from the very first page." —*Laura Zigman*

"Strewn with idiosyncratic perspectives and eccentric characters... alternately evokes lively laughter and anchoring sympathy." —*BlackBook*

"Davies's subtle observations about life and strategic lack of romanticism make for an impressive and thought-provoking work...a fun and memorable read." —*Booklist*

"This is indeed a love story, a genuinely modern tale of good intentions and bad manners, and though Harry may not be much of a charmer, his roller-coaster story is charm itself." —*Newsday*

"*The Frog King* takes the coming-of-age-of-a-young-writer-living-and-self-destructing-in-New-York genre to its highest level. It's so funny, timely, and smart that the fact that it's really a love story sneaks up on you, till it's too late and you're really sucked into the tragicomic romance. Broken hearts, lives in ruins, and a little bit of redemption—what's not to love?" —*Newcity Chicago*

ALSO BY ADAM DAVIES

THE FROG KING
GOODBYE LEMON

Dear Marie Arana,

Sorry I wrote in your book.

Best,

Adam Davies

MINE
≥ALL≤
MINE

ADAM DAVIES

Riverhead Books

New York

RIVERHEAD BOOKS
Published by the Penguin Group
Penguin Group (USA) Inc.
375 Hudson Street, New York, New York 10014, USA
Penguin Group (Canada), 90 Eglinton Avenue East, Suite 700, Toronto, Ontario
M4P 2Y3, Canada (a division of Pearson Penguin Canada Inc.)
Penguin Books Ltd., 80 Strand, London WC2R 0RL, England
Penguin Group Ireland, 25 St. Stephen's Green, Dublin 2, Ireland (a division of
Penguin Books Ltd.)
Penguin Group (Australia), 250 Camberwell Road, Camberwell, Victoria 3124,
Australia (a division of Pearson Australia Group Pty. Ltd.)
Penguin Books India Pvt. Ltd., 11 Community Centre, Panchsheel Park, New
Delhi—110 017, India
Penguin Group (NZ), 67 Apollo Drive, Rosedale, North Shore 0632, New Zealand
(a division of Pearson New Zealand Ltd.)
Penguin Books (South Africa) (Pty.) Ltd., 24 Sturdee Avenue, Rosebank, Johannesburg
2196, South Africa

Penguin Books Ltd., Registered Offices: 80 Strand, London WC2R 0RL, England

Copyright © 2008 by Adam Davies
Cover design by Benjamin Gibson
Book design by Tiffany Estreicher

First edition: August 2008

Library of Congress Cataloging-in-Publication Data

Davies, Adam.
  Mine all mine / Adam Davies.—1st Riverhead trade pbk. ed.
    p. cm.
  ISBN 978-1-59448-314-1 (trade pbk.)
 1. Police, Private—Fiction. 2. Women college teachers—Fiction. I. Title.
  PS3604.A953M56 2008
  813'.6—dc22

                                                      2008001000

PRINTED IN THE UNITED STATES OF AMERICA

10 9 8 7 6 5 4 3 2 1

For Esther

Those two fatal words, Mine and Thine.

—Miguel de Cervantes

The Awful Truth

I am now going to tell you a secret. I am going to come clean. How can you ask someone to marry you if you're living the big lie? You can't, not if you're one of the good guys. Not if your last shot at happiness after years of sitting alone in darkened rooms, waiting for a bullet, depends on telling—it's a hard word—the truth. So tonight before I pop the question I am going to tell Charlie everything, but I am going to rehearse it on you just this once, before the real confession, to see how terrible it sounds. Here it goes. The dirt on Otto Starks. The life strife. The biohazard. The awful, unavoidable truth of it is:

"I am not a talent scout for the New York Mets."

Through perforated bulletproof glass the Guere-Wobe K'plua mask stares back at me with an ancient, implacable intelligence. It is made of wood, cloth, raffia, and has cowrie shells for eyes. Its conical headpiece made out of ivory and bone makes it look a little garden gnomey but it also has something really soulful going on. Understanding and omniscient.

These African K'plua masks are protectors and judges. Their enormously oversized heads, dominated by glistening, all-pupil eyes, are supposed to keep spiritual watch over their families. But they also maintain karmic scorecards and decide who is permitted entrance to the promised land.

It's a good avatar to practice on.[1]

I will get so written up if I am caught violating proximity, so I peep around the corner to make sure Herkimer isn't passing by on an Evac Recess. Herk is the closest thing I have to a best friend. He's a new hire at Janus, just six months, but I feel like I've known him forever, and although he would never report me, I'd hate to put him in an awkward position. But so far, so good: no sign of anyone. I double-check to make sure no one's installed any audio on this thing, then lean in as close as I can without tripping the prox-alert cloud and spill the rest of it into the K'plua's enormous turtle-shell ears.

Those three weeks in February? I was not in Dubuque taping a high school phenom's big twelve-to-six breaker. Last Christmas, when I bolted the house at one in the afternoon and didn't come back until after New Year's? I was not called away to perform a battery of psych evals on a former NFL quarterback looking to make the jump to the mound. Spring break? I was in Yokohama, all right, but I was not calculating the big league potential of undersized Japanese singlers. In fact, I have not once scrutinized college kids at batting practice or analyzed the barehanded fielding of awkward grounders on the torn-up lots of the Dominican Republic. I have never had

---

1 It inspires that feeling of awe and moment, true enough, but I'm probably also fishing for a benediction: I feel like if I can convince a freaking K'plua that my deception isn't so bad, then maybe Charlie will be able to forgive me, too.

a legit follow. I don't know how to determine a fringe, average, or definite prospect. I don't know any of it. Talent scout for the Mets just came out of my mouth that spring day I met Charlie. I'm glad it did, though. It has made everything plausible. Why would anyone doubt that I was out trolling all time zones on behalf of the Mets? It accounts for the irregular hours, the time away. Plus it affords a certain black-ops secrecy. I always tell her that contractually I am not allowed to talk about what I do on scouting trips. Just the way it is. Sorry, Charlie.

But this story is just my cover, my headliner, my Clark Kent.

I down a couple of quick cyanide tabs—I know, I know: I'm working on it—and brace myself for what I say next.

"I am a pulse."

The Life

As soon as I utter that word I gasp and reflexively hold my breath. At ninety it tickles. At one-eighty it pinches. After four minutes[2] my lungs go taut and my eyes feel stretched out like an overtuned guitar string and I have to let it go. Coast still clear. No sign of Herk. Schermer and his asshole friends aren't doing rounds. I can still hear the dieseling groan of the rooftop AC unit four floors away and if I concentrate I can hear one of the stoolies riffling the pages of his girlie magazine. He's got

[2] God, I am out of practice.

the radio on low but I can make out a staticky ad for that new Covet perfume.[3] I even detect the electricity crackling in the walls. All normal sounds. No one has heard me.

So I screw up the guts and say it again. Out loud.

"I am a pulse."

I am sure Charlie won't have heard about pulses. Most law-abiding people haven't. Being an art historian, she may have heard another term for us floating around. There are a million names, and you hear them all on the job. Pulse, body, mack, Johnny, pinker, voice, vox, squealer, jagger, spoiler, eyeball, sitter, squatter, asstimer, watcher, fido, spook, caspar. Different names for the same thing. If you are a national government who wants to hang on to your military secrets, if you are a plutocrat with an extensive personal collection of bronze Shang-dynasty water-buffalo-themed *kuangs*, if you are a multinational corporation who wants to keep what is yours yours, then you need to put a pulse in the room—a human guard with a finger on the button when the high-tech talent disables your safeguards and penetrates your compound. To say that we are elite security guards doesn't quite cover it. We are the reason why the Crown Jewels still belong to Great Britain and why warheads haven't shown up in Iran. We are also the reason why every crime story you've ever seen or read is either hilarious or just plain stupid.

Herk and I have a few favorites:

Mission: Impossible. It's cool, all right, when Tom Cruise and his badass crew infiltrate the government complex as firemen on a call. But when they crawl through the air shafts and Tom gets lowered on a trapeze from the ceiling vent so

3 Siren says: "You know you want it. What will you do to get it?"

as not to set off the sensors in the floor and then sets about "hacking into the system" it's hard not to snicker. Do you think that if the US government is going to pay millions of dollars on a custom system of thermosensitive receivers, pressure-sensing floor plates, and multiple retinal-scanning hydraulic-sealing door locks, they are not going to hire a pulse? I'm not kidding—one mediocre pulse in that room with his finger on the button and Tom Cruise and his Supercuts hairdo are history.

This film also gets major demerits for the use of the air shaft. I mean: the air shaft. The *air shaft*, people. Is Brian De Palma in third grade?

Entrapment. Don't get me wrong, Sean Connery is a classy bad guy, and Catherine Zeta-Jones is an elegant and fascinating thief with smooth moves, but you know the big scene with the lasers around which Z-J does her sexy thief yoga? If you were the retention strategist on that one, would you honestly make the laser pattern just irregular enough for a swimsuit model to cha-cha around? Or would you simply make an impenetrable network of evenly placed lasers at six-inch intervals? Is that such a toughie?

Once again, a single pulse in a chair and Z-J is doing downward dogs on Rikers.

Ocean's Eleven. I feel bad about debunking this one. The movie is so much fun. And suspenseful. There's nothing more terrifying to a pulse than thieves making off with a MacGuffin and taunting the client while they do it. However, in the case of Clooney and Pitt et al., it is also ridiculous. Naturally they do a slick job of bypassing the safeguards and getting into the vault. But then they "loop the tape"—again, here I must suppress a guffaw—and engineer a clever way out dressed as SWAT guys. Smart, but—can you feel it coming?—even if they blew the power to the entire state of Nevada they would have been snagged by a pulse in the vault armed with a child's bicycle bell.

Brrring brrring! You're busted.

While I'm at it, let me dispel some other security myths. The first thing is air shafts. Let's just get this one out of the way. No facility on earth that is serious about MacGuffin containment has air shafts big enough to crawl through. They have a series of smaller ones, vulnerable to nothing larger than a specially trained ball python,[4] so unless you're pulsing a really crappy site (such as the one I'm at tonight) you don't have to sweat the air shaft.

Trained dogs cannot be bypassed by throwing steaks at them. Some guy did this to my late, beloved Pinkerton and he got an assful of teeth.[5]

You can't fool a pulse by showing up dressed in the same uni and pretending to be a last-minute replacement for a colleague who called in sick. It's just ridiculous. There's a strict protocol for call-ins and every pulse at Janus knows each other. We aren't interchangeable. The second we see an unfamiliar face on-site it's button time.

---

4 Don't laugh. One guy, Simon McCord, tried this twice. He tried it once on Schermer, which garnered him low seven figs of Ashcanners, and once on me, which garnered him five years in stir upstate. Not that I'm bragging or anything.

5 Pinky wasn't an imposing dog—just an Australian shepherd mix—but he was smart and steadfast and developed a bit of a reputation after the Frankie "Nickels" Bozzuto bust. Sometimes I think my recent demotion was caused in part by Pink's death. Sure, the Rat Burglar is obviously skilled, and yes, he has gotten the best of me the last three times, and I suppose technically I've already been cut considerable slack after so many hits, but the truth is I have simply been off my game since I lost Pink.

It's hard to cudgel someone and not kill them or cause serious brain damage.

Only stoolies do predictable, thief-friendly rounds. Pulses don't break sight line with their MacGuffin unless they're on a rare Evac Recess, in which case they get covered by a floater. When necessary to do a round—or if you're overstaffed on a particular gig—you bob and weave, and you never follow a sked.

And I know I probably shouldn't be saying this so publicly, but: it's never the green wire. It just isn't. Maybe it's the red, maybe it's the black, maybe it's the yellow. It could very easily be the chartreuse wire with magnolia piping and purple doily-esque filigree, but it's never green. Every time some bluethumb tries to cut the green wire to bypass the system it ends up in one quick arrest.

I know. You're thinking: why should I believe this guy when he has received two Desuetude Warnings in the last eight weeks? Why should I listen to someone who has been downgraded from solo to partner to backup? Why should I put any faith whatsoever in the opinion of a pulse who has set a Janus record for permeability with three hits in the last nine months? Why should it matter to me that old Otto has screwed up so royally that this job, this lousy job pulsing third-class, six-figure tribal artifacts, represents his last chance to improve his standing at Janus and save himself from being sent back out to the colonies?

You should listen because I am an exemplary cautionary tale. I used to be the man. Just look at who I used to be only one year ago, when Pinkerton was still alive, before I became a punch line, before I started finding rattraps in my locker, before the goddamn Rat Burglar—

The cowrie shells and sacrificial pigment stare at me in a

menacing way. There's no fooling a K'plua. You might only be worth mid-six, fella, but you're sharp. You know I'm stalling, don't you? All right, all right, all right already. The hard part is over. I've said what I had to say about being a pulse. Now down to business.

I pull the ring out of my pocket and get down on one knee.[6] A false alarm would pretty much guarantee demotion, but when I propose I'm going to be nervous[7] so I need to simulate that as closely as possible if I am going to get it right. So I risk it. I lean in so close to the glass that my breath fogs it up and I can see the proximity cloud glowing red.

"Charlie," I say out loud. "Charlita. Charlita Sophia Izzo. Will, ah, you..."

What I hear next makes me jump. I go sprawling backwards and my legs kick the shelving that supports the mask. It's a seri-

---

6 I have a whole routine planned for this—I have been obsessing about it for months—but can't decide if it's sweet or disgusting. I fear it's disgusting, however, and I can't bring myself to talk about it. I haven't breathed a word about it to anyone. I haven't even made one nibstroke about it in my journal. You think I'm going to elaborate here?

7 Oh all right. If I can't overcome the nerves here, how can I possibly do it in front of the flesh-and-blood Charlie? I'll just pop a few saxitoxin to give my courage a jumper and...So, I've got this car, a K-Car, a 1987 Plymouth Reliant (oh the irony), a POS from my stoolie days that is always breaking down. Whenever we drive it anywhere it makes terrible noises—sometimes grinding, or percolatory, or tussive, or explosive, who knows—and Charlie always gets worried and makes me pull over and inspect under the hood. I don't know the first thing about engines but it makes her feel better to get a diagnosis, so every time when she asks me the same question—"What is that sound?"—I make something up. "That is the sound of the XK-B11 modulator unit pressurizing; nothing to worry about," I tell her. Or, "That is the sound of the butterfly inserts discharging carbon; we'll just let them cool down and desalinate for a second." One time while I was pretending to tinker I noticed that in the engine compartment there is a small plastic

ous impact. For a moment I can't tell if the mask has moved. I brace myself for the squeal of the alarm, but it doesn't come. When I recover—I am so lucky—I turn around, and there he is, the last guy in the world I want to see.

Schermer.

Make That Four

I don't know what I did to make this guy hate me. Maybe it's because I always outpoint him on our comps. Or because I'm the one with the signature busts.[8] I think maybe there is some class hatred going on, too; Schermer comes from a long line of distinguished pulses and has the pedigree, but I'm the one with the gift, and—until recently—I've been the one getting the prestige gigs. One time when he was being snotty to me

enclosure that is just large enough to contain a velvet box. My plan—can you feel it coming?—is to act like we are going on an errand, but secretly I'll have her bags all packed for a weekend at this getaway spot in Connecticut, and while I'm driving I'll pull over to investigate a worrisome noise. From the engine bay I'll extract the ring and walk it around to her side of the car. "Know what that sound is?" I'll say, shaking the box as if it's an intransigent component. Then when she gets out to look at it, I'll say, from one knee, "That is the sound of our future together." Is that disgusting? Is it repellent in every way? I honestly can't tell. But it's what I want to say, and if you aren't going to have the guts to abide by your gut when you propose, then what good are you?

8 Simon McCord comes to mind. As do Crummy Markovich, Deacon Breedlove, Pituitary Jones, and the biggest bust in decades, according to *Retention Sciences Today*: Tony "Kong" Mavrogordo and Frankie "Nickels" Bozzuto.

after I again posterized him on the tests, I called him Mr. Honorable Mention, which, in fairness, didn't help make friends.[9] Whatever the reason, he's been after me from my very first day at Janus. When the Rat Burglar rolled me the first time (seven figures' worth of twelfth-century Khmer reliefs from Angkor Wat: ouch) using a heavy dose of Kolokol-9, Schermer filled my locker full of rattraps. I came back from the job, opened my locker, reached in without looking and about a dozen rattraps exploded everywhere. I got two broken fingers and he didn't let anyone forget it for months.

Ha-ha, right? What a riot, this guy.

He did something like this after every hit. They were all annoying, but do you know what really hurt? After Pink died in the line of duty, guess what I had waiting for me in my locker? An enormous pile—I mean the mother lode—of dog biscuits. That isn't even a joke. It has no setup. It has no punch line. It's just plain old mean. And just like Schermer: The only thing in the world you love just died? Well, here are some of his snacks! Get it? Get it?

God I wish Herk had been there.

And that he were here now.

"Yes!" Schermer cries again from the doorway, mouth glistening, arms flung wide. He does a tippy-toe kind of love-struck dance, smoothing across the floor toward me. I'm still tangled on the concrete and he descends on me, sort of wrapping his arms around my head and making smooching noises. "Yes, I will marry you, Otto! I thought you'd never ask! But"—and here

---

9 I might also have alleged that he "fellates tubes of Chapstick." I don't know if he has a lip gloss habit or what, but his mouth always looks like he's been bobbing for chicken fat or orally stimulating jars of petroleum jelly or something. Not an exaggeration, but not judicious of me to mention, probably.

he emits a melodramatic burble while chewing histrionically on his fingernails—"what will we do to survive? How can we live on the wages of a . . . *stoolie*?"[10]

I try to shrug him off me but Schermer is stronger than I am and it takes me a few tries. When I finally get free I'm breathing heavy and can tell I'm blushing. In the struggle something hit my nose and I can feel my eyes starting to water. This makes me feel like I'm about eight years old.

"Boy, that was a close one," Schermer says. "If you had tripped that alert it would have just about finished you off as a pulse, wouldn't it? That would be a real shame."

"Shouldn't you be making rounds?" I say, trying to make it as sneery as possible.

"I wonder what would happen if I were just to touch it. . . ." And he tries to reach past me and poke the glass. I swat his hand away just in time.

"That's not funny, Schermer."

"It sure would be awkward to explain a false alarm if somehow the cloud got stimulated—" And again he makes a stab over my shoulder at the K'plua.

"Cut the shit."

"Or if the bossman knew you were going to break cover to your girl?"

"Stop it."

"Make me, Starks," he says, making fists. "You fucking pill-popper."

This is a touchy subject. Pulses are required to wear imperfs—imperforables, synthetic aramid fiber blend bodysuits that are flexible but impenetrable to needle puncture. Janus thinks

---

10 That makes a dent, all right.

this is a good idea because we are so often the target of tran-
quilizer guns. Only infrequently do you see a pulse get shot at
with a bullet; in an environment that is as loaded with motion
sensors as ours, it attracts a lot less attention to have someone
slump into a sleeping pile. Exploding flesh sets off the sensors.
Hot blood trips the therms. You get the idea.

But to me imperfs seem like a bad idea. They promote a false
sense of security. They don't save you from getting slipped a
mickey in your coffee. They are obviously useless against airborne agents. And because they are not hooded they leave the
neck and face exposed. If I were sharpshooting talent I'd just
smile and think, "Well hellooooo, jugular."

So I never wear them. Instead I have devoted the last fifteen
years of my life to cultivating immunities to every drug you
can name. I was born with the gift, it's true, but in an industry like ours you have to work at it. At breakfast I have coffee, a bran muffin, and a heavy dose of vecuronium. For lunch
it's usually tuna fish and whatever muscimol I'm on. At dinner I like to mix it up with propofol or tsusensan or gamma-
hydroxybutyrate or whatever. And then throughout the day it's
neurotoxins or paralytics or tranqs galore. I'm even doing my
best with nixolophan.[11] I inject them, breathe them, swallow,
transdermally patch them. I can outbeer the entire offensive
line of the Giants. I can shoot up with all the junkies on Tenth
Avenue and breeze through any field sobriety drill you throw
at me. You should see my piss tests. It's a lot to keep track of, but
it makes a hell of a lot more sense than wearing what basically

---

11 A badass paralytic known in pulse circles as "Nix" because, brother, once
that sucker is in your bloodstream and staring down your site 1 voltage-
gated fast sodium channels, there is not one thing you can do about it. You
are going to be paralyzed permanently, and it is going to hurt.

amounts to an enhanced wet suit. I don't honestly know why my uppers have been giving me so much grief about it.

Schermer makes another move on the K'plua. This time I shove him away, hardish, and then, just like that, it is totally on. He makes a strong, windmilly move. I counter with a violent lassoing motion, fist aloft, that doesn't connect with anything.

"Buttons down," I say in the best high-noon voice I've got.

"Buttons down," Schermer agrees. We slide our buttons safely away and start circling each other in deep kung-fu stances, making threatening movements—dog-paddle punches, minatory half-kicks—that look like an angry, disco-style hokey-pokey.

The good news is that I am saved from throwing, or catching, any punches.

The bad news is that my savior is a very sudden, very painful sensation of pressure in my bowels. Instantly I double over and collapse on the concrete. Before I know it my knees are drawn up to my chin and I'm lowing like an animal in a slaughterhouse. It feels like my intestines, suddenly molten, are braiding together into the nautical knots that I have been studying so hard: my duodenum is now an anchor bend, my colon a boom hitch.

With indelicate language Schermer indicates that he considers my inexpedient moaning and breakdancery writhing to be unsportsmanlike in the extreme. He circles me a few times, renewing his invitation that I get up. I cannot, and do not. He impugns my character, my mother, my ignoble pulse bloodlines, offers me a last chance, then advertises that failure to right myself in a timely manner will precipitate a number of punitive kicks and, very probably, induce him to start "throwing some knobs." Most of my brain function is busy sorting the urgent signals of pain being sent from my gut and the only verbal response I manage is a series of sad, stuttering groans. I am able to apprehend his leg pulling back, his boot glinting, the offroading Vibram treads of his sole. I squeeze my eyes shut in anticipation of additional pain—a nearly incomprehensible idea—but when I open them again I see that gravity has performed a miracle. Schermer is now prostrate alongside me, his face turned away, immobilized.

Protruding sprightly from his neck, just above his imperfs, is a red-tufted dart.

Behind me I hear well-padded footsteps. I fight and beetle until I have rotated enough to see the figure drilling under the shelf supporting the K'plua. Even from the back I recognize the Rat Burglar immediately. The easy, assured movements. The arrogant, matadorlike attitude of indifference. He isn't muting the drill. He isn't using any monitors, just touch. And his deportment at the MacGuffin is the same paradox it always is: sacred and ruinous. He behaves as if he's at an altar, but one he must desecrate. It is at once reverent and sacrilegious. I can't explain it any better than that.

Another Rat Burglar cue: he doesn't even bother to look over, to check on me.

I don't know what he's given me—or how he got it in my system—but it's bad. It's not a tranq or a paralytic or anything I've ever had before. I've got a grim feeling it's acid. Or polonium-210. Dimly I wonder if this will be my last job. I have a vision of the *Clean Getaway* sailing off into distant tropical waters without me, Charlie waving goodbye from the bowsprit, obscured by prisming sea spray until she finally disappears like a beautiful wraith.

With a sharp metallic buzz the shelf bottoms out. The K'plua drops, the prox-cloud undisturbed. It is almost unbearable to watch for the fourth time as the Rat Burglar sprinkles a few darkly pigmented animal hairs on the floor—his calling card, by now a redundant gesture—and deposits my MacGuffin in his bag. Before it disappears from view I can discern the K'plua's expression. It looks righteous; it looks pissed. Maybe it expected this of me.

Or maybe this is its way of expressing its opinion of my deception of Charlie.

My button, I realize, is only a few feet away. Although my stomach produces nauseating waves of gastric and muscular distress when I move an inch, I force myself to reach out an arm toward it. If I am going to die tonight, I think, I am going to bring the Rat Burglar down. I extend far enough to get a fingerpoint on the edge of the device. For a few agonizing seconds a finger tickles the edge of the hard plastic but then a gloved hand enters my line of sight, clasps the button, and slides it away like a puck. He bends down, putting his face very near to mine. He is wearing paint under his mask, naturally, so I can't determine ethnicity, and his only odor is ammonia. Normally at this range my olfactory is so precise that I can discern what brand of deodorant someone is wearing, what kind of toothpaste they use, what they had for lunch, what hair product they have on, whether they take light or heavy starch. Sometimes I can even tell where they might live—close to the river, say, or near fish markets. At close range, I can pretty much detect and parse any emanations someone produces; it's so reliable I can ID them out of a lineup blindfolded. But this guy has basically bathed in ammonia; I can't figure out anything.

That's clever of the Rat Burglar, and exactly what I expect of him. What isn't so swift, however, is that he gives me a good look at his eyes and I see that he is wearing darkly colored contacts that cannot conceal faint flecks of blue.

So, I think, he has blue eyes. That's a valuable piece of information.

If I live long enough to tell anyone.

Then the Rat Burglar does something strange. He reaches out and presses two fingers to my neck. At first I think he is going to strangle me, but he doesn't. He is checking on my heart rate. He keeps his fingers there for a long time, maybe thirty seconds, then he nods and gives me an affirmative pat. Next he inserts a dextrous hand inside my pocket and extracts the velvety box. It pops open and suddenly the Rat Burglar has Charlie's ring out. He slides it on a black-gloved finger and holds it up to the light, rotating it critically, inspecting. With every vestige of strength I have left, I try to lash out at him. It took seven years of subservitude in the colonies before I got the gigs that paid for Charlie's ring—literally my blood and sweat—and I'll be damned if I'll let him take it without a fight. The rupturing feeling in my stomach, however, reduces my offensive to a spastic bucking-bronco number that seems only to amuse the Rat Burglar. He takes his time appraising the ring, then obviously decides it isn't worth stealing, reinserts it into the box and again into my pocket. From his bag he extracts a roll of something that looks, incredibly, like toilet paper, places it gingerly beside my head, springs up and starts walking away to a hole in the ceiling from which a rope is hanging. Insult to injury, I think: he came in through the air shaft. Another excruciating flare of pain ignites and blackness descends on me in a compressive, seismic wave. This is it. I am going under.

The last thing I think is why is he after the K'plua? It's only six damn figures.

The last thing I feel is something undignified happening in my pants.

Heaven, or: Last April at the Frick

Pulses are obsessed with dying. Probably dozens of times I have heard locker-room talk about how you lose control of certain bodily functions, but I had hoped that the inglorious trouser activity might occur after you had lost your senses. Apparently not. But I am grateful for one thing: the parts of my life that flash before me are of Charlie.

I met her at the Frick. One of my ex-MacGuffins, a Boucher, was on display and I felt lonely for it one day midweek, so I stopped by. I must have been really entranced because I didn't hear her behind me. I was only vaguely aware of a headnote of white ginger and tiara flower with some suggestion of petit-grain. I was so engrossed in the Boucher that the odor seemed like an olfactory evocation of the painting itself. My brain just didn't process it as a separate stimulation. Then I retreated a few steps to get a fuller view of the painting, bumped into something, and realized that the source of the floral odors was a beautiful woman in a white summer dress.

I meant to apologize but found myself syllabically stranded. You could have fit a shoebox in my gaping mouth. Pulses don't get out much in general, and I certainly have never been much with the ladies. I'm not deformed or anything, I'm just more accustomed to talking to paint-and-canvas women than flesh-and-blood ones. The last time I even dared to use a line on a girl I was seventeen. I had spent three months nursing a crush on this teller at the drive-thru when I finally pulled up to her window and, with all the sunglasses-on-nosepoint suavity I could muster, said, "I would like to make one withdrawal and one deposit, please." "Yes?" she said, sounding bored. "I want to withdraw *you* from the banker's box and deposit you in a restaurant with me, tonight. Say sevenish?"

It worked, believe it or not, but the night ended in failure. On her front step, the door cracked open invitationally behind her, she leaned into me, her beaded lashes louvering her eyes, her lips parted and pliant,[12] and I didn't get it. I could read every single freaking optotype on the eleventh line of a Snellen test at fifty freaking feet but I could not read, at point-blank range, these signs, these obvious, guileless signs. I didn't even get it when she asked if I wanted to come inside to "see her coin roller." At that critical doorstep moment—a moment every teenaged boy dreams about—as she turned and went inside, looking at me over her shoulder and giving me a walk that she didn't learn at Miss Porter's, I said, "Nah, I've got a first period tomorrow. I'd better go. I'll call you later."

That was how shrewd, how slick, how perceptive I was.

Or maybe: am.

And then just ten years later, at the Frick, in front of my Boucher, there I was with this incredible woman, experiencing a massive sensory overload. Olfactory cues and visual stimuli were cauterizing my brain—a dim part of me kept wondering how I had not heard her behind me—and I was unable to formulate a comprehensible sentence of introduction. "Hello," I could have said. Or "Nice day for a museum visit." Even "Do you like art?" would have been preferable to the stunned, saucer-mouthed silence. But language was beyond me. I felt mesmerized and arrested, as if viewing my own car

12 "Looking," I should say. "Pliant *looking*."

wreck. I was lockjawed—don't laugh; it's true—with a vision of pure love.

Another, competing feeling was a bolt of dread; i.e., "I've been staring at her for a long five silent seconds and if I don't say something soon she may walk away from me and never come back."

It grieves me to report that I did not conquer this fear. I remained mute. But someone else wasn't afraid, and he might have just saved my whole life. A homeless guy clothed partially in the patched skin of a ruined umbrella and sporting several wool hats teetering on his head in a nesting, Russian-doll fashion approached Charlie and held up an empty 8" × 10" picture frame to her face.

"A picture…," he said with *Masterpiece Theater* gravitas, "of loveliness."

Then it happened. She laughed. I laughed, too, and was restored to my normal, fully verbal state.

From that moment Charlie and I moved through the museum together as if obeying a little-known law of physics: when two forces collide while among pink, cavorting putti and lush, idyllic grottoes it results in indissoluble bonding. We walked among the Fragonards, the Sargents, the Vermeers. Together we got nose-close to the canvases. It probably looked like we were being connoisseury—ostensibly we were inspecting impasto—but really we were employing a pretext to move within inches of each other's face, each other's mouth.[13]

---

13 At that range I could detect pomegranate and carbonation on her breath and rosemary and mint and something else, something mysterious and warm, in her hair. The polished leather of her shoes. Crushed grass and pollen—had she walked through the park?—and a hint of dewy, fresh sweat.

We pointed, we stared, we talked.

In front of one of Ingres' odalisques I discovered why I hadn't heard her behind me.

One of the things I hate about museums is the conveyor-belt attitude of some people. They act as if it's a competitive event. "Classical antiquity, check. *Vroom!* Medieval armaments, gone! Renaissance, Enlightenment, all you Dadaists, gotcha! All done! I'll beat you to the café and finish my cocktail before you even place an order!" It makes me nuts. But Charlie was different. I hadn't heard her simply because she hadn't moved. She had been standing behind me the whole time, totally still, totemlike, absorbed.

A dumb reason to find someone additionally irresistible, maybe, but no one else I knew—not even other pulses—could stand still that long and *watch*. Just like me. For the first time in my life there was someone who saw things, literally, as I did.

But we talked more than museums.

Charlie loved the *pfffft* sound of a freshly opened soda can pop-top.

If she adored a book she would never read a second by the same author because she was too frightened of being let down.

Her father wanted a boy so much that he named her "Charles Izzo." It was only through relentless lobbying that her mother succeeded in securing "Charlita" as a variant, but the feminized version was limited to mainly mother-daughter dialogue, and it never became ratified by any documents. Birth certificate, driver's license, school records—everything—were all under the name Charles. For a few uncomfortable years he even called her "Chuck," a mistake that I made only once.

Every time she goes to this one bodega she gets accosted by the same Puerto Rican guys. At first they were trying to pick her up but when she didn't respond to their overtures in Spanish they started berating her for not speaking her mother tongue. She tried to explain that she's from Malta, that her language is closer to Arabic and Italian than to Spanish, but their English isn't so hot and they never get the idea. They yell at her every time. When I asked her why she kept going there she said, "Alas, it is the only market around that carries Coco Rico."

"So?" I said.

"It is the only soda that, ah..." She cleared her throat awkwardly. A sheepish smile was offered. "Well, it has...superior...acoustical properties. You know. When opened."

The slight boomerang bend in her nose came from an accident she had at age twelve. She was trying to flirt with a high school boy by riding her bike along the top of a stone wall. The boy was waiting on the curb for the bus and she rode along above him, waving gaily as if he were a sailor returning from sea. She passed by, only one hand steering the bike, juddering on the uneven stones until she hit a loose one and: smash. She executed a very sudden half-pirouette/half-pike, stalled momentarily in midair like a cartoon, then bellyflopped onto the pavement, breaking her fall with her face, an assault spearheaded by her nose. She didn't get the guy.

Charlie grew into her clumsiness as if into an allergy, and by the time I met her she had become a danger to herself and anything within striking distance. She is always knocking over stacks of cans at the grocery. Once she tried to put together a bed frame and bloodied her forehead. I discovered her on the floor, on the verge of tears, tools scattered around her like importunate pigeons. She tried a second time to mate the pieces and again struck herself in the face with the flat metal edge, which propelled her over the verge. Another time she set off an alarm at the Czartoryski Museum by headbutting *Lady with an Ermine* while closely inspecting one of the poorly retouched fingers ("a digit that belongs on E.T., not the duke's mistress") and, while being ushered out, klaxons wailing, she knocked over the urn containing the ashes of El Cid. Only the quick swandiving of an alert security guard saved her from disgorging the true grit of the Campeador all over the place. The Krakow paper ran a headline that said, DA VINCI AND EL CID SURVIVE TIME, EROSION, HITLER—BUT AMERICAN SCHOLAR?

This sort of thing happens a lot.

The one time when Charlie isn't clumsy is during sex. Can I say this? Normally her body stutters, no doubt. Her left/right motor isn't synchronized; she trips, she lurches in a zombie gait, she steps on the accelerator instead of the brake. She is an inveterate dropper of keys through subway grates. She endangers millennia-old masterworks. All true. But when she is naked she undergoes a wild, nearly Ovidian change. She becomes superkinetic, fluent, dancerly. When I surprise her in the shower, a hard-on banging around like a weather vane in a cyclone, she doesn't rip the curtain or claw down the shampoo caddy. When she is innocently brushing her hair—thick with curls, fragrant with some odor that I can never fully parse— and I clutch it like a bouquet of flowers while rubbing that spot on her hips, she does not drop the brush or crack a knee on the table. When we fall to the carpet she doesn't jab me in the ribs. Or elbow my skull. Or nearly enucleate me with a jagged fingernail.

Her fingers are articulate, certain.

Her hips are dextrous and undulant.

Her body is all reflex, full of grace, rife with the purity of its own movement. It knows, as it knows at no other time, exactly what it wants to do. And it does it.

How does it happen? How does she attain this transformation from smash-prone klutz to sex ballerina? I don't know, but sometimes, when I've had a little too much naloxone or pancuronium bromide or norisol or something and am feeling high enough to permit myself some fantasy, I can't help thinking, wistfully:

Maybe it's me?

>≺

Considering Charlie's all-around wonderfulness and my nearly record-setting sparsity of female contact, why am I so cowardly about popping the question?

Part of the problem is that, outside of centuries-old artwork, I don't have anybody to talk to about it. And I have no frame of reference. I have almost no memory of my mother and father together, and I don't have any friends with real girlfriends to speak of—Herk's Goldfish Girls don't count[14]—so I don't know what is normal and what isn't. I am limited mainly to sitcom wisdom on this, which, according to a show I saw recently, says that to men engagement is terrifying because it is a visceral reminder of mortality. You are about to become engaged to be married, to just one person, with whom you will presumably spend the rest of your life and produce offspring, who

[14] More on them soon.

are really just second-draft *yous*, said the hipster on the show, future yous, man, set to replace you after you kick it. Who needs that? Not me, said the guy. I don't want to have a kid successor. I want to *be* the kid.

I'm not sure his logic applies to me, necessarily—I metabolize visceral reminders of mortality every day, and they are much less pleasant than the strokable Charlie Izzo—but I still have the same fear. I've got no problem pulsing a site I know has a very good chance of being targeted by some of Azar's trigger-happy talent, but man, when I crack that velvet box open it creaks like the coffin and terror makes the words in my throat turn into cement.

It's also true that practically everyone I have ever loved has died a painful death. That does not exactly provoke the urge to certify another love.

The counterargument to this is Charlie herself.

When I grit my teeth in my sleep she rubs my jaw and makes me stop.

When I'm depressed she cooks me Maltese meals with names I cannot pronounce.

She even makes me want to take it easy with the succinylcholine chloride.

So why don't I just spit it out, already?[15]

---

15 I have made one attempt. Technically. I'm not sure it counts, but it was three weeks ago, when I had just been assigned the K'plua job and things were looking up. I called the hotel, packed her bags, whisked her away in the reliably unreliable Reliant, and pulled over when she asked what that noise was. I pulled out the velvet box, started shaking it, and, from under the hood, said, "Do you know what that sound is?" Charlie said, "What is it?" and then, suddenly, I froze up like I had scarfed fifty milligrams of Nix. "Nothing," I said. "It's nothing." I can't explain it. It was just total G-lock—bang, freeze, done—and I haven't tried since.

I don't know. Since I've met Charlie I have logged about five thousand hours of time sitting alone in dark rooms, thinking of almost nothing else, and I still don't have the answer.

In the museum, Charlie also told me her mother died when she was nine. Before the accident her mother was opening a party supply business and she had just received a huge order of balloons. Their house in Long Island was filled, in some places floor to ceiling, with countless boxes of them. After the accident her father could not bear to get rid of the balloons, but he also wouldn't let anyone open them. So Charlie grew up in a house full of aging balloons that she was never allowed to touch. Sometimes, late at night, she would come home to find her father drunk in a chair, bringing the navel-like opening of the balloons to his mouth tenderly, as if in a kiss, and blowing them up. Then he would cradle them in the darkness of the room and whisper to them like children.

When Charlie grew up and left the house he moved to one of those California towns that had legislated against meats, trans fats, and synthetic materials. No rubber, he thought, no balloons.

He organized his whole life—abandoned his whole life—to kill memory.

She told me this in the dark of the Frick's screening room, as an educational reel was rolling. There was no one else in the room—it was two p.m. on a Tuesday—and I could see her eyes slick with threatening tears. I could smell the salt and water. I could detect her respiration catch, her heart rate accelerate. I almost reached out and touched her bare shoulder.

I was this close.

Instead I told her about my own family grief.

When I was a kid my parents and my brother, Tobias, were killed in a botched robbery of our house in Connecticut while I was on a sleepover at a friend's. I told her what I remembered about my family—my mother playing the guitar on the porch, my father's fridge in the basement with Pabst Blue Ribbons stacked like bars of gold in a vault, Toby's corduroy pillow that made his face corrugated with wrinkles for half an hour every day when he woke up. But I did not tell her that this was one of the reasons why I wanted to become a pulse: to stop people taking what didn't belong to them, whether it's a Jasper Johns or sensitive government documents or the lives of the people you love.

I also didn't tell her that at age eleven I discovered my gift when, miserable and depressed and living in my third foster home in five years, I tried to end it all by downing a bottle of Somnipro Plus with a fifth-of-bourbon chaser only to wake up six hours later, a little foggy but very well rested.

Something else undisclosed: for the first time in my adult life I was interested in something other than an eight-figure MacGuffin. I wanted to pulse Charlie herself. I wanted to protect her. I wanted to be her personal pulse.

When she asked me what I did that allowed me to escape to the Frick on a weekday it just came out. "I'm a talent scout for the Mets." And for the last twelve months I've had to stick to that story. It makes me feel bad to lie to Charlie, but it also makes me feel a little James Bondy. Dangerous. And what choice do I have?

≽≼

If I had a second chance, though, I would tell her everything.

≽≼

It's a small museum: it had to end.

We walked out onto the sidewalk. Her body tugged south down Fifth; mine lurched north. I had a job uptown—one of my first jobs after the Frankie Nickels bust, eight-figs of Neo-Classicists in a private collector's facility—and I was going to be late. So I was fretting over that. Additionally unnerving was the valedictory moment itself. I was once again arrested by a powerful paralyzing force—it was like my first major Pavulon hit—and I heard myself mumbling something about it being nice to meet you and good luck with classes and may all your pop-tops be fizzy. Then, with a crabbed, flipperlike wave of resignation I turned and started limping away.

After three feet I regretted it. After five I hated myself intensely. After ten I knew I had made the biggest mistake of my life.

But again a third party saved the day.

I have already noted my olfactory percipience? I can affirm that my other senses scarcely score less well on Janus's comps. My sense of smell, obviously, is nearly unchartable, and therefore my taste scores are enviable. Visual acuity tests out above "fighter pilot." And auditory—well, modesty prohibits me from elaborating. Suffice to say that from nearly fifty feet away, with my back turned, and even with the ambient noise of the street—revving engines, tires abrading the asphalt, the plaintive bleating of a truck's reverse-siren—I overhead several aggressive voices overlapping Charlie's. Petitions for money were made, rejected. Imprecations were issued and footsteps accelerated in a way I knew, without turning around, indicated that the owners of the voices were now following her. Charlie iterated that she had nothing, which provoked more jeers and denunciation. And then the clincher.

From my position, nearly around the corner, with the vociferation of afternoon Manhattan thrumming in my ears, I heard Charlie say, "Hey, get your hands off me!"

Before I knew what I was doing I had wheeled around and saw Charlie surrounded by a crowd of guys. I was outnumbered 3:1 and outweighed by about 5:1. But they were openly pawing Charlie. They had pushed her into a hedge of blooming honeysuckle. One of them pinioned her arms while a second yanked her purse off her shoulder and a third made lewd clasping gestures with his hand near the opening of her dress. It was broad daylight. It was unbelievable.

Also unbelievable: I was now streaking toward them, full speed ahead, fists clenched in a businesslike way.

Even by my standards of visual acuity what ensued was a blur. I fell upon them and started flailing. The only punching I had ever done was in my aerobic kickboxing class, and the instructor's loudspeaker beat-counting was so firmly embedded in my psyche that I swung away at Charlie's assailants while counting out loud.

"And a-one!" as I threw a sinking cross.

"And a-two!" while looping a hard hook.

"And a-three!" when I scooped an uppercut.

When I stopped momentarily after my first onslaught—"And breathe, two three four"—I realized there was no need for another; all three attackers had been literally floored. They lay scattered about the pavement like spare change, emitting noises of remorse and surrender.

I guess I didn't know my own strength.

With a shaky hand I pulled Charlie to her feet. With a Parkinsonian quiver I returned her purse. Her dress was torn and her shoulder was bare. Her hair was garlanded with wands of honeysuckle and nectar. Again I smelled the flowers and grass, the rosemary and mint. Again I detected the leather of her shoes and fresh sweat. And when she leaned into me, face upturned, adrenalized and frightened and wild, clutching my collar and pulling me down, pressing her beautiful mouth to mine, I realized I had been right:

Pomegranates.

I would give everything I have to taste them again.

New Punch Line

Apparently, to get a second chance at life I needn't give up everything I have, merely the sum total of all dignity I have accrued during my lifetime. I wake up on my stomach in the dedicated pulse subacute-care unit with a tech—how can I put this?—wiping my ass. The odor, my abject babylike position, ass-high, and the mortifying heat and viscosity laminating everything south of the belt line eliminate any doubt about what has transpired.

"Hey," I say to the tech as he goes about his ungentle business. "What do you think you're doing? We haven't even been properly introduced."

"Hunh?"

"Don't you think you should at least buy me dinner first? Or take me to a show or compliment my shoes or something?"

"What?"

"It's O.K.," I tell him. "You don't have to do that. I can take it from here." The tech shrugs and tosses me the box of moist wipes. Fine by him, I'm sure.

Delicately I peel up from the bed and teeter behind the curtain, where I continue in private my disgraceful ablutions.

"How long have I been out?"

"Nearly two hours."

"Jesus," I say through the plastic sheeting. "They hit me with some kind of soporific I don't know about?"

"No, you suffered some extracranial nonpenetrating trauma." When I stare at him blankly he says, "A nasty boo-boo. To your squash. Presumably when you fell over. Conked yourself out."

"Well, in one way, I guess I feel lucky to be alive. I had no idea what hit me. My stomach felt like it was on fire. Thought it was some kind of acid."

Before I get his "Nope" I am pretty sure I hear a snicker.

"If it was a tranq it's got weird side effects."

"Not a tranq," the guy says, a warble in his voice.

"Some kind of poison I don't know about?"

"Nope. It was nonlethal."

"I didn't feel a dart."

"Wasn't one."

"Airborne?"

"Nope."

"I don't get it."

"It was an old-fashioned pill. Someone got to you."

"How would someone get to me?"

The guy shrugs.

"Well," I say. "Go on then. What was it? Lay it on me."

After a silent interval I peer out from behind the curtain and see the tech vibrating with mirth. When he regains motor control he says, "You were temporarily debilitated by acute muscular seizure induced by a sizable overdose of ingested pachylax."

"By *what*?"

After a few poorly suppressed giggles the guy manages to bear the bad news, a tidbit that will, I'm sure, be the highlight of Janus headquarters gossip for weeks to come. "Pachylax," he repeats without the equanimity you hope for in a bedside manner. "Elephant laxative."

⇒⇐

There's no getting around it: after my vitals check out stable at the SAC unit I have to report to Po-Mo at headquarters. On the long interborough ride the escort team doesn't hide it very well. They try to swallow it down, or cough over it, but I can hear their jaws crunching, their vocal folds tensing. They want to laugh so bad. I almost tell them it's O.K., just get it over with, but instead I try to concentrate on how I'm going to explain this one to the boss.

Nothing useful comes to me.

Half an hour later I'm at headquarters being logged in by security. None of the unies looks me in the eye, and after the usual checks and inventory I'm cleared for entrance wordlessly. After two corners and three different hallways I stop and wait another thirty seconds. Those guys know me, and my range, and I know they are going to wait a while before saying anything. After ten seconds there's nothing, ditto twenty and thirty, but then, finally—right when I think I might be in the clear—they all crack up.

Even the unies know. Perfect.

Another record I've set: the only pulse ever to be a punch line to a stoolie.

The machine scans me in and I slink into division. Mercifully it seems fairly quiet. Everyone at dispatch is at their desks, heads bent over schedules with phones plugged in their ears. The comp facility isn't running any tests and the windows are all dark. I'm able to breeze past the frosted glass of the admin offices—Po-Mo's is vacant—and before I know it I'm in the locker room. It's empty, thank God, and still smells of fresh body odor and the saline shots that pulses use to keep their eyes fresh on double shifts, so I must have just missed an outgoing crew. I suppose I was due some sort of luck today.

I pull on the handle and my locker creaks open. Taped to the inside of the door and the back panel are clippings of my more exalted accomplishments as a pulse—the award celebrating my three-year record of taking highest honors in industry-wide comps in Salt Lake City; my first at the Endurovigil Sleep-Deprivation Sit-Off; the newspaper clipping of the bust nearly a year ago that brought down Kong and Frankie Nickels—but they aren't reassuring. They seem almost quaint, as if from a bygone era. When I finger the corner of the article about Kong turning state's evidence against Frankie Nickels I realize that the powerful jolt of nostalgia I'm feeling is a bad sign: I'm already thinking in the past tense.

But it's not as bad as the feeling I get when I am confronted, as usual, with the brochure of my sailboat taped, like a centerfold, to the back of my locker.

Early in our relationship, maybe a month after that day at the Frick, Charlie told me about her secret fantasy of sail-

ing away to someplace where no one would find her. She
was having trouble getting tenure; no one was interested in
her research;[16] she was living in a miserable little studio in
Ozone Park that she was too embarrassed ever to let me see.
She wanted out. She wanted a new future, one that was wide
open, one without conniving colleagues and the years of grad
school debt that were heaped upon her. So powerful was her
longing that she had even tried to teach herself how to sail.
She couldn't afford lessons, she told me, and she knew that
probably she would never even be able to charter a boat, but
she couldn't help it. She wanted to learn, and so she had spent
months and months reading books and renting how-to videos
from the library. She knew, in principle, how to jibe and tack
and navigate without instruments. Eventually she included me
in these drills, and we began quizzing each other on terminol-
ogy and etiquette, technology and vexillology, you name it.

Some couples play House. We play Boat.

In the pulsing business there is an old industry dream called
the clean getaway: you work long enough to get the big gigs
and then after a few years of heavy commissions you call it
quits before you suffer anything irreversible.

And one night, while struggling with a timber hitch, it
occurred to me that what Charlie wants is her own kind of clean
getaway.

---

16 Her specialty—wouldn't you know it?—is the Rat Burglar. She will say
that it is "limits of first- and third-world diplomacy and legal, moral, and
fiscal issues in cultural patrimony." Or something that sounds a lot like
it. I don't really understand her research, but I do know that she supports
the Rat Burglar because he "restores" artworks to their countries of origin,
which is a stance that has earned her the enmity of her department and just
about every museum worker in the country. And, naturally, nearly every
pulse on earth, including this one.

I had never envisioned getting away on a boat, but then again I had never imagined being loved by anybody. The next day I coaxed from her the exact type of boat she wanted, called up the manufacturer, and emptied my life's savings on a deposit for a slick fifty-five-footer, a Najad, built to order, trimmed in handcrafted, unstained African mahogany, and loaded with all the oceangoing tech you need to leave everything behind and sail away with the woman you love.

After the celebrity of the Frankie Nickels conviction and my triumph at Salt Lake City I was supposed to earn enough in six months to pay for the whole thing, but then the Rat Burglar rolled me the first time on the Angkor Wat job. I didn't get that commission, obviously, and a month later, on the same day I got passed over for my next assignment, Najad called to say they needed a payment for the next phase of construction, so I took out a hefty home equity loan on my apartment. I remember confiding fearlessly in my journal that it would be no problem. One bad mark on an otherwise unblemished record at Janus. I'll just take out this loan and pay it back just as soon as I get my next gig. Only on my next gig (a priceless, 4,400-year-old statute of King Entemena, Sumerian ruler of Lagash) the room I was being paid to keep unempty was emptied forthwith by you-know-who.

A few months later I got a call from Najad indicating they needed another installment. I didn't have it. The only thing I could think about was what had happened to some other veteran pulses. Two years ago a guy at Janus was injected with a refined dose of cyclosarin, a nasty G-series nerve agent; unfortunately, he lived for two days. Another guy got hit with some kind of synthetic hemotoxin that was roughly four times more virulent than that of a Russel's viper; within forty-five minutes he had basically blistered, clotted, and hemorrhaged to death.[17] Jimmy the Hat is always scalping some pulse some-where. I didn't want to wait for any of that. So I took out the maximum allowable cash advances on my credit cards. The rates were exorbitant, but I figured, what the hay, I'll just pay them back on the next gig.

I never imagined it would happen again. But it did, and rap-idly. The third time in under a year. (A little cluster of alabaster vases of the goddess Inanna: yawn.)

That didn't look so great on the old résumé.

That didn't have Charles Saatchi calling me up at home.

The credit card bills kept coming. As did notices from the bank. Najad informed me that if I defaulted on payments my contract would be nullified and they would sell the boat to someone else. I had visions of my future sailing away with-out me.

What could I do?

I called Deke—the only moneyman I knew. Deke, who doesn't have an office but always seems to be on the corner when you want him. And when you don't. Deke, who doesn't bother hiring muscle because he likes collecting debts himself, using pliers in a way that I don't want to talk about. Deke, who would no doubt be displeased in the extreme to discover that I am not a talent scout for the Mets but am in fact a top-notch pulse and have personally accounted for the arrest and incar-ceration of at least five clients with outstanding debts.

---

17 This sort of thing isn't limited to pulses, either; it's no treat, I'm sure, for Frankie Nickels to be serving time in a maximum-strength facility while paralyzed from the neck down. Maybe I'm a sucker, but I can't help feeling bad for him. Sometimes I'm even tempted to go visit him, to bring him some brownies or something, but then I think that he worked for Azar, and was a colleague of Jimmy the Hat, and I think of what Jimmy did to Kong. And what he did, just one week later, to Pinkerton.

Deke: either my best chance or my worst chance, but certainly my only chance.

The next day Deke gave me the money. I gave the money to Najad. And now the boat is mine. Well, Deke retains the title until I pay him off, so I can't luxuriate in the thrill of ownership just yet. For the time being the *Clean Getaway* is stuck up on stilts in a boatyard.

But soon, I keep telling myself. Soon.

When I was the accolade-laden Otto Starks of a year ago none of this would have been a problem. After a few big-time gigs I would have just paid Deke off and sailed away, bada-bing bada-boom. But now that I'm on lousy mid-six jobs with crappy commissions, it's complicated. I still owe Deke a harrowing amount of money. The commission from the K'plua job wasn't going to come anywhere close to getting even, of course, but it would have been a good-faith gesture. And the successful pulsing of that job could have gotten me the gigs I need to get even with him and make sure I don't end up on the wrong end of his pliers.

Now I don't know what will happen.

Grimly, tenderly, as if reading a last letter from someone I had loved and lost, I untape the Najad brochure from the back of my locker, fold it up, and put it in my pocket. If security is going to clear out my locker today, I'm going to make sure I have this with me. At least I'll have a souvenir.

"Where have you been, young man? Your mother and I have checked every shitter in the tri-state area. We've been worried sick."

The voice has the sound of heavy machinery dieseling underground: Herk. He holds up a camera and there is a flash like sheet lightning as he snaps my pic. He is always spending his commissions on tech gadgets and I've grown accustomed to him snapping, beeping, and flashing at me all the time. Most of the time I hardly notice it, but he's been going nuts with this camera for the last two weeks and it's beginning to get to me. The last thing I want is the cleaning out of my locker recorded for posterity.

"Oh God," I say, surprised at the surprise that everyone's been able to sneak up on me lately. "Has everyone on earth heard about it?"

"No, no. Not everyone," Herk assures me. He makes contemplative, arithmetical gestures with his fingers, as if the numbers are too high to calculate without aid. "Drop the nine, carry the one…"

"All right, all right," I say. "Funny."

"What are you looking at so hard in there? Nudies of Queen Latifah?"

Herk is big. Really big. His big mouth often gets him into fights, and he often gets out of them by standing up. That's the size of his size. I mean, he has *loom*. One time at the Snug Bar some guy tried to start something with him. Standing up and blotting out the light from the bulb overhead didn't discourage him, so when the guy started pushing Herk, he enclosed the guy's hand in his. Gripping a beer bottle, the guy's hand inside Herk's was so small it looked like a child's grasping a sippie cup. "You're about to make a very bad mistake," Herk said, smiling. "Why don't you just go on home?" But the guy wouldn't be discouraged. He unwisely cocked his other arm and started launching a punch that never got off the runway. Herk, still smiling, just squeezed and: smash. He shattered the bottle by crushing the guy's hand over it. Beer and shards of broken glass went everywhere, but primarily into the fleshy parts of the guy's palm.

If Herk ever gets tired of pulsing, I always tell him, he'd make great muscle.

Anyway, probably because of his own impractically enormous body Herkimer only admires larger ladies. Tall is good, sure—he has pics of Gabrielle Reece all over his locker—but big and tall *both*? Now you're talking. His number one is Queen Latifah. He has an ongoing crush on Mrs. Hulk Hogan. Ditto postmenopausal Elizabeth Taylor. It's part of the regulations that Charlie cannot ever meet Herkimer, but I have shown Herk a million pictures of her, and he thinks her build—all cheekbones and slenderness and whippetlike muscle—is laughable. "Pretty cute," he said, "for a splinter with tits and hair."

"Yeah," I say now, unwilling to tell even Herk about the sailboat. "Sort of."

I pop a couple of tabs of dendrotoxin, just for the nerves. Herk sees it but doesn't say anything. Like everyone else, he thinks my method is weird, but he's not one to talk. He's a devotee of some kind of Taoism that I've never heard of. He thinks that saliva is the "Golden Elixir" of life and that by swallowing it a thousand times a day it will increase his resistances. He engages in "testicle breathing" and thinks that body hairs are antennae that receive signals from the universe around them. "Gotta lubricate the receptors," he'll say as he consumes his lunchtime avocados and Spam. "Don't laugh. It's follicle food, son. Why do you think your hair pricks up when there's trouble? What do you think goose bumps are, man? They're God's Distant Early Warning system."

He also is very touchy about undressing in the locker room in front of other people. Even in the hottest weather he won't take his shirt off or roll up his sleeves. He says it disrupts the purity of the signal or something. Personally I think he's nuts—give me a consistently applied regimen of toxin desensitization any day—but I'm grateful that he doesn't make fun of my method.

"If it makes you feel any better, your ass isn't the only big newsmaker today. There's a big new job up for grabs."

"Oh yeah?" I try to sound interested.

"Dream job. A fucking grounder. This Japanese guy, Nakamura, wants to ice it for a week for some Stateside buyer. Eight figs."

"A one-week hold?" I say, perking up despite the fact that in twenty minutes I probably won't work here anymore anyway. "For eight? You sure?"

"It's a two-man job. Solo plus a floater. I know you're not cleared for a solo, but a floater on a one-week job for eight? You know what the commission on that would be?"

In my head I do the math. The cut, even for a floater, is good. Really good. Enough to get Deke to keep his pliers in his pocket.

"Otto?" Herk says, snapping his fingers. "You following this?"

"What?"

"I know today was number four for you. I know it's grim. But it's just a stretch of bad luck, man. It can't keep up. You're the best pulse here. Everyone knows it."

"With the worst record."

"Well, who's got the biggest-profile gigs? You. That makes you the favorite target, right? No wonder you're getting hit."

"I haven't had top-shelf gigs for six months. The K'plua was mid-six. Tops."

"You're missing the point. Comps for this Nakamura job are tomorrow. You always take the top score. Take top score again and they have got to give you at least the floater, right?"

"So what if they do, though? I'm sure the Rat Burglar would just get me again. What's the point?"

"Cheer up, numbskull. You *want* the Rat Burglar to make

a move on you. That's how you're going to get your career back."

"How? With cunning reverse psychology?"

"Just pulsing to term isn't going to get you back your career, Otto."

"Who says I want my career back?"

"Oh no. Oh Jesus. Please—please, for the love of Sally Struthers—do not tell me you're still thinking about a clean getaway. How many times do your mother and I have to have this talk? No Santa Claus. No Tooth Fairy. No Fraggle Rock. And no fucking clean getaway."

I don't say anything. He knows I want out of the business— we've had this argument many times, and many times he's made his views clear on the subject of the viability of the clean getaway—but I've never told him about the sailboat. If he knew I had gambled money on it—all my life's savings, in fact, plus money I don't technically have—he would freak. And it's no fun being near a man Herk's size who is freaking.

"Look," he says in a makepeace voice, "at least in the short term you need your job, right? You're not going to get reinstated to solo just by pulsing one job to term. You're not going to get a fucking whiff of solo because you go one-and-four instead of oh-and-five. Is Herk right? Hell yes, Herk's right. You need to do something dramatic. You need to put an M-80 up Janus's ass."

"And what is said M-80?"

"The Rat Burglar, naturally. You need to take down the Rat Burglar."

Even though I'm the butt of this joke, I can't help laughing at it.

"Sure. Why not? I'll put that on my list. Laundry, milk, return movies, and, oh, yeah, bring down the most successful talent on earth. Right. Oh, but just one thing—how the hell am I supposed to find the Rat Burglar when Interpol hasn't, when MI-5 hasn't, when the FSB, DST, SISDE, FBI, CIA, and various mobsters haven't?"

"You've got an advantage they don't have. You know where he is going to be."

"Oh yeah? Where's that, smart guy?"

"The same place you are."

I think about this for a second. It's true. I've never thought about the Rat Burglar's affection for me as a tactical advantage.

"So I'll probably see the Rat Burglar if I ever get a gig again. Then what?"

Herk makes a gun gesture with his hand, fires it.

"Oh no," I say. "I'm not shooting anybody. You know how I feel about guns."

"Just one pop—"

"No. I don't want to *pop* anybody, Herk. I don't want to off anybody. I don't want to cap anybody. Got it?"

"But it's self-defense."

"He's never actually tried to kill me, quote unquote. All the juice he's used has been nonlethal."

"What's the difference? He's killing your livelihood. What do you think happens to burned-out pulses? You think you can find a lot of good jobs out there for people who can sit on their ass for seventy-two hours without sleeping? Really. Where will you go from here? A nice comfy stool somewhere? Is that what you want?"

"I don't want to shoot anyone. I don't even know how to shoot a gun."

Herkimer again makes a gun gesture and squeezes a finger to illustrate how easy it is.

"It won't make a difference anyway if Po-Mo fires me today."

"Well, right. If that happens. Sure. Or if your balls shrivel into Raisinettes."

"Is this your idea of a pep talk?"

This time my senses don't let me down. I hear Po-Mo's assistant coming a mile away to fetch me. Before he exhales I know what words his breath will make and before his facial muscles flex I can see the satisfied smirk.

The J-Mart Employee of the Year Pleads His Case

My boss, Everett Polizzi-Molanphy—Po-Mo—sits in his chair, with his back to me, staring out the trompe l'oeil window while steepling his fingers archvillainously. For a long time he sits like this, as if there were a view to admire. He's trying to make me sweat, and it's working.

"Do you know why I hired you, Starks?" he says, without turning around, as if I am too unpleasant for viewing. "Do you know why I brought you in from the colonies?"

"My aggregates at the combine?"

"Your interview. Remember what you said?"

Of course I remember. I told Po-Mo about the burglar who killed my family. I also told him about what happened in the Chaffee Planetarium when I was thirteen.

I was on my fourth foster family, the Zlolnierzes, Poles who didn't like the Germanic name Otto and insisted on calling me

Potap, and if I didn't respond when they addressed me I got it with a plastic bag of drainage gravel. Back then, I told Po-Mo, the only thing I wanted—besides the lives of Mom and Dad and Tobias back—was to be left alone. Preferably in the dark. Preferably in silence. I went to movies, but two hours later I had nowhere to go. I went to the woods at the reservoir, but there were kids from school. Finally I discovered the Chaffee Planetarium. There were no janitors, no ushers. No one cared if you stayed for eight consecutive shows. Almost no one else ever went there. It was dark. It was quiet. It was solitary. It was perfect.

One day two other people showed up, a guy in overalls and a little girl, who I at first thought was his daughter. The guy had taken steps to assure discretion; they were sitting on the far side of the planetarium, he had scared the girl into silence—the whole time she didn't utter a syllable; she didn't move one muscle in self-defense—and he even laid his jacket over their laps. He almost got away with it.

But he hadn't counted on someone with my audiometry.

Over the susurrus of the air-conditioning I heard the metallic creak of a zipper disjoining, tooth by tooth, in the darkness. I heard a tiny, frightened inhalation of breath and I knew, instinctively, even at fourteen, what was going on. I was too scared to confront the guy myself but I could see them, and I knew they couldn't see me, so I tiptoed to the doorway and, with my heartbeat roaring in my ears and sweat cabling down my back, I flicked on the light and yelled at the top of my lungs. The guy sprinted to the door, past me, knocking me down, frantically working his fly. Security got him at the revolving door. In no more than thirty seconds the whole thing was over.

That was it: my first bust.

The girl's name was...well, I shouldn't say. But his name

was Eugene L. Sikes, and he was her uncle. It had been going on for six months, since the day of her ninth birthday. But it wasn't going to happen anymore. Not after I heard it. Not after I flooded the room with light.

Let me tell you: flicking on the switch was a powerful gesture. It sounds corny, but in that moment before I flicked that switch in that darkened planetarium, with the silvery pinpricks of light glittering overhead, I felt a rush of something like supernatural possession; something was moving through me and it turned me, at least momentarily, into someone else. Not the guilt-ridden sole survivor of the family Starks, not the kid who keeps switching schools, not the kid who feels the most alone when around other people, not the miserable Potap, cowering before a bag of drainage gravel. I didn't have a name for this new person, but I felt bigger. Courageous. Better.

And in that moment I had a superherolike epiphany. I had been given hyperdeveloped senses for a reason: I could use them for the power of good. I could use them for protection. As soon as I was old enough I got a job working as a uni in a parking garage and I worked those kinds of jobs—even nights during college—for the next seven years. Seven long years in the colonies: at Upper East Side boutiques, JFK terminals, downtown hotel lobbies, private parties, front desks in Midtown offices. I worked part-time for a minimal wage and no benefits, broiling in polyester slacks and blazers and knit ties, doing my best to ignore the condescension of the professionals and bartenders and first-class passengers, the resentment of the custodial staff. Of course, there was the constant threat of violence, too. A shoplifter or pickpocket is a more unpredictable, hazardous character than professional talent. They don't know what they're doing. They make mistakes; they don't have exit strategies; they think the only way out is a knife slash or gunshot.

It was hard, unprofitable, demeaning, dangerous work, but I kept up with it for seven long years, without complaint or blemish, because I knew one day I would get a shot at the big time: being a pulse.

When I got that chance, three years ago, and was interviewing with Po-Mo, I told him that I couldn't stop that burglar from taking what didn't belong to him: the lives of my family. But I stopped Eugene L. Sikes, all right. And I will stop anyone else who tries to come into my goddamn room and take my goddamn MacGuffin. You can count on it, I told him. Sure my scores are great, but that's not why you should hire me. Look at me, Mr. Polizzi-Molanphy. Look me in the eye. And listen to this.

I wasn't just born to be a pulse. My life was spared—and my family died—so that I could be a pulse. And I swear to you that I will never lose a single MacGuffin. I will never let anyone take what doesn't belong to them.

Now, as I rock uncomfortably on my feet in front of Po-Mo, I assure him that I remember.

"Good. I'm glad. And do you remember who this person is?" he says, throwing a stack of bound papers at me. Opening it, I see that it is my file.

OTTO J. STARKS

119 Orchard Street, No. 7, New York NY 10002

(212) 523-6803

Professional Clients

Philip Morris[18]	Hatakeyama Museum, Tokyo
Lockheed Martin	Übersee-Museum, Bremen

18 Before you say anything: I was young; I was poor; I needed the money.

Adrian Sassoon, London

Dept. of Defense[19]

Albert Sarraut, Phnom Penh

Archaeological Museum, Sarnath

Sotheby's, NYC

Cloudsplitter

Museum für Völkerkunde, Basel

Musée Guimet, Paris

Bodleian Library, Oxford

Christie's, NYC

Galleria degli Uffizi

Orley & Shabahang, NY

Personal Clients

Suge Knight

Richie "Hammer" Lizardo

Ganz Collection

François Pinault

Guilford Montcalm Tennant

Earl Fistbeiner, Jr.

Elton John

Miuccia Prada

Liliane Bettencourt

August von Finck, Jr.

Immunities (short list)

- all naturally occurring neurotoxins from agotoxin to zaxodoxin
- all batrachotoxins, including 100% immunity to Phyllobates terribilis
- all cyclopeptides, monomethylhydrazines, coprines, muscarines, ibotenics, psilocybins
- anesthetics, intravenous and inhaled and ingested, including:
  - propofol
  - barbiturates
  - midazolam
  - nitrous oxide
  - isoflurane
  - xenon gas
  - etomidate
  - benzodiazepines
  - ketamine
  - enflurane
  - sevoflurane
  - gamma-hydroxybutyrate

19 The job that pushed me into the art market full-time. Talent, at least those who don't work for Azar, are reluctant to kill you—attempted robbery is an easier rap than murder—but spies and terrorists? They don't care. They'll shoot at you. And they'll hit you. And it will hurt much worse, and for much longer, than you think it will.

- tsusensan
- burundanga
- iocaine powder

- paralytics, including but not limited to:

- vecuronium
- pancuronium
- mivacurium
- rocuronium
- atracurium
- cistracurium
- succinylcholine
- curare
- Perrelet
- picotine
- norisol
- grisogonol
- nixolophan[20]

Notable Busts

Simon McCord[21]   Rona "the Body" Bedzilnik

Crummy Markovich   Zed[22]

---

[20] A bit of a whopper, actually. No one really has an immunity to Nix. What makes it such a nasty customer? Nix has incredible bioavailability—nearly instantaneous—and the antidote requires several applications at thirty-second intervals, which means that the cure often loses the race to the fast-acting toxin. So if you've got any last words before your entire body is paralyzed, you'd better spit them out, pronto. It's brand-new, too, a hybrid of the natural maculotoxin found in blue-ringed octopods and some kind of synthetic. You get all the pain and paralysis of the former but, thanks to the latter, not death. If you want to paralyze someone for the rest of his life, and you want to do it with maximum discomfort, Nix is for you. I've been working hard to build up a resistance, but because it's so new, and a hybrid, it's tricky. I'm only up to one ten-milligram pill, and even that amount makes my lips and tongue tingle with numbness. So I really shouldn't say I have an immunity to Nix. Even saying "resistance" is a stretcher. It's a work in progress.

[21] Attempted to use trained ball python to infiltrate air shaft; busted when I discovered the snake coiled under heater for warmth.

[22] Drilled up through concrete flooring; I detected vibrations through bare feet on the tile.

Marty & Benji Estrovece   Dallas Spicer[23]

Deacon Breedlove[24]   Boki Fujiwara[24]

Pituitary Jones[24]   Frito Kriskstein[24]

Frankie "Nickels" Bozzuto and Tony "Kong" Mavrogordo[25]

Now, as I stand in my boss's office and look back over the file, I can't help smiling in fondness for the good old days when all the top talent feared me, when I had a perfect retention record and was getting top gigs all over the world, but that sends Po-Mo the wrong message. He interprets it as cavalierness.

"Is there something funny? Am I missing it? Maybe I don't have the greatest sense of humor—maybe I'm not getting it, Starks—but you tell me, is there something funny about losing almost thirty million dollars for Janus clients in nine months? Does that sound like a knee-slapper to you?"

23 Failed to lubricate the soles of his shoes and when he tried to walk across tiles that had been sprayed with movie butter—an old favorite of mine—I heard, from several rooms away, the sticky, riplike sound of rubber separating from adhesive.

24 Cut green wire.

25 My best boldface names. They both worked for Azar. Frankie Nickels was New York's premier talent and Kong was top tech support. Frankie had the drop on me, but I heard the nickels shift in his pocket overhead. That was his signature device: leaving nickels at the site of the job. As a kid Frankie would shoplift some big-ticket item and leave a pair of nickels behind so he could tell the cops, "Hey, I wasn't stealing! I was buying on deep discount!" Juvie humor. Anyway, when I heard the change overhead I was all over the button. I didn't even have to look up. There was brief hand-to-hand (hand-to-paw, really: after getting punched in the mouth I assumed a strategic defensive posture, which to the untrained observer would look much like closing my eyes and curling up into a ball while Pinky got himself a mouthful of pant leg that delayed Frankie's getaway long enough for the back-up

"No, sir," I say, abashed.

"Me either. Look. You know I like you. You're one of the most promising pulses I've ever seen. Despite what Detective Nunes thinks—"

"Who's he?"

"She," he says. "Cheryl Nunes. In charge of the investigation."

"What happened to Fritzy?"

"Off the case."

"What do you mean off the case?"

"He was moonlighting."

"Doing what? Killing baby ducks?"

"Seems the city wasn't paying him enough to investigate; the Rat Burglar paid him better not to."

"I hadn't heard this."

"So far it's an internal affairs matter. The chief doesn't exactly need any more bad Rat Burglar press after all Fritzy's bad arrests, does he?"

"So Nunes is his replacement?"

He nods. "Going back over Fritzy's ground. Which includes you—"

"Me?"

"—but when I think back on that interview, when I look

---

to surround the building). He fled and ended up falling from the roof and breaking his spine. Kong was apprehended two blocks away, in the van, and cut a deal with the DA, who then convicted and sentenced Frankie Nickels in record time. Two days later Kong goes into a public restroom alone and comes out minus his hands, courtesy of Jimmy the Hat. Normally Jimmy uses his knives to remove a portion of a victim's head—he "takes off your hat." That's his modus. In this case, however, taking only Kong's hands was not a mercy. He wanted to advertise the message: this is what happens to you when you roll over on Azar.

at that file, when I think of those busts—and when I think of Frankie Nickels cooling upstate—I like to think that you're not...*involved* in the thefts."

"Involved?" I say, feeling something screw down in my gut. "What does that mean?"

"I prefer to think that you're just having a bad spell. I prefer to think that maybe you're fatigued for...personal reasons. Or maybe for...pharmacological reasons."

I think: oh no. Here we go again.

"I've told you a thousand times, haven't I? Haven't I told you to quit with the pills? Didn't I tell you that no one—not even you, Starks—can take all that juice? Didn't the guys in tox tell you the same thing?"

"Yes," I say sheepishly.

"Didn't they tell you dozens of times?"

I nod.

"Haven't they been telling you that for months?"

I nod again.

"Did you do it? Did you quit?"

"Yes," I say, stupidly.

"You know I read the tox report, right?"

"Oh."

"Starks, empty your pockets, please." Onto the table I unload a logspill of bottles and hypodermics and a few torpedo-shaped suppositories. "What is all that?"

"Flintstones?"

Po-Mo picks some up and rolls them in his hand. "Isoflurane? Grisogonol? *Phyllobates terribilis?* What is all this for?"

"Headache," I say hopefully. "Runny nose?"

"You got anything in here for recovering thirty million bucks? I know you're a college guy, Starks, so I'm sure you can

follow this.[26] Janus gets clients because we have an impec-
cable record of MacGuffin retention. Good news for us is no
news. But when something like this happens"—and he throws
a newspaper clipping whose headline I have time to see says
something about the Rat Burglar and the dearly departed
Khmer reliefs—"it's the opposite of good news. And when it's
the same talent rolling the same pulse…"

"The media has my name?"

"No. But they have Janus's, don't they? Do you know what
they're calling us?"

"I don't really follow the news, boss. I mean, what they call
news nowadays…"

"I'll quote it for you, then. From Doreen Doherty, Patriot TV."

"Come on, boss. Patriot TV doesn't even count as news. It's
just tits and teeth—"

" 'Janus, Inc., one of Manhattan's Big Three specialized security firms, has lost another objet d'art to the Rat Burglar, who
has been raiding its facilities with such ease and regularity it
looks less like robbery and more like shopping. One industry
insider from rival Invigilator Corp. confided in us that the Rat
Burglar himself refers to the embattled Janus, Inc., as his favorite store—J-Mart.' "

---

26 I was an English major because a) I liked sitting around in dark rooms by
myself and b) I craved the stories of other people. My thesis was on Dickens;
I couldn't stop reading about him because all his stories are, one way or
another, about the lifesaving power of family. If I couldn't have my own
family, I thought, I can at least have Oliver, Nicholas, Pip, Little Nell. Senior
year I even won a Fulbright to study "the role of family and forgiveness in
Indian literature," but I turned it down because I also got offered a job as a
uni at the Larco Museum in Lima, a well-known feeder program for pulses.
Still, I regret not taking the Fulbright sometimes. Like right this very second, for example.

When I say nothing to this Po-Mo repeats it. "J-Mart, Starks! And you're the employee of the year!" He exhales a ragged breath of disgust. "I don't know how else to say this. The stock is down nine percent. We are in danger of not making our earnings projections. And when the media gets hold of the K'plua, well...The long and short of it is the board wants you out, Starks. Can you think of any reason why I shouldn't do it?"

"Because you know even though I've had a rough patch lately I still have it? Because you wouldn't send me back out into the colonies after investing all this time in me? Because you're more of a people person than a bottom-line guy?" When Po-Mo's dark and stony expression goes darker and stonier, I try another tack. "Because it's an administrative pain to fire me?"

"An administrative pain? It's a shitdrizzle, Starks. Shit. Drizzle. But that's what the board wants. And even though you're my guy, I've got to do it. Unless—" He rubs his face briskly with his hands as if scrubbing to get something—my failure residue?—off his skin, and says, "Unless...you've got something...up your sleeve."

In my head, in clarion surround sound, I hear the train-rumble of Herk's voice urging me to say: I can get the Rat Burglar, boss. I can bring him down. And I'll use a gun.

But I can't say it. I can't kill anyone. I can't even utter the syllables.

"Boss," I say, "please just let me test. Not for solo. Just for floater. I need this. I'm desperate. And I promise I've still got it, boss. I can prove it with the comps. You've got to let me try."

Po-Mo sighs with something like defeat, then waves his hands angrily in front of his face as if dispersing a cloud of pesky insects and says, "Just...go on, Starks. Get out of my office. Get out of my sight."

When I turn and am at the door, with my hand on the knob, Po-Mo says, "Wait. Freeze. Don't turn around. What anomalies are on my desk?"

I was hoping he might ask me this. It's a test—a crude plastoperceptivity test—to determine the ability of a pulse to identify suspicious irregularities within a pattern that could indicate a foreign presence in a secure environment. It means he's curious about my faculties.

"Your name plaque is askew. Under some papers is a book on bilberry extract as a vision enhancer. One of the bulbs in your lamp is out. The cap on your Orangina is loose and the sticky-looking smear on your blotter suggests you might spill it again if you don't tighten it up. Your stapler has a torn-up staple in it; it's probably jammed. There are a few multicolored jimmies—you know, shots, sprinkles, whatever—on the carpet by your trash can, from which I might infer that you've gone off the diet, sir, and that you tried unsuccessfully to dispose of the evidence. And there is an e-mail from the directors on your screen regarding the status of my employment—"

"What?" he says, alarmed, grabbing his monitor and looking at it hard, as if making sure it's not transparent. "How did you see that?"

"The reflection off your glasses, boss. I hope you don't play poker with those suckers on." Now he takes off his bifocals and stares at them in his hand, almost in shock, as if he had pulled a living animal off of his face. "Anyway, you've got an e-mail from the directors on your screen. I can't read everything, but I see my name in the subject line along with the words 'termination protocol,' but you haven't responded to it. At least not yet. Which I like to think means that you still have enough confidence in me to—"

"That'll be all, Starks. You can go. Make sure you submit your write-up on the retention failure before you go."

"Does that mean I can test for the Nakamura job tomorrow, sir?"

"Can you give me one compelling reason why?"

I give him the only thing I can think of that he wants.

"Boss, if I don't take the top score by fifty points"—I can't suppress a gulp when I say this; I always take first but I've never taken it by such a huge margin—"I'll save everyone the trouble and resign. I won't make a fuss. I'll just disappear. But please, you've got to give me a chance. All I've ever wanted to do is be a pulse. Ever since what happened to my family. Ever since that day in the planetarium. All those years in the colonies. You gave me a chance then; give me a chance now. Please, boss. I don't have anything else."

"If you're late, you're fired. If you're early, you're fired. If you breathe the wrong way—"

"I get it. Thanks, boss. I won't let you down."

I try to shake his hand but Po-Mo doesn't move to accept it. Instead he says, "You know, Starks, a little birdie told me you were going to break cover to your girl. If that were true, it would make the administrative process of terminating your employment a lot easier. You know that, right?"

I wouldn't say I feel good. My stomach hurts too much for that, I am still the record-holder for permeability at Janus, and although other people probably can't detect anything, my olfactory informs me that I still literally smell like shit. My own shit, no less. But as I exit Po-Mo's office I realize, with joy, that I have escaped headquarters without suffering any of Schermer's pranks. I am still employed. Soon—within an hour, I hope—Charlie will be coming over. Tomorrow I'm going to test for the floater position on the Nakamura job. I have a shot at the clean getaway. I'm still alive.

It's a good place to start.

Reminder

There was a time in my life, not so long ago, when I would have been amazed to be pulled rapidly to the ground, backwards, in a deep, gravity-compliant, limbo-like arc by a pair of pliers gripping my earlobe. A year ago, perhaps, an innocent age blissfully unacquainted with the grief caused by the death of a beloved pet, or the debilitating effects of a massive overdose of elephant laxative, or the specter of unemployment and insurmountable personal debt. But not now. Now I only note, with an academic detachment, the many varieties of pain involved in the transaction, the most salient of which is the scalding sensation produced by the textured teeth of the pliers clamping down on the tender fatty tissue of the earlobe, but there is also an awareness that instead of simply detaching from my skull, as I dearly wish it would, my ear is following the pliers with great alacrity toward the hard concrete of the sidewalk outside my apartment in Clinton Hill.[27]

27 I moved to this neighborhood in Brooklyn from the Lower East Side three years ago, when I first started at Janus. I wanted to be responsible; I wanted to get a cheaper place, save money, build for the future. And at first it was great. The place was bigger, cleaner, brighter, but, I realized quickly,

By a small margin I am coherent enough to discern an additional pain, a complex emotional one composed mainly of humiliation and amazement caused by the fact that I have once again failed to hear someone behind me.

As my skull accelerates toward the asphalt, I think: what use are these ears?

When I encounter the ground, and incur my second concussion of the day, I smile politely at my assailant and say, as cheerily as possible, "Hi, Deke. I was just coming to see you." This does not have the pacifying effect for which I had hoped. Apparently this is an utterance that Deke hears routinely, and its familiarity has bred a contempt that is expressed instantaneously by the torque-heavy twisting of the pliers.

Electrified by pain, and incapable of saying much more, I scream, in such a rapid-fire repetition that it sounds like a kind of deranged war cry, "Moneymoneymoneymoneymoney!"

Deke, who must entertain so many agonized egurgitations that he has cultivated a dentist's facility for interpretation, comprehends my meaning instantly and relaxes the pliers. He does not let me up, however; he holds me to the ground, pinned in a posture of absolute submission, hovering over me. Up close, I notice that he has the sad, calm eyes of the truly violent, eyes that have seen it all, done it all, and therefore know what's coming, and how much it will hurt.

Deke tilts his head quizzically, showing me his ear, flaunting

it is also much quieter. I started missing the cacophony of my old street. When you're a pulse with so few friends, and so much of your time is spent in absolute silence, you long for the noises of other people. Consequently I find myself hanging out in my old neighborhood all the time—I'm always at the Snug Bar—and whatever money I save in mortgage payments I lose in taking late-night cabs back to Brooklyn when I finally, reluctantly, hangdoggedly go home.

it, I think at first, but then I am able to comprehend through the stupefying pain that he is making a gesture that is meant to invite speech. He is encouraging me to repeat myself, and I am only too eager to please.

"Money," I say, sticking to the vitals. "I have some. Will have some."

"How much?" he asks casually, as if inquiring about a menu special.

"Plenty."

"How much precisely?"

Reflexively I utter the figure that will be due the floater as commission upon full execution of the Nakamura job.

"And you want to do the right thing with it?" he asks, squeezing the pliers.

With my earlobe ensnared, nodding is out of the question, so I contort my face into an expression that I hope conveys affirmation. Deke nods as if proud of a student who has hazarded an adventurous guess at a difficult problem. The pressure diminishes, the curtains of pain in front of my eyes momentarily pull up, and I am able to breathe.

"When?"

"Soon," I say, committing another faux pas. Apparently this is yet another statement Deke is weary of hearing, and down go the curtains. I'm not sure how much time passes but eventually his vise grip lets up and I am able to gasp for oxygen.

"When precisely?" Deke asks tonelessly.

It's hard to do the computation when my head is so preoccupied routing signals of agony, but I think: today's Thursday, the Nakamura job starts next Saturday, one-week hold, figure another week for the clowns in payroll...

"Three weeks!" I blurt. Then as the pliers relax, I unwisely say, "Four absolute max." Seconds later I am recanting. "Three-threethreethree!" I repeat until Deke releases me and under-goes a facial spasm that might be a smile.

"Three weeks, then," he says. Then he repeats the figure I quoted as the floater commission, which, without the influ-ence of pliers, now seems optimistically large. It's possible I carried a nonexistent one or messed up a decimal. I was never any good at math in school, much less math under duress of torture. "I'll pencil it in."

Then he pockets the pliers, stands up, pats his chest and inhales pleasantly, as if savoring the first flowers of spring, and produces an envelope that he toys with like a bauble.

"I know I have a reputation," he says, almost apologetically, turning the envelope over in his hands. "I know people say things. But don't worry. If you're late I won't kill you. I try not to kill clients. It's bad business."

Then he tosses the envelope at me. When he's gone I pull myself up and open it. The blood pounding in my ear is deaf-ening and my vision is blurring with tears, but even in the shadows of my stoop I can make out the details of the crowded Indian restaurant in the photograph. There are a bunch of those faux gold diva lamps everywhere, pictures of Shah Rukh Khan almost kissing Kajol, innumerable hanging talwars and images of dancing Hindu gods, and, at a distant table in the back, sitting with a big guy in a deep red turban that matches his shirt, nearly out of focus but with a circle drawn clearly around her face with an X cut through it—like crosshairs—is Charlie.

Auto-Nav

It turns out that the earlobe is a pretty vascular area. As I inspect myself in the bathroom mirror I can't help but think about its similarity to the lips; both are filled with tender collagen and, under pressure, both swell prodigiously with blood. What was once a tidy, buttonlike hemisphere attached cheerfully to my ear is now an engorged wad of livid flesh that sags like an obscene tropical blossom. The skin is embrailled with the textured markings of the pliers' teeth and it is so tortured by the passage of blood that I can see it twitch minutely with every heartbeat.

Not exactly inconspicuous.

I can't conceal this from Charlie with makeup, as I do with the various puncture wounds that I typically incur. I've never had an injury like this before, so I'm not sure how to proceed. The only comparable bruising I can think of is a hickey, and even though I recall hearing in grade school that you can "brush them out," after fifteen agonizing minutes with Charlie's stout-bristled paddle, I reluctantly conclude that you cannot brush out a devastated earlobe.

Ruefully, I concede that I may have to ice it, a step I hate to take because it requires a trip to the freezer, which is where Charlie has stockpiled a cache of top tiers of wedding cakes. Apparently it's a tradition for a newlywed couple to save this part of their wedding cake—the one with the action figures on it—for their one-year anniversary. For some reason, all of

Charlie's friends have entrusted her with the guardianship of these cakes. I'm not sure what it is about them that makes me so sad[28]—all those soldierly figurines in glossy black and white, leaning in toward each other—but I can hardly stand to look at them. I haven't told Charlie this—I'm afraid she would think it is dumb; even I think it's dumb—but lately it's gotten worse.

I try to shake it off by popping a couple of tabs of Hemofex, a branded schedule one blood agent to which I'm still pretty new, so it stings. Just like I want it to. Enabled by pill-courage, I plow into the kitchen and force myself to confront the freezer. As if about to dive into dangerous water, I hold my breath, yank open the door, focus hard on not focusing at all on the couples, and grab all the ice I can.

As I apply the pack to my earlobe I sit on the stool next to Pinky's dog bed—I haven't had the heart to throw it out—and flip through the pages of the current *Retention Sciences Today*. There is a "Where Are They Now?" item on Kong and Frankie Nickels—it's the two-year anniversary, after all[29]—and there is a piece on the growing violence of Azar's men,[30] but the cover story, wouldn't you know it, is none other than Detec-

28 A plausible theory is jealousy: all those other guys had the guts. They have made their clean getaway with the woman they love.

29 Frankie Nickels is still paralyzed from the neck down, and still serving time. Kong, once the finest tech support in the business, is now employed by the Geek Squad. In the interview he says if he still had his hands he'd strangle everyone who comes to the counter. "If one more person makes me say the word 'reboot' I'm going to go absolutely batshit," he says. "I swear to God."

30 Recently, in Seattle, a pulse was found dead and scalped, "clearly the work of Jimmy the Hat, hitherto known to work only on the East Coast." The killing is notable not only because of its longitude but because this

tive Cheryl Nunes. The article makes no mention of Fritzy's corruption and his many false arrests; it merely says she has been "newly appointed" in the Rat Burglar investigation. The production quality of the magazine is not high, and the light is poor, but Nunes appears to be a wiry woman with startling blue eyes and a complexion like washable glue. She looks cold; she is wearing a shabby trench and hunching up like a hardened *frileuse* even though the picture is taken indoors. Despite the cloudless sky outside the window she has an antique full-length umbrella hitched over her arm.

I'm just reading about her tracking down tithers in Graz[31] and exterminating a *tombaroli* racket in Salerno[32] when I detect outside my door, on the exhausted strip carpeting, the familiar light, clumsy, rhythmless footfalls. I can almost smell the odor of hot plastic and ink she will have from the photocopier; on her hair will be the burned chemical smell of industrial solvents that the university cleaning crew uses every night; her clothes will have the fuzzy suggestion of polyester and public transportation from riding the bus; there will be the polished leather, the rosemary and mint, the jungle-like perfume of her body. I can hardly wait.

There is enough time to stash the mag and my pills but I'm

time the typically missing scalp isn't missing. The medical examiner discovered it in the pulse's stomach, masticated and partially digested: before executing him, Jimmy had made his victim eat his own hat. The value of the MacGuffin? A measly three hundred thousand dollars.

31 Tithers: talent who steal works with no intention of selling or fencing them. They merely cash in on the 10 percent reward offered by insurance companies for returns. This has become a popular strategy lately because it's so tough to prosecute.

32 Nifty.

not able to jot down anything about pachylax in my journal. I am just able to slip it under the cushions on the sofa before the ringer buzzes. Frantically I check to make sure there aren't any spare vials or hypos lying around, then I fling open the door and there, leaning against the frame, her black curls tightening in the humidity, is Charlie.

"Someone call in an order of *ta' l'Armla*?" she says, dangling a plastic bag that radiates the scent of vegetables, peppery goat cheese, and eggs. But I also smell something sweet—honey icing and biscuit—and sure enough, from behind her back she produces another bag and makes a suggestive pendulum movement with it in front of her chest. "And if you're good, I brought some *figolli* and a video of sailing disasters caught on tape."

Charlie is naturally a gesture-maker, a gift-bearer, but she seems to have a nearly paranormal knack for bringing me home cooking whenever I've had a bad day. After the Khmer reliefs I got a steaming pot of some kind of spicy fish soup and rice whose name I can never remember but which rhymes with "Gargamel." When I lost Entemena I discovered on my doorstep a plastic container with a note attached that said Charlie would be stuck in departmental meetings all night but here was "fennek" in a red wine sauce. On the night when the Rat Burglar stole the mediocre Inanna vases she showed up with a book on water safety skills and some kind of pastry things stuffed with dates.

How does she do it? How does she always seem to know when I need something like a home-cooked Maltese dish whose name I cannot pronounce? Could anyone else intuit this? I doubt it. When I think about how she is always doing these things I am nearly overwhelmed with guilt about the way I have lied to her.

And—God help me—about how I've involved her in this thing with Deke.

"You're too good to me," I say, meaning it more than she knows.

"Very true. But later," she says, putting the bags down on the table, "you might be afforded the opportunity to express your gratitude."

When she wraps her arms around my neck, and tilts her face up to mine, pursing her lips into the shape of a pink-brown butterfly, prekiss, I amaze her by emitting an agonized shriek.

"Sorry," I say, displaying my ear. "I got...hit by a, uh, foul ball."

"Ouch," she says, squinting at it. "It looks awful."

"It only hurts when my heart beats."

"It's got some...strange markings on it. What *is* that?"

"What's what?" I say innocently.

"Those things. Like a pattern."

"Oh, that must be the stitches from the baseball."

"It doesn't look like stitches. It looks like some kind of weird cross-hatching. Like diamond-shaped or something."

"Oh yeah," I say, trying to think fast. "It was a, uh, minor league ball."

"Hunh. Well, let's put some ice on it. And get you some Tylenol."

For me, trying to treat an injury with an over-the-counter analgesic is like trying to extinguish a forest fire by spitting at it, but I dutifully swallow the pills and do my best to act relieved by it. I make a deeply satisfied, gustatory sound, as if swallowing a particularly refreshing carbonated beverage, and smile with gratitude.

Charlie bangs around in the kitchen, reheating the dinner while whistling to herself, but she seems to know something else is wrong, and when I decline her offer to practice constrictor knots on the line she brought over she can't help asking.

"Yeah," I confess. "Today I lost a...prospect. The team was really counting on this one. And he got away. Thanks to the fucking—" I nearly blow it. By a fraction of a second I choke back the *r* in Rat Burglar.

"Yankees?" Charlie says, saving me from myself. "Again the damn Yankees?"

"Yeah. Fourth fucking time this year."

Contemplating my dim and dangerous future provokes from my gullet a pathetic, waterlogged sniffle of grief.

"Hey," Charlie says, "it's O.K. Things will change. I know they will." Then her expression brightens; she has an idea. She inserts the video of sailing disasters and fast-forwards. "Hey. Look at it this way. No matter how bad it was today, it can't be as bad as this guy's day."

The screen shows an enormous oceangoing sailboat, maybe seventy feet, clippering along at top speed, making a beeline, in broad daylight, for an immense cargo ship. The voice-over informs us that this is the perilous result of "entrusting your passage to an auto-nav system while entertaining your spouse belowdecks." Seconds later the ships collide, the smaller one shattering into a million pieces of jagged composite, as a terrified, naked couple leap over the stern while orange life preservers rain down from the deck of the steamer like some kind of life-sized ring-toss game.

Charlie laughs conspiratorially at this, pointing vigorously at the screen, encouraging me to partake in the jollity—and normally I would; I can't get enough of this kind of thing—but suddenly the sight of a beautiful sailboat going down, down, down has a very real, very personal, very doomlike aspect.

When Charlie realizes what a poor choice of cheer-up strategy this is, her face landslides into such an apologetic, helpless expression that I can't help, finally, laughing. She starts to say something—she was dumb, she didn't mean it like that, she wants me to crack the last can of Coco Rico—but I pull her down to me.

Charlie's fragrance is different today. Underneath are the usual notes, but presiding over everything today is a powerful odor of peony and black cherry, and when her hair falls over my face and I am nearly suffocated in it, I realize this must be a new purchase. Charlie's inveterate clumsiness extends to indextrous misapplications of perfume, especially new ones whose atomizers she hasn't mastered. A crop-dusting like this on another woman would flay my odor receptors and induce a terrible headache, but it's Charlie, and my brain is already awash in pleasure chemicals. The silk of her blouse is slick and slides against my body. Her pelvis begins to surge into mine but something sizzles on the stove and she tries to pull away.

"But dinner," she says.

I don't let her up.

"The stove."

I renew my grip.

"It'll burn."

"Put it on auto-nav," I say.

She does. Then, standing in my kitchen, facing me with her legs spread apart like a gunslinger, with her eyes all pupil and her heartbeat pulsing hard in her jugular, she looks so fierce it's hard to tell if she wants to fight me or fuck me. When she unbuttons her blouse, when she hulas out of her skirt, when she thumbs out of her bra and panties, it is tender and intimate, but her face is brazen and reckless, nearly martial, as if issuing me a dare.

She undergoes the transformation. She has the grace.

Then, for the third time today, I lose track of my surround-
ings. I try to blink out of it, but it's no good. I am totally locked
in. When she moves across the room, presses her naked body
against me, and puts her warm mouth on mine, my five senses
go insensate to everything else—the eerie carless quiet outside
my window, the wilted carpet crushed beneath my toes, every
object and light source in my visual field—and all I see hear
smell touch taste is Charlie.

Our Greatest Hit Hits Again, or: Who Is the Rat Burglar?

Afterward, as we lay together on the bed, with the blades of the
fan overhead cutting stroboscopic ribbons of shadow into the
ceiling, our skin dampening the sheets, Charlie and I stumble
into it: our all-time, triple-platinum, greatest-hit argument.

The Rat Burglar.

When I get up to go to the bathroom Charlie makes the mistake of turning on the TV and there she is, Doreen Doherty,
Patriot News telepromptress and all-around bigmouth, brack-
eted by an intake pic of the K'plua and the familiar graphic of
a whiskery rodent beneath a dramatic floating question mark,
recounting in excoriating detail the events of this afternoon.
She has everything but my name. She has the location of the
facility, the properties of the mask, its value, its owner, the fact
that the mysterious thief disabled two security agents. Detective Nunes is not available for comment. Neither is Po-Mo but
Doreen quotes a formal statement from him saying that Janus

has no formal statement. In the pic, the K'plua's expression is, if anything, even more hurt and reproving and Doreen's manner is, if possible, even more smug than usual.

Without fail, every time the Rat Burglar does a job, Doreen covers it, her pudgy cheeks appling as she blabs away about the haplessness of "J-Mart," and I can never stop myself from saying something. I know I shouldn't. There are plenty of reasons why I shouldn't, among which a) there is no explicable reason why a baseball talent scout should have a beef with the Rat Burglar or Double-D, so b) it therefore unnecessarily raises certain suspicions that could lead to complicated conversations, and c) it is never nice, while in the company of one woman, to call another woman a "slutty, ignorant, obese cretin capable of only the cheapest, most irresponsible, slapdash, jingoistic 'journalism' and who has wardrobe people who dress her funny." Even if it's true.

Tonight I resolve to be better. In the bathroom I bunker the space under the door with a rolled-up towel and plug my ears with facecloths but I can still hear Doreen and her guests discussing the Rat Burglar. One voice is the academic. I can tell by her phonation, which is both faucalized and mucusy, with strident accentuation and wet vowels that make it sound as if her voice is mayonnaise squirting out of a plastic packet. Plus she has the full-stop terseness of hauteur, as if she knows the soup du jour and you have absolutely no idea.

In other words: she is annoying me already.

The other speaker has an accent that aspires to identify itself as British-American of unspecified but probably aristocratic derivation[33] but which succeeds only in designating its speaker as art-world-phony. It belongs, I can tell despite the

33 Think Cary Grant times ten.

terry cloth I am forcing deeply into my aural canal, to Arthur Quackenbush, head of Signature, a second-tier auction house from whose employ I have been dropped.

In other words: he has annoyed me for a long time.

As have the words that have become Doreen's catchphrase, which she utters after introducing her guests: "But America, who *is* the Rat Burglar?"

Then comes Patriot TV's familiar machine-gun report and, simultaneously, bullet perforations underscore the Rat Burglar graphic. Canned applause roars over the wire.

It makes me sick to see how much people love their criminals. It was bad enough when the Gottis got their own reality show, but in the last couple of years the Rat Burglar has eclipsed even that standard of perversity. Although he is reviled by many—the media, the authorities, the entire art world, anyone with two brain cells to rub together—to some he has become a cult hero. Such is his celebrity that those five famous words—"Who is the Rat Burglar?"—have attained a pop-culture ubiquity. In bars, on dates, at the watercooler, they are invoked as if they were a jingle. There are innumerable Web sites devoted to theories of identity. An Elephant 6–like all-girl indie band, the Hard Twenties, has a hit song dedicated to the Rat Burglar called "Steal *Me*." And Crimies, a brand of trading card that features infamous mafiosi, gangstas, snitches, hitpersons, muscle, gaffers, talent, et cetera, has the Rat Burglar's infamous blank-silhouette mug shot valued at three Frankie Nickels or two Jimmy the Hats. I ask you: does that make any kind of sense?

"Well, Doreen," Quackenbush informs the telepromptress, "as you know, there has been a tremendous increase in art theft in recent years. It's not a new phenomenon—the total dollar value of art looted during the Holocaust is put, conservatively, at twenty-five billion—but I think part of the reason for its recent surge in popularity is the media coverage of the record hammer prices we are seeing for various single works. If a thief can rob a bank for, say, a hundred million dollars, he must contend with the logistics of carting away all that cash. Hardly a one-man job. A hundred-million-dollar painting, on the other hand, is a tempting, and portable, prize.[34] Traditionally art thieves have been bunglers or, at best, opportunists—the hapless thieves who damaged Munch's *Scream* so severely come to mind, as does the Louvre worker Vincenzo Perrugia, who literally walked out the door with the *Mona Lisa* under his coat. The work of the Rat Burglar, however, is meticulous and precise. It shows an intimate familiarity with security systems of all sorts and, as we saw in Paris two years ago, he has considerable physical prowess.[35]

"I don't think it would be inappropriate to look to someone outside of the art community. Perhaps with a military background. It is not inconceivable that the Rat Burglar could have experience in espionage. Or, perhaps, a branch of law enforcement."

"Fascinating," Doreen says.

34 I hate to say it, but Quackenbush is right. Recently a Klimt, *Adele Bloch-Bauer I*, sold for $126 million—a tempting target for any talent looking for a one-stop haul.

35 After stealing an El Greco from the Louvre the Rat Burglar was chased through the Tuileries on foot by French police. The gendarmes found the painting, cut from its frame and hanging from a branch in a small enclosure. They approached it, searching for signs of damage, and then, according to the report, "the tree came alive." Three of the officers were knocked unconscious; a fourth, the victim of a debilitating kick to his leg, said that the tree became a hulking figure "well over two meters," swathed in black, who rolled up the canvas and, swinging it playfully like a cricket bat, sauntered off through the garden "without even doing us the dignity of running."

"Forgive me," says the academic. "The who might be in law enforcement?"

"The Rat Burglar."

"I believe you mean the Polecat, Arthur."

Quackenbush groans.

"What do you mean, Dr. Spivey?" says Doreen.

"Unbelievable," says Charlie.

In that mayonnaisey voice Spivey adduces reasons why everyone has it wrong about the Rat Burglar.

"The sobriquet 'Rat Burglar' derives from the calling card, as everyone knows. But the popular claim that the hairs are from a rodent is erroneous; the hairs actually come from a *Mustela eversmanii*—a steppe polecat."

"Same thing as a rat," says Quackenbush.

"Actually, it's a different family altogether. Different genus, different species. It's more closely related to a cat than to any kind of rodent."

"Well, Janice, a rat by any other name is just as rotten. The upshot is that the Rat Burglar, the Polecat, whatever you want to call him, is one thief who needs to be put out of business."

"This may come as a surprise to you, Arthur, but the Polecat has never stolen anything."

For the first time, Quackenbush and I share something: a feeling of outrage. I can't help unplugging the towels and opening the door to stare at the TV as Dr. Spivey goes on. Charlie, naked and garmented flowerlike in the folds of sheets, sailcloth-white against her skin, like a Christo wrapped in cotton, is also agog. She looks personally affronted by the TV, as if it has just slapped her with an antenna.

"This is ludicrous," says Q. "He's stolen hundreds of millions of dollars of art!"

"Such as?" inquires Spivey.

"*Ashurbanipal Hunting Lions* was in the British Museum before it was stolen—"

"Not stolen. Restored. Restored to the Malik National Museum in Tehran, whence it came before it was looted. And where it belongs."

"The Getty's entire Incan collection, down to the last spondylus figurine—"

"Was returned to the Museo de la Nación in Lima. Again, to its proper country of origin."

"The El Greco at the Louvre, for which they paid five million dollars—"

"To an ex-SS officer who had 'commandeered' it from a Jewish family in World War Two, Arthur? The *Pole*cat liberated it and returned it to the surviving children of the family. Again, these are not thefts, Arthur, unless you consider their unlawful possession by foreign museums thefts. They are restorations."

"This is craziness," says Charlie. "I can't believe it."

"Me either," I say, feeling suddenly very chipper to be in agreement with Charlie over anything Rat Burglarian. "Nuts!"

"All those works were lawfully purchased in good faith with proper certificates of authentication," says Q.

"Which you can write up in crayon, for all museums care."

Doreen ushers them back on topic so swiftly I can almost hear the producers yelling in her earpiece.

"Well, Doreen," Spivey continues, "the clue to identity— and the only clue ever left behind by the Polecat—are the hairs. A steppe polecat is similar to the American barn weasel, but considerably more rare. Why, if you were the Polecat, would you go through the trouble of using such a hard-to-find item as your calling card? It is inconvenient, certainly, but it also makes you vulnerable to being traced by the authorities, as there are few outlets from which you can attain the hairs of a steppe polecat. Why would you risk that? The only sensible explanation is that the steppe polecat contains some sort of valuable message or metaphor."

"Such as?"

"Unlike Arthur, I believe the Polecat is a member of the art community. The items targeted for restoration are much too specific to be the work of anyone but an expert. And as an expert, I know that the Polecat is aware that the only important representation of a steppe polecat in art is in the cave painting of the Upper Paleolithic. In these works animals are always associated with gender—'male' animals such as aurochs, bears, mammoths, horses, and 'female' animals such as reindeer, fish, various types of felines. The iconography is consistent: the 'male' animals always encircle the 'female' animals, as if to protect them, or exclude them. There is only one exception to this patriarchy, and it is the polecat. A 'female' animal, it is often corralled in the usual manner, but in some instances you will see a polecat penetrating the demarcation made by the male animals. You can interpret this as a transgressive act, or an act of privilege, but what is undeniable is that the steppe polecat's only salient image in art history is that of a female agent penetrating into the male world. And I ask you, what is more masculine than thievery? What is more male than crime, or, as Arthur points out, fisticuffs?"

Charlie gargles a turbid imprecation at the screen.

Doreen says, "So you are saying that you believe the Rat Burglar—"

"Polecat."

"Is a woman?"

For a long moment there is just dead air. The split screen shows us Quackenbush. His jaw drops. My jaw drops. Charlie's jaw drops. We look like synchronized swimmers working on a questionable new move.

"That's right. And if we look at what the Polecat is accomplishing in Iraq, where looting is..."

Charlie is the first to recover the power of speech.

"This is outrageous."

"I know!" I say, still completely amped to be in agreement with her. In fact, I am so pleased not to be arguing with Charlie about the Rat Burglar this time that my reaction to what is transpiring on-screen sounds more joyful than I mean it to.

"This is beyond credulity. This is just beyond...beyond."

"Beyond beyond. Right. I think so, too."

"I can't even..." And Charlie makes strangulation gestures at the screen.

"Same here!"

"I hate that miserable Spivey."

"Me too! Oh man, this is great!"

"That thesis she is espousing is mine."

"Mine too!" I say, comradely and bright. Then, one moment later, "Wait, what?"

"That is my argument. Mine. I sent Spivey a paper for publication in her journal on this very subject, making the same exact arguments, using the same exact examples, and she gave me a pass. A thanks-no-thanks. She said the same stupid things that my department head told me. I could practically hear her laughing when she wrote the note. And now she has the gall to come on TV and pretend it's her scholarship. It's simply...rank...plagiarism."

Needless to say, I am vexed. I had thought, briefly, that Charlie was coming around to my side. Probably because of the day's events, I am not capable of exercising the restraint that is normally required to dodge the subject. I sense a flare-up coming. Before it occurs, however, there is a moment when I can still pull back, but I don't. Whenever I have this argument with Charlie I always lose my cool. Probably it's because she's a professor and is accustomed to polemics and I most often argue with two-dimensional characters painted on canvas, but I always end up feeling wrong. And not just in a factual way. I feel as if everything I have ever done since that day in the Chaffee Planetarium is wrong. Like my whole life is wrong. Which makes me tetchy, and tonight, even though I have a dreadful checkmate feeling, I am incapable of stopping myself. So we have at it. Boy do we ever. We argue over whether it's theft, who has the moral/legal/financial right to various works, and, like all of New York City, like the whole country, we argue over those five words: who is the Rat Burglar.

My dialectic is not characterized by dignity and sangfroid. When Charlie affirms her belief in the Polecat business, I make cheese-gobbling noises to which I append, with a finger pointed at the TV, "Rat!" When she expounds on the economics of the museum industry[36] I can't resist making an overbitten, gnawing gesture. When she says something further about war and the abuses of first/third-world diplomacy,[37] I hold my hands up to the TV in the manner of a B-movie director parsing a scene and reiterate, "Filthy rat!"

---

36 Annual income from museum admission far outstrips ticket sales to all sporting arenas of all sports combined; of course museum boards have a vested interest in acquiring and retaining their works, she says, regardless of how they are attained.

37 Often the thieves are diplomats or journalists or soldiers who have immunity or privilege or power by fiat. What is a country like Benin to do when British troops help themselves to their sacred gold? What could Egypt do to stop Napoleon from taking the Rosetta Stone? Has diplomacy helped the Greeks recover the Parthenon Marbles?

But the real goat-getter is what I do when Charlie is giving me a précis on the state of things in Iraq[38] and the beneficial role that the "Polecat" plays in returning cultural treasures to their countries of origin: I make a gun gesture, squeezing off a few self-righteous rounds, and say, "I'll tell you what someone needs to do. They need to shoot the fucker."

Charlie makes a mortified, goose-faced look.

"Oh, Otto. You can't mean that."

I am presented with another prospective pullback moment. Again I ignore it. I fire off another imaginary fusillade and say, "I'd do it myself. Shoot him dead dead deadski."

My childish potshots aren't helping. Neither is my blood-lust. A third problem is my hard-on.

While Charlie gesticulated at me/toward the TV/to the heavens, the sheet fell away from her. Her hair is pulled back, half in a kind of haphazard, semicoiled, nearly Grecian bun, and half trailing down her strong back and over her beauti-ful collarbones and between her breasts. When she shakes her head at my disetiquette, her hair and skin spray fragrance into the room, making my dick twitch with interest.

As soon as I feel it I issue immediate orders for detumes-cence, which, of course, only make it worse. It's like vascular quicksand: the more I fight the worse it gets. There aren't many places to hide when all you're sporting is a towel, and the sight and smell of Charlie naked, her mouth moving at me, is too much, and soon I have an aching, full-salute erection, an excla-mation mark made flesh. It won't go away, it won't diminish, and, worst of all, it won't quit pushing at the knot in the towel.

---

38 She says it's the most widespread looting since World War Two. She also says something about who is doing the looting, but I'm not really listening. I'm deafened by outrage.

I'd like to help it, but I can't. Charlie is plenty beautiful under normal conditions, but when she's angry, when she's fired up about something, then look out. She is absolutely irresistible: proud, passionate, vivid with life. It's thrilling even when we're arguing about a subject that rankles as deeply as the Rat Burglar.

Weird? Perhaps.

Convenient? Certainly not.

As I have never been in this situation before, I have no precedent to use as a guide for conduct, and so I choose simply to ignore it. Which isn't easy. If there is one thing an erection wants, it's attention. It isn't reasonable. It strives. It filibusters. It demands to be heard. When I feel the towel slipping it seems to me that I have two options: sue for peace with expedition, or try to nuke the whole thing and storm off before I am disrobed.[39] Alas, I do neither. I just stand there as the towel unwraps, falls, snags momentarily and spinnakers proudly in space for a few rebellious seconds, and then slips to the ground.

To those of you for whom this is a novel experience, let me assure you: arguing with the woman you love—in fact, endorsing the murder of the cherished idée fixe of the woman you love—while wagging at her in an imperious manner both finger and cock does not conduce to peacemaking. No it does not.

The debate screeches to a halt and Charlie looks me up and down, scoping head to hip—confounded, yes, amazed even, ensnared in some kind of curiosity as if viewing an incomprehensible Dada painting.

In the silence of her contemplation the TV babbles on about theories of identity. Doreen has moved to the street and is polling the average citizen. The nominations are imbecilery:

39 Although how this is to be accomplished in one's own home is not clear.

Colin Jepson, a jewel specialist. Dez "the Clock" Keeler, a former member of the intelligence community. I hear a Crummy Markovich or two, and while it's true that Crummy has blue eyes, he's also about a hundred pounds heavier than the Rat Burglar. There's a Simon McCord, even though his ball pythons have all been remanded to the custody of a children's zoo and he's serving ten to twelve upstate. Someone else thinks it's Pituitary Jones, an absurd nomination not only because he doesn't have the skills[40] but because I have reported many times that the Rat Burglar is nearly twenty inches shorter than the seven-footer, no matter what that French cop says.

But what really gets me is when Doreen holds the mike up to a guy's face and he says "Jimmy the Hat" while making a swashbuckling gesture meant to evoke the flourish of Jimmy taking off someone's hat, a pantomime that produces in me both marvel and disgust: first the Rat Burglar gets all that cult celebrity and now Jimmy the Hat, a bloodthirsty killer who scalps people and dismembers innocent dogs, gets people on the street raving for him like a rock star and impersonating his murder style like it's the freaking Macarena.

I am also outraged because while, yes, it's technically conceivable that the Rat Burglar could be Jimmy the Hat,[41] it is insulting to me to suggest that muscle could roll a pulse with my qualifications. It is my professional opinion that Jimmy the Hat couldn't rob a tip jar, much less the Prado.

The imputation offends my entire canon. I have had enough. That it is impossible to manifest an air of injured majesty while

40 PJ, after all, cut the green wire.

41 Jimmy the Hat is like the J. D. Salinger of muscle; no one has ever positively identified him and there are no existing photographs; his only ID is the image of a hat with a knife thrust through, Cupid-arrow style.

arguing with a mutinous, questing phallus pointering about the room does not stop me from trying. Huffily I snatch the remote from Charlie and shut off the TV.

But Charlie protests—she isn't done watching; this is her whole career being stolen right in front of her on national TV—and thrice I am offered a chance at détente and yet again, as in some biblical parable of pride and consequences, I refuse it. I do not surrender the remote. She grabs at it, with surprising alacrity, and obtains a handhold. A brief struggle ensues, which terminates in me losing purchase on the remote in a way that causes my hand to slap, accidentally but with considerable force, the gracile angle of her jawbone where it meets her ear.

Charlie makes a tiny sound, so remote it sounds as if it's a deep subspace signal picked up by outdated astronomical machinery. It's unclear if her emission is of injury or rage. She rubs her jaw. Her eyes, dilated to wet black nickels, stare at me in a way I hope they never do again.

My heart beats like a drumroll, torturing my earlobe.

But, incredibly, the words that come out of my mouth aren't of apology. They approximate: "Well, you should have listened to me."

Which isn't what I mean at all.

What I mean is, "I fear for my career. I am terrified that I have endangered your life. I am humiliated by my on-job performance and am regularly mocked by my colleagues. I feel emasculated by all of the above, and by the fact that I am too cowardly to propose to you. The source of all this, ultimately, is the Rat Burglar, whose work, by a cruel irony, you happen to champion. These stressors have joined in a perfect storm of personal anguish that made me assert myself in some bullheaded way, for which I'm sorry. I need you to forgive me, and to listen, for I am going to tell you everything, the whole truth of my life, so that you can understand. That is what I need, I now realize. I need you to understand. I need you to hear the truth of my life, understand it, and love me anyway."

While I am trying to formulate a facsimile of these sentiments Charlie dresses,[42] regards me and my deflating erection one final time with an air of inscrutable electricity, panthers down the hall, and disappears from sight.

When she's gone I don't have any feeling of victory or justified indignation. I don't consider my views on theft or ownership as solidified or vindicated. I don't congratulate myself for having the courage to endorse Herk's idea that someone should kill the Rat Burglar, even if I didn't one hundred percent mean it. Instead, as I sit on the corner of my ravaged bed, alone in my room with the sense-memory of Charlie's body heat fading from my skin, her fragrance dissipating, I feel only that the Rat Burglar has stolen something else from me.

I'm the Mang?

The next day I ace the comps. They don't post scores until the end of the day, after everyone has tested, but I can feel it. I nail the plastoperceptivity module. I correctly deduce the telltales of all the various talent and muscle. I identify the odor

---

42 So rapidly that she doesn't bother to locate her bra in the shipwrecked bedding.

signature of every toxin.[43] I'm totally up-to-date on who's who in mobland.[44] My visual is both sharp on the detail segment and instantaneous in the kinetic samples, and I record few, if any, saccades. Taste is solid, haptic strong, olfactory rocks. In fact, I am so jazzed I do this great thing on auditory. When I've got the headphones on and we're down to decibel fractions, I spy on the attendant in the booth behind me by focusing hard on a metal joint in the wall molding that gives just enough reflection to make out which button he's going for. Before the guy even presses it, I stick up a left hand and say, "Left!" When I see him go for the other one I shoot up a right and say, "Right!" For a few tries he obviously thinks I'm horsing around, or just playing the odds or something, but when I get it right every time, before he lays a finger on the button, he freaks.

He's thinking: subjects sit at a table facing a wall with their backs to the attendant. How is this happening? But I play it innocent, and it makes him nuts. It's probably not nice, but I have so successfully channeled my bad Charlie energy into positive comps-taking energy[45] that I can't help myself.

I am so amped, in fact, that when I encounter Schermer and his asshole friends—in this case, Murgos, Iovine, and

---

43 Tougher than it sounds. A lot of these toxins are engineered to avoid detection. Usually only the newest ones, ones that have yet to be refined, have any odor. Nix, for example, is instantly recognizable. It smells like a potpourri of sperm whale feces and hamster vomit. Even Schermer can get that one.

44 Also no easy feat. Now that Azar has killed so many of his rivals there are a lot of underlings adrift and looking for freelance work. It's tough to keep them all straight.

45 Herk would be proud.

DeLesseps—it doesn't really bother me. I apprehend them when I push out of the air-conditioning into the heat of the parking lot. My time slot was late in the day, and it's already dark outside, but Schermer et al are discernible by their snickering. I consider flipping them the bird but I think of Herk's Taoist pacifism and just smile at them with what I hope appears to be the indulgence of a patient adult indulging the antics of a bunch of squealers rioting at the kids' table. Even when they do their defecatory pantomimes—Murgos putting his palm-heels to his mouth and blurting out a farty noise; DeLesseps making unmistakable propeller-like eructations; Iovine sticking out his tongue and flapping it against his lips, producing a raspberry-style flatulence while aiming at me the business end of his gastrointestinal tract—I keep composure.

Normally I crumble at moments like this, but tonight I am all rubber and they are so totally glue. I just grin and nod, as if to say: I can bear any puerility you generate, for I have just made the comps my bitch, and it will be I who works the Nakamura job, not you cretins.

Part of my unusual invulnerability is due to my performance, no doubt, but I am also buoyed by the sense of triumph I feel from my locker still being free from adult sanitary napkins or containers of Imodium or whatever Schermer usually thinks is funny.

I hazard a hope: maybe things are turning around for me.

Maybe I've paid my dues. Maybe I get this floater gig, give the commission to Deke, get the damned title, and sail away into my future with Charlie.

Maybe I get my clean getaway after all.

I am so pleased with the novelty of my coolness that it takes me a few moments to process the noise originating from over by the Reliant. Even at a distance, through the darkness of the parking lot, with the struggle and complaint of the BQE in my ears, I discern the sound of a brass-tipped umbrella crunching in the gravel. When I get to my car Detective Nunes looks the same as she did in her photo spread. Grim mouth, alert blue eyes, her shoulders hunched up as if struggling against a strong wind even in the breathless summertime air. She smells of stale menthol and rayon and gasoline and pencil shavings and body odor and fear: the precinct.

"Otto Starks?" she says.

I grunt.

"Cheryl Nunes. I'm taking over the Rat Burglar investigation."

"Hunh," I say as if it's news to me. Totally dull, irrelevant, nonthreatening news.

"I've been trying to clear up some gaps"—this word is freighted with innuendo; she knows I know about Fritzy sitting on the investigation—"and I'm hoping you can help me with some things."

"I already typed up a report for Janus," I say. "They'll forward it. Can we do this later?"

"We can wait to discuss the events of last night," she says. "I'd just like some quick background. I'm sure I don't need to tell you that you are uniquely qualified to provide insight on the Rat Burglar." When I don't respond immediately, Nunes says, "Ever hear of the Polecat?"

"The what?" I'm not sure why I lie about this. It's just instinct, and I instantly regret it. It's not a good way to start a relationship with a person trained in detecting prevarication and guilt.

"How many other Janus pulses have been hit by the Rat Burglar?"

"None."

"To your knowledge, how many years has the Rat Burglar been active?"

"Several. At least his calling card has only been on record for a few years. There are infinite other jobs he could have pulled without using that signature. After narcotics, the black market in stolen and looted art is the most lucrative in the world. There isn't exactly a shortage of talent."

"When has the thief been most active?"

"The last year."

"Interesting. O.K. Now I'm going to read you some items. You tell me what you know about them. What do you say?"

In this light Nunes has a complexion the color of burned mashed potatoes and pinched, too small eyes, like shoelace holes, that get smaller when she looks at me.

"I'd really rather go home right now. I've had a tough couple of days."

"Hemofex?"

I sigh with resignation. A woman who is so meticulous she carries her umbrella on cloudless days isn't going to be deterred because I make a turn-key gesture. I tell her what she wants to know. "It's a kind of cyanogen chloride. A blood agent."

"Lethal?" she says, her gaze seeming to shift in and out of focus. She has hardly looked me in the eye once. She seems to be addressing my shoulder, then my waist, then my feet. It's unsettling.

"It's a schedule one chemical weapon," I say, as if she just asked me if I enjoy oxygen. When she stares at me I say, as patiently as I can, "Yes. It's lethal. Extremely."

"Not to you, though, apparently."

To this I just shrug. The less anyone knows about my gift, the better.

"And how about Perrelet?"

"Trade name for a commercialized V-series nerve agent. VX, specifically."

"Lethal?"

"Oh yeah."

"Triphosgene?"

"A pulmonary agent. Pulmonary edema is induced by even a small quantity, within minutes. Also schedule one."

"Anything else notable about them?"

The only way Nunes could know this is if she has been looking into my file, either with Po-Mo's assistance or via a court order. Not good.

"I was hit with all of them, if that's what you want to hear, yes."

"When?"

"I don't know. My first year at Janus. Azar's men, mainly. Frankie Nickels hit me with four shots of triphosgene on his last job. I had a sore throat for weeks."

"So pre–Rat Burglar?" she says, addressing my lapel.

"Yes."

"How about Kolokol-9 and norisol and oxonone?"

"Kolokol-9 is the latest iteration of Kolokol-1, the psycho-chemical gas used to such poor effect in the Moscow theater siege. Nine is much cleaner. Norisol is another incapacitating agent. Ditto oxonone."

"Lethal?"

"No. None of them. And all have benign side effects. And before you ask it, yes, I was hit by all of them by the Rat Burglar. And I'm sure you know all about pachylax."

Nunes's face reveals nothing.

"So pre–Rat Burglar you were subject to all lethal toxins."

"Not all…"

"Some lethal, some non," she concedes. "But during that time you had a perfect retention record. Spotless. And then along comes the Rat Burlgar and in about nine months you get rolled three times—excuse me, *four*—by the same thief, who uses only nonlethal drugs. That's an awfully considerate brand of thief. How would you account for something like that?"

"The guy's just getting lucky. He probably guessed that since none of the lethal drugs were working on me, I hadn't worked as hard on the nonlethals. And he's right."

"There is no video footage of the Rat Burlgar. No audio. No hair. Not a flake of dandruff. No DNA whatsoever. No evidence of any sort. Convenient, no?"

"I've given you a physical description. And," I say, "if you read my retention failure report, you'll see that he has blue eyes."

Nunes ignores this. "The Rat Burglar has never been stopped. Never caught, never foiled, never left any useful clues. In every other case of attempted burglaries of sites you were working you were able either to facilitate the apprehension of the thief or to make observations—truly remarkable observations—that led to arrest and conviction. But with the Rat Burglar you haven't been able to provide, well, anything. Why is that?"

I say nothing. With some cops this is enough. This time it isn't.

"Something else I've had a hard time figuring out. The Rat Burglar takes you for a tribal African mask valued at less than half a million dollars when at the same facility, not even two rooms away, another pulse—a less qualified pulse, according to Mr. Polizzi-Molanphy—is sitting on over ten million dollars' worth of artwork. But instead the Rat Burglar chooses your room, and your mask. How would you explain something like that?"

"Perhaps he has a crack problem. Maybe he's bad with numbers. Could be he is a genius with door locks but not so bright about the criminal underworld. How the hell should I know?"

"I'm going to have to disagree with you there, Starks. It sounds like an inside job to me." Nunes's eyes go small and fierce, bird-bright. "And that makes you the most favorable candidate."

She's not wrong. Something smells like shit in Denmark, all right, and it's me, figuratively and literally, but I do my best not to get it.

"Me?" I say. "You like me for this?"

Nunes stabs a cigarette in her mouth, lights up, exhales on me. Schermer and those idiots can't hear the dialogue at this range, but they see me cough and that makes them yuck it up.

"Like you? Right now I love you for this, Starks. Right now you're my leading man. You're my favorite. You're my goddamn prom date."

"If I'm a mang[46] on jobs that have totaled twenty million dollars, why aren't I living the life? Do multimillionaires drive K-Cars? Do we beg our bosses for our jobs? If I'm the inside man, then what am I doing with my haul?"

It is then that I realize that Nunes's roving glance is not merely a personal foible. She has been checking me out, and, I now see, I am not the only one with visual acuity. She reaches out and extracts from my chest pocket the Najad brochure I salvaged yesterday from my locker. It is in vivid full color with the comprehensive digital workup of my boat, complete with the name stenciled across the transom and everything.

"Good-looking boat. These things go for, what, a couple

---

46 Robert Mang, a retention engineer who famously used his knowledge of alarm systems to steal $65 million worth of Renaissance figures from a Vienna museum.

mil? That's a lot of boat for a pulse who's been downgraded to backup, don't you think?"

It occurs to me that if Nunes compares my bank records to the money I've put down on the boat, there will be certain discrepancies. Part of me wants to come clean to her about Deke right now, but my relationship with him isn't exactly legal, and I'm already close enough to getting the axe.

"*Clean Getaway*? Interesting name. There's a term for that."

"Irony?"

"Appearance of guilt."

Again I say nothing, hoping that silence conveys not guilt but disdain for the ludicrousness of this line of questioning.

"Know what they do to pulses in the joint, Starks?"

"Do people honestly still call it the 'joint'?"

"I could arrange to have you in the same ward as Frankie Nickels. I know he'd love to see you. How do you feel about that?"

With one hand Nunes plays with the butt of her handgun. She pulls it half out of the holster, then reinserts it. It's only a gesture. Not really a nervous tic—I cannot imagine Nunes being nervous—but maybe a habit of security, making sure it's still there. Or available for immediate withdrawal. But I am so terrified of guns—even theoretical guns—that the sight of real gunmetal from a real gun, in someone's hand and half out of its holster and glinting in the weak light of the overheads, makes me quail. A car backfires and I try not to flinch but the chorus of howling from Schermer's corner of the parking lot tells me I fail.

Then I make a mistake. I'm terrified, naturally, the way anybody would be while facing a gun and considering jail time with Frankie Nickels, but I don't want to look it, so I resort to using a line I heard Herkimer utter once when he was getting chewed out by Po-Mo, but when I say it—"Doesn't make me want to write a letter home to mama"—I garble it unintelligibly. Plus it seems, after I utter it, that it does not exactly make any kind of sense.

"Don't try to talk tough, Starks. You're not smart enough."

Again, my gut tells me it's wrong, but I can't help offering another desperate Herkism. Again it makes no sense. "Putting butter on it don't make it taste no better."

Nunes's smile is thin and straight and unpromising, a slit of light under a closed door.

Then I make a related mistake. The voice that comes from the general direction of my mouth, and which sounds remarkably like mine, says, "There's only one problem with your scenario, Nunes: no evidence." As soon as it's out, I realize I have just uttered criminalese for "I am one hundred percent guilty and I double-dog dare you to find out how I did it."

Nunes sighs with something akin to disappointment, as if she knew very well this would be the outcome of our discussion and is a little bored by it. "Give me the Rat Burglar and I'll make sure you don't do any time. That's the only protection you're going to get. But this is a one-time offer."

"But I don't know who the Rat Burglar is. I'm not involved," I nearly plead.

"I'd rather have him, Starks, but I'll settle for you if I have to."

"I'm just a pulse!"

"Give me a better option than yourself, Starks, or you're going down. Your choice." Stunned, I say nothing. After a long, portentous silence, Nunes shrugs, turns on her heels, and, leaning on the umbrella with her back hunching up against a nonexistent wind, starts crunching away through the gravel parking lot.

Me vs. the Goldfish

One of the many downsides of living a double life is that it's hard to get close to anyone and you therefore have very few people to confide in when the sudden, mortifying need for it materializes. It doesn't help if your girl is still angry at you about last night and does not pick up the phone, even after three emasculating calls within ten minutes. Neither is it very useful if your only good pal also isn't summonable. I sort of wish I could call the K'plua—he would know what to do—but that isn't a productive line of thinking. The only thing I have left is the Snug.

The Snug is a mime bar on Stanton. In some ways it's a weird choice for a down-and-out pulse—there is nothing more depressing than a bunch of deadbeat mimes streaking their whiteface with tears and gasping with shame when they get drunk enough to drop out of character—but it's in my old neighborhood and it gives me a chance to walk my old streets. Also, no one from the biz would ever slum this low, so it's safe for Herk and me to meet here.

Sitting on a stool in the corner, dropping zaxodoxin and Antabuse into the conga line of shots in front of me, I try to think my way out of it. I can't. I look at my reflection in the mirror behind the bar. I don't like it. Neither does the mime hovering over my shoulder. I know this guy. The nosiest, he considers himself the alpha mime and likes to do orangutan-like impersonations of Herkimer when he isn't looking. Now he is clasping his hands prayerfully under his chin and making lip-smacky gestures while pretending to swallow shots in an attitude of despair.

Fucking mimes.

Then his face is obscured in the darkness of a shadow I know by heart.

"Hey, Herk," I say. "Where you been? I've been calling you all night."

"Sorry. Had a date with a Goldfish.[47] Phone was off. But the date went bad and I decided that I needed some Trace time." Herk whistles at Tracey but she is still mad at him from the last time he was here and she just keeps on slicing those lemons. "Besides, I wanted to see how you did today. I mean, I know you always boot glute on the tests, but you know—"

"I've been off lately, you mean."

---

[47] Six months ago, after a big rainstorm, Herk found a goldfish in a puddle on the sidewalk, gasping for breath. There was no broken glass or anything, no plastic bag nearby—it was eerie, displaced, like something out of a Magritte. Then Herk saw the pet store with the open window. He scooped the fish into his water bottle and confronted the clerk at the register, who confessed that they had discarded it because it developed a kind of rash or fungus or something that made it unattractive and that could conceivably be spread to the other fish in the tank. So they just threw it out. Sidewalked the sucker. It required all of Herk's self-discipline not to throw the guy out onto the sidewalk, too, and make him gasp for air. Instead he took the fish home and put up an ad on Craigslist, telling the story of the forsaken goldfish and pleading for an adoption. He even attached a picture of the puddle where it was found and one of himself holding up the fish in a glass bowl. The ad provoked over a hundred responses in its first day, nearly all of which were from single women, and many of which featured touched-up photos of themselves and heartfelt avowals to foster the poor little guy. It was then that Herk realized what he had stumbled onto: pure womanizing gold. From that first ad Herk got twelve dates with women whom he

"Trace! Jesus! Come on!" he calls out. The mimes all crane at Herkimer, their painted faces doughnut-mouthed at the outburst. The alpha mime makes wailing expressions and prostrates himself on the bar, begging for a drink from Tracey. But Herk acts like he doesn't see Alpha. Even the little muscles around his eyes don't flinch. His Taoist calm is absolute.

"Yeah," he says to me. "Basically."

"Well, not today," I say tonelessly. "I rocked it."

"Yeah?"

I shrug.

"You get confirmation, then? They already release scores?"

"Anytime now. Waiting on the text."

"Trace!" Herk again waves at Tracey, who is now ignoring him by breaking up clots of ice with the scooper like her life depended on it. He produces his new camera from his pocket and zooms in on her with smirky, prehensile interest. "God, that woman's a pain but I love watching her bend over those bottles. Look at those tits. You could breast-feed China with those tits."

"She's got to be sixty years old, Herk."

"But she's still beautiful, man."

He shakes his head as if witnessing a sublime revelation of the universe.

"She's married," I tell him.

"Six foot. At least. Maybe six-one. And look at that grip

could screen for size. In the intervening months this snare provided him with nearly countless sentimental women won over by his guardianship. He calls these women, with some ungenerous condescension, his Goldfish Girls, and there are so many that when he tires of them and tosses *them* out onto the sidewalk, he often has to work hard to dodge their stalking. Which they do. Like Herkarazzi.

strength. I bet she could crack coconuts with those hands. Aloha, right? I mean, *aloha,* baby."

"She doesn't even like you."

"And look at that ass. I'd like to chew on that like a plus-sized piece of ass jerky." He makes a squinty expression that is a mixture of frustration at his drinklessness and carnal admiration for her stature.

"Well, that's great about the comps," he says after he snaps a pic and gets it out of his system. "That's the first step in catching the fucker."

"Sure. Next stop for the Rat Burglar: Rikers Island."

"You don't sound too thrilled about it."

"No, I am. I've just got some...personal shit going on right now."

"All this time you've had a personal life and you haven't told me?"

I'm about to spill it to Herk but am foiled by the intercession of a former Goldfish whose name neither of us remembers. She attaches to his arm and ingratiates herself by offering her drink, which he downs. That buys her the ticket for entry, all right; she nuzzles his shoulder with her breasts and it's open sesame. He puts his arm around her. She says something she thinks is too quiet for me to hear, puts on her best Olan Mills smile, and offers her bosom for the camera.

Disgusted, I pop a few Perrelet and take another shot. I'm untouched by the liquor, naturally, but after the pills I've got a little buzz working, and at first I don't notice Alpha behind me, pantomiming swallowing a handful of pills and rubbing his stomach. What else can you do with a mime?

"Fuck off," I tell him.

As the Goldfish giggles and poses, my cell vibrates against

my leg with an incoming text. The subject heading says NAKA-MURA RESULTS.

Schermer: 694. Starks: 687. Herkimer: 641. Ellis: 640. Iovine: 636. Murgos: 630. Sharp: 569.

At first it does not compute.

At first I think it's a typo.

Maybe that six should be an eight? Maybe it's the result of sloppy penmanship; they didn't complete the double loop for that first digit. That makes sense: 887. Or maybe it's an inverted nine: 987. The six is right by the nine on the keypad, isn't it? That's possible, right? I keep waiting for it to change, but it doesn't.

My heart crumples like a piece of tinfoil and rattles around inside my chest.

The cell vibrates again and a second envelope swoops into the screen.

C me 1st thing Mon morn. PoMo.

I don't even look to see what I'm popping. I just squeeze the lids off the bottles and throw them back. There are so many pills in my mouth I can't get them down—there are so many pills that Kobayashi would have a hard time getting them down—and I choke on the wad and spit it back up onto the bar, making a Pollock-like spray of bright multicolored pills and milky spit.

Three of the pills, I see, are long, red, torpedo-shaped ones: Nix.

Thirty damn milligrams' worth. A record for me. Probably a record for Guinness.

Fuck it. I lube my throat with a gusher of whiskey, claw up the mess of them, Nix included, stuff them back in my mouth, and force it all down. This time they go. It only takes about fifteen seconds for me to feel the sting.

Oh yeah, I think. That one's going to leave a mark.

It hurts plenty but it doesn't distract me from the score. I feel as if a trapdoor has opened under my feet and I'm falling, falling, falling. Where do I land? Where else. On another stool. That's the ghost of Otto future: a fucking stoolie. That's what they should have as my gravestone. Not a cross or angel or obelisk or anything cool like that. Just one huge stool. Facing a fucking monitor like an underpaid, underappreciated, underchallenged jackoff with a girlie magazine and a bag of Combos.

Alpha notices what's transpiring and starts rubbing a knuckle in his eye socket with his mouth sagging in faux grief. Boo hoo hoo, he mimes. Then he swallows invisible pills, gulps an invisible shot, and recommences his silent sobbing. When he sees me clench my fist he mocks that, too. With one hand he wipes away weepy eyes, with the other he puts up a feeble duke.

"Hee-HEE!" goes the Goldfish.

Between the asshole mime and the braying sex laugh track behind me I feel both confused and tormented, a straight man caught in a Beckettian scene. My eyes perceive Alpha but my visual cortex processes it as Po-Mo, Deke, the Rat Burglar—all my failures—and I snap. For the second time in my life I throw a punch that is not an aerobics-class punch. It's all business. It's all malicious intent. It's a hard sinking left that appears to have admirable speed and targetry until, that is, it skims over the air above his head and twists me around in a swirling triple axel that sends me to the ground.

Alpha looms above me, making that face and throwing a fey drumroll of impotent punches. As I feel the sinus sting that heralds chaotic, prolific, playground-style tears, I see, at the edge of my visual field, a sudden movement and all at once the mime's neck is ensnared in Herk's fist. Alpha, who probably weighs two-twenty, and isn't dainty, leaps to his tiptoes in a sprightly rain dance of pain, thrusting up his chin in search of oxygen.

"Why don't you mime on someone your own size?" Herk says evenly.

With his chin the guy makes an eager, nodlike movement.

"What was that?"

Alpha nods again, wordlessly.

"I'm sorry, but I can't hear you." Through the fabric of his shirt I can see Herk's clublike forearm flex, making Alpha's eyes gush waterworks. The guy makes fending-off measures, clutching desperately at Herk's sleeve, which reveals skin halfway to the elbow—a violation of unfathomable Taoist principles—but it's only for a second. Instantly Herk increases his vise-grip and says, "I don't like it when people mess with my shirt, friend. It interferes with the signals, you know what I mean?"

Alpha makes a toadlike noise of compliance and speedily relinquishes the sleeve.

"Now, I think you owe my friend an apology, and I'm beginning to interpret your silence as bad manners." Herk squeezes again and from within his grip come several gristly popping noises. "But I'd like to offer you another opportunity to do the right thing. Now, what were you saying?"

Alpha makes a few agonized balloon-squeaks.

"Come again?"

"O.K., O.K.," Alpha manages. "I'm sorry. I'm really sorry."

Having made Alpha commit the most humiliating act of

submission, Herk lets him go. When he flees out the door Herk sends the Goldfish on her way, rights my stool, gives me a hand up, and invites me to sit.

"What's all that about, then?"

"I didn't get top score."

"Say what?"

"I got second."

"I thought you nailed it, buddy."

"I did. I swear I did. But I guess I didn't. I can't figure it."

"Hey, don't look so sad. There will be other gigs. It's not the end of the world. Right? Maybe your receptors were just down. You been eating avocados like I told you? You been downing that Spam?" Then, when he sees my expression, he says, tenderly, "Or were you distracted by...that personal shit you were about to tell me about?"

I can't take it anymore. I blab. I blab big-time. I tell Herk everything: the *Clean Getaway* on stilts in the boatyard; Deke keeping the title until I pay him off; the fight with Charlie; my cowardice regarding the proposal; my do-or-die agreement with Po-Mo; Nunes. Everything.

It's a little bit terrifying to hear all of it spoken out loud, but in another way it feels really good. I suddenly feel much less alone.

"Ouch," is all he says at first. Then, when he's stabilized: "So who took first?"

I pry out the word.

"Schermer."

"That talentless, shystie, Blistex-blowing motherfucker..." Herk's face knots in outrage. "How?"

"Beats me."

"That cumsock has never come within twenty-five points of you."

"I know. But that didn't stop him from laughing at me in the parking lot when I came out after the tests."

"That sheepfucker...wait. He was where when?"

"Parking lot. After my comps. At, I don't know, eight or something."

"His comps were this morning. Early. I saw him after mine. At ten."

"So?"

"Why would he still be at the office eight hours later? And why would he be laughing at you before any results were in? He's never laughed at you about comps before, right? He's never had anything to laugh about, has he? He's Mr. Honorable Mention, isn't he?"

"Maybe he was laughing about the pachylax."

"If he knew about the pachylax wouldn't you have had dog shit in your locker?"

I shrug. "Probably."

"How sure are you that you nailed the comps?"

"Pretty sure."

"Well...don't you get it?"

"Get what?"

"Schermer is on-site long after his slot. He's laughing at you before the results are in. He outpoints you for the first time ever. Are you connecting these dots?"

"Not really."

"Jesus, Otto. Maybe Nunes is right. Maybe there is a mang. But it isn't you. It's Schermer."

"Get real."

"Think about it. Schermer knows the pulse world inside out. He was at the same facility for the K'plua job. He distracted you, right? He was the floater on the Angkor Wat job. Entemena. The Inanna vases. He obviously has access to your locker. How tough would it be to switch one of your pills for pachylax?"

"Not that tough, I guess."

"You keep a written record of your tox resistances?"

"I do, actually. I have a journal. I make notes in there."

"You use a code or just plain English?"

"I guess I have a kind of shorthand but it's not Pepys or anything."

"What?"

"Nothing. I'd say it's ninety-nine percent intelligible."

"You ever keep it in your locker?"

"Sure."

"Well, that would explain how the Rat Burglar always knows precisely what toxins to use. Wouldn't it?"

"Do you know what kind of background checks Janus makes?"

"He's always had it in for you. So why not?"

"I just don't know."

"Well, let's go find out. If he's the inside man then you can clear your name. Hell, maybe you'll get the Nakamura job. Get Deke off your back. Maybe even get that boat."

"How are we going to find out if he's the inside guy?"

"How do you think, dumbass? Look for proof."

"Where?"

"Jesus, Otto. Where else? His apartment."

"Breaking and entering? You know we're pulses, right? Not talent? Do you even know how to pick a lock?"

"How tough can it be?"

"I don't know, Herk...."

Herk eyeballs my groin, making a suction noise that suggests raisinlike shriveling.

"Have you been listening to what I've been saying to you?

Do you understand that Nunes already suspects me? Do you think that getting caught breaking into Schermer's apartment is going to make me look innocent?"

Herk is getting impatient with me. It's hard for a man his size to hide his physiological response to elevated emotional stimuli. He didn't display even a molecule of sweat while throttling the mime, but now, as he is getting frustrated with my reticence, I can see dewy beads of water forming on the whiskers of his upper lip and the inverted U at the hairline of his brow. I can nearly hear his veins and capillaries constricting, the blood congesting.

"You know what? You're a great asstimer. World-class. Maybe the best I've ever seen. But Otto, your whole life is asstime. You never *do* anything. The universe isn't going to save you because you said pretty please. It doesn't reward slackasses. If you don't do something to prove your innocence, to get this inside guy, whoever he is, guess what? You are going to get fucked. It's not a hypothetical. It's not a probability. It's not a fucking Miss-Cleo-says-the-future-is-cloudy-so-who-knows-what-will-happen. It's for real. It is going to happen. It's guaranfuckingteed."

"Herk..."

"Look at that girl," he says, indicating the Goldfish. She is still working it, smiling at Herk from the other side of the bar, striking supposedly photogenic poses. "She's not just sitting around on her ass, feeling sorry for herself and rubbin' her nubbin. She's making an effort."

"She's pathetic," I say. "She's desperate."

"You're desperate, Otto! You two have that in common. What makes you different is that she is doing something. Not to brag on my own cock rock or anything, but she wants me, and look at her go. You have been in love with Charlie for a year; you have bought the ring; you have almost bought the boat—you're trying to start this whole new life—and yet you haven't popped the question? And your career, your freedom, and maybe your life are in danger—hell, Charlie's life may be in danger—and you still aren't doing anything? Does that make her pathetic or does it make you pathetic? Because from where I'm sitting, dude, you're the one with the Raisinets."

Herk toasts my glass sarcastically with his. He is upset with me enough to hit it harder than he means to and it makes a loud, clear, ringing note like a boxing bell, but it's impossible to tell if it indicates the start of something or the end.

Size Matters

Herk is my ICE,[48] my Linderman,[49] my Cosa Nostra, my Secret Service guy itching to jump in front of the bullet. It hurts to hear him speak ill of me, so I take the only logical and emotional action of which I am capable at this vertiginous moment: I run away. Double-time. With my head awash in poison, my eyes stinging with toxic fumes, my mouth smelling of sperm whale feces and hamster vomit, I stagger out the door and crabwalk to the corner of Pitt and Stanton, where I make a defeated semaphore at passing cabs. One finally stops and I try to convey my destination by making a steering-wheel

48 In Case of Emergency—a big deal for pulses.

49 The bodyguard from *My Bodyguard*, obviously, not the Long Island onion czar.

gesture and saying, "Orchard," then, with sadness, I realize I no longer live there, so I try to say, "Clinton Hill, Clinton and Greene," which also doesn't get much of a response. The trouble is that all the Nix I just shotgunned is suppressing respiration and making my lips feel as large and dead as a pair of suitcase handles, both of which give me an Elmer Fuddian accent that makes it difficult for the cabbie to decipher my meaning. While the meter runs, I administer the first dose of antidote. The delay doesn't exactly smooth things over.

"For the last time, where to, pal?" says the cabbie.

Thirty seconds later I garble at him.

"Where?"

Another injection, another thirty seconds later, I try again.

"Where?"

A third dose and yet another thirty silent seconds don't make him any pleasanter. Finally, as the guy froths in the front seat and spins around in a way that suggests he craves physical access to my person, I just write the address down on a receipt and present it to him, eyes downcast like someone trying to placate a wild animal with a nonthreatening offer of food.

"Fucking people," he says.

I am out of it enough not to notice how long it takes to get home, or how circuitous the route, but the fare glowing at me on the meter convinces me that we've taken the scenic route. It's possible we took the Brooklyn Bridge *and* the Williamsburg Bridge. Too weak to argue, I push a wad of bills of unknown denomination through the slot. I wait for a certain amount of time for change. I might have some coming. I might not.

Inside my apartment I don't fare much better. I follow a track that terminates at the wall, which is also where my nose close-encounters the plaster, leaving a bright red spot on the paint. It is involuted, flowerlike, and because my brain is so distracted by the chemical maelstrom raging in its neurons, it takes me a long time to realize how bad it hurts.

The answer is: bad.

Bad enough to require ice, which is in itself additionally painful: the wedding cake action figures are in there. But my brain is sufficiently fricasseed to forget about that until I open the door and see those schmucks staring at me. One of the women is definitely smirking at me and her groom, Chester Wellington III,[50] is giving me the eye.

I yank Chester off his pedestal and give him a punitive squeeze. At first I feel massive and powerful, like a Polyphemus in those old stop-action films grabbing Claymation mariners and biting their heads off. The exultation and the analogy are short-lived, however, for when I grip Chester he does not beg for mercy nor crumble into plastic dust, and when I insert his head into my mouth and clench down nothing gets severed, although my teeth do crack in a painful way.

Plan B is a dressing-down. You think you're so cool, I tell him. You think you're so cool because you've actually done something. But you're just a piece of plastic. And you're still an asshole. An English jerk. A bumlover.

Chester is unruffled by the pronouncement.

I give consumption another shot. I shove him as deep into my mouth as I can. His grape-sized head tickles my epiglottis and his legs protrude from my lips and I shake him violently like a dog with a rag in its jaws. This doesn't produce a notice-able response in Chester but it does in me. The combination

---

50 A name given by Charlie, who thought that he matched precisely the appearance of the hypothetical English gentleman that in her childhood she fantasized would want to marry a Maltese girl from Long Island, about which I cannot help feeling just a teensy bit jealous.

of Nix-laced toxins scouring my bloodstream and the way I am jiggling my braincase like a can of paint in a shaker generates a sudden irresistible urge to regurgitate, which I do, like a drunken cadet, in the sink.[51]

As this marks the inaugural puke of my whole life, I try not to reproach myself for my imperfect aim but I cannot help feeling generally negative about the whole enterprise. I am debating the merits of my InSinkErator vis-à-vis Chester's head when I see something startling: the old sport is anatomically correctish. He has a meaningful bulge in his zipper zone that is, honest to God, precisely the size and shape of a Raisinet.

That sobers me up.

And it makes me realize Herk's right. I don't do anything. I just prevent. That's what a pulse does: makes sure nothing happens. I'm a Sit Alone In a Dark Room guy. A Night In with a Book guy. I'm the guy who works up to the proposal and then shies away. "Do you know what that sound is?" I say from under the hood of the Reliant on the side of Lafayette. Then Charlie says, "What is it?" and I go, "Nothing."

In short, a chicken.

Static cling.

A trouser void.

I can talk all the Joseph Campbell I like, but the final fact is: Raisinets.

While squirming with the discomfort of self-examination I catch sight of my reflection in the metal of the refrigerator. It hardly counts as a reflection—most people wouldn't even register it as a blur—but I can see everything in excruciating detail. What I crave right now is some peppy outrage. A defiant, dauntless, possibly violent, You Looking at Me? moment. But

51 Mostly.

instead of a raving De Niro staring back at me in the metal I see only a bobblehead of fear and cowardice and inertia.

Then I start feeling another, non-Nix tingling. It starts in my gut and spreads up my spine like a constrictor vine. It has heat. It has thrust and purpose. It is, I realize, anger. Motile anger. Resolute anger. Get-up-off-your-ass anger. Revolutionary anger. It's not an exaggeration to say it is tumescent anger.

God it feels good.

With some difficulty I locate my cell, force my Nix-numbed finger to dial Herk's number, and, while moonwalking on a small, slippery quantity of out-of-bounds egesta, I slur angrily into the mouthpiece, "What's Schermer's address?"

Life of Crime

"You spare some, pretty lady? You so pretty you look like Michelle Pfeiffer and shit. Come on, Michelle Pfeiffer, you don't need that extra change in your pocket. All it do is go jingle-jangle-aing and make people stare at you as you walking with those fine legs of yours, and you don't need no more men staring at those stems than you already got. Am I right?"

I have been outside Herk's apartment on the corner of Eighty-ninth and Second for nearly twenty minutes, waiting and listening to this homeless guy with a burlap bag and a long-necked shovel sitting on the curb and spare-changing people. He's petitioned me five times, even though I gave him a dollar the first time he asked. I am not usually a sucker like that, but I am nervous about breaking into Schermer's and feel, like an underqualified[52] character in a Greek myth, that it would be a good idea to propitiate something, even if it's a nut with a shovel.

It's hot enough to deliquesce cardboard, but mainly I'm slicked in the sweat of tortured morality. The prospect of getting caught breaking and entering is worrisome, of course, but I also feel a deeper, stomach-based, karma-centered dread about it. My whole life I have dedicated myself to upholding the law and it seems very weird—like my yin-yang has short-circuited or reversed its charge or something—to be committing a crime now to prove my innocence.

I may not be doing the right thing, I tell myself, but at least I am doing.

The light on Eighty-ninth turns yellow and the blond woman shifts on her feet, preparing.

"Come on, Michelle Pfeiffer," he says, making creepy murder-movie scratching noises on the pavement with the tip of his shovel. "Turn around. You know you want to. Turn around and Catwoman back to me. Give me what I deserve. Give me what I don't deserve. Give me—"

The light goes green and the guy nearly prostrates himself, clawing and scuttling after her, but the woman is already gone.

"Bitch!" he yells, banging his shovel. "I didn't mean none of it! You're no Michelle Pfeiffer! You're Teri Garr, lady! You're Sissy Spacek!"

A hand attaches to my ankle. The homeless guy, writhing like a crushed insect, has me in a vise-grip and is weeping

52 And likely doomed.

into, and possibly purging his nose on, my sock. I whirl around and see that under everything—soiled Depression-era cotton overalls, sans shirt, a tattered and grease-stained stadium jacket, duct tape shoes, reversed bomber hat, heavy woolen gloves—the dirt-smudged face contorted in grief is Herk's.

I yank my foot away as if pulling out of a sinkhole.

"What the hell are you doing?"

"Hey buddy," he says happily. "Hand up?"

"Do you want to tell me what's going on?"

I pull Herk up and he leans in to me, conspiratorially, which isn't easy to take, as he smells like he looks.

"We're going to break into George Schermer's apartment!" he yells.

"Jesus, shut up!" I try to shake him by his lapels but he doesn't move a gratifying amount. "What are you trying to do?"

"See?" he says happily, looking around him at the crowd of people waiting for the light. Then, privately to me: "They don't give a shit. That's the beauty of it. When you're homeless it's like you're mute. No one listens to a word you say. And, if they can help it, they don't look at you either. Since what we're about to do—what *you're* about to do—isn't strictly one hundred percent legal, I thought it would be good if we discouraged people from looking at us." He pumps his fists, mock-victorious, and, ululating, makes lively humping motions at a guy in a sharp, English-looking suit, who pretends he doesn't notice anything. Then, again, to me: "See? What do you think?"

Herk uses his camera to zoom in on the guy's ass, upon which he dirty-dances at very close range, but the guy just keeps on inspecting his folded newspaper as if nothing is happening.

"I think...," I say, blinking, "I think you're a genius."

⇥⇤

Thanks to the supplies Herk had the foresight to bring along in his burlap bag, I am now attired in an oversized, duckbill-orange raincoat that looks like it has been used for fifty years or so in the service of mud-puddle gallantry to women with sharpened stilettos, one of those foam hands fixed in a Number One position that you see at sporting events, and a flaccid tam-o'-shanter with an enormous, anemone-like ball. I have also been put in charge of the shovel, which I use as a walking stick, pointy side down. We smell of unchecked biological processes, airplane glue, and fortified wine, but we are able to cruise completely unimpeded down Second Avenue. People say nothing, avert their gaze, mambo out of the way. We even split a phalanx of tourists loitering outside of Elaine's trying to get a look at the Thursday night posttheater crowd.

"How do we know he's out?"

"Checked the schedule. He's on a gig till midnight."

"That doesn't give us much time."

"Enough."

"You sure you know what we're doing?"

"Trust me."

Suddenly, half a block from Eighty-sixth, Herk skids to a stop, yanks out his camera, and zooms in on the corner.

"Oh shit." He spins around, hiding his face. "Tell you what. You keep going. I'm going to cut over a block or two and meet you there. You got the address. See ya!"

"Wait. What is it?"

Herk sighs with something like defeat.

"Janice DeMayo," he says, as if the name should mean something. "Ex-Goldfish."

"Which one?"

"Under that awning. Brown hair, these beautiful blue eyes, an ass that shakes like a doublewide maraca."

"She big?" I say, searching for her in the crowd.

"Like a sexpot manatee, dude."

"So you went out with her once. So what? Let's go."

Herk shakes his head vigorously.

"Why not? What are you, fifteen years old?"

Herk won't even turn around.

"She probably won't even recognize you."

"Can't take that chance, bro."

"What did you do that was so bad?"

He shrugs. "She's got a sister. A big big sister, if you know what I mean...."

"Oh, Christ. Don't be such a baby. I don't even see anyone that looks like her, and we don't have that much time."

I yank on Herk and, slowly, like a tree being uprooted from wet earth, he starts to give.

"One condition. You go first. Go down to the next block and use that vision of yours to tell me if the coast is clear. And give me your hat." Immediately he presses my tam-o'-shanter to his face, exposing only his dirt-camouflaged eyes, and breathes in relief. "That's better."

"Good. Let's go, already."

I cross Eighty-sixth, cast about for the Goldfish in the intersection and on the corner, see no sign of her, push down another block, search again and again see nothing, and wave Herk in.

"Thank God the hard part's done. Now let's go commit a crime," he says, making my heart wince.

⊰⊱

"What are we going to do, dig our way in?"

We are outside of Schermer's building. It's nicer than I expected. Doorman, underground parking, balconies. Through the glass of the lobby I can't see an infinity pool or peacocks running around but you get the idea that the management is looking into it.

"Or are we knocking out the parking attendant? Please tell me we're not knocking anyone out. I'm not going to—"

"Relax. There is no attendant. Just us and the parking gate. Now use that zoom of yours and tell me if you see any cameras in there."

Through the bars of the garage I scan for cameras. It's poorly lit, and the concrete castings, support beams, and overhead sprinklers make it tough, but I don't see anything obvious.

"Not that I can tell, anyway."

"Good enough for me," he says. "Now just wait a few minutes for the foot traffic to die down . . ."

As we sit there, being ignored, I ask Herk what's else he's got in the bag.

"*A-Team* stuff. Spray paint if there are cameras. Ski masks. Lock pick. Dirt—you want some? Bottle of Night Train. Good and Plentys. Game Boy, if we get bored. Glock. You wanna do a Mad Lib?"

"A what?"

"Mad Lib. They're easy. You just—"

"No. Glock. I thought I heard you say 'Glock.'"

He pulls the matte-black handle out of the bag, finger perilously close to the trigger.

"This?"

"You brought a fucking gun? A gun, Herk? Are you insane?"

"People often shoot at burglars, you know."

"We're not burglars! And we're not shooting back at anybody!"

"If someone shoots at you, you might change your mind."

"You're aware that most people who carry guns end up getting shot with them?"

"Then I recommend you don't give the gun to another criminal."

"We're not criminals. And just . . . just put it in the bottom of the bag, all right? I swear to God."

Even though I am, on a conscious level, aware of the ludicrous histrionic nature of the gesture, I find myself wringing my hands. In a sour flash of irony, it occurs to me that a gun would fit snugly inside such a gesture.

A long angry minute of silence passes.

"Do you want the dollar back that you gave me?" Herk says apologetically, nudging me in the ribs with the folded bill.

I sigh. I can't stay mad at Herk. He's an idiot, but he's also my only friend.

"Nah," I say. "Put it to the Night Train fund."

There is a lot of foot traffic, and for a while there's nothing to do but sit. "Herk," I say, "who do you think the Rat Burlgar is?"

"Aren't you sick of that question?"

"I just want to know your opinion."

"I don't know, man. Could be ex-military, I suppose. Not just anybody could have taken down those four French police unarmed."

"You could, probably."

He shrugs.

"Who else?"

"Who knows?" Herk says. "None of the names you hear make much sense. Not Dallas Spicer."

"Not Gurcop."

"Not Bolivar," Herk says, "not Oyama, not Keeler."

"Those guys all have brown eyes."

"So?"

"On the K'plua job I saw that the Rat Burglar has blue eyes."

"Oh. How about Doghouse Reilly?"

"Green eyes."

"Webster?"

"Brown."

"That Danish guy with the magnets has blue—"

"Dutch," I say.

"What?"

"The magnet guy is Dutch."

"Same thing."

"Herk, Danish is Denmark. Dutch is the Netherlands. The magnet guy is from Amsterdam."

"No, he isn't. And Amsterdam is in Holland, fool."

"Holland is a province of the Netherlands."

"You're out of your mind."

"Honestly. The magnet guy is from Amsterdam, which is in northern Holland, which is a part of the Netherlands. Where they speak Dutch. And some Flemish."

"You're such a clownus. They don't speak Flemish in Netherfuckingland."

"Oh yeah?" I say. "Then where is it spoken?"

"Flemland, dumbass."

"You're an idiot."

"Look, forget it, Carmen Sandiego. It's not the magnet guy anyway."

"Well," I say, "who else you got?"

"Pituitary Jones and Frito Kriskstein have blue eyes."

I snort. "Those guys cut the green wire."

"You kidding me?"

"No. They cut the green wire. It's like they never went to thief school."

Herk laughs out loud. It sounds like a Mack truck running over rumble strips.

"Dummkopfs."

"Seriously."

"Well shit," Herk says suddenly. "You know who's got blue eyes?"

"Who's that?"

"Nunes."

"Who?"

"Cheryl Nunes."

"Don't be dumb."

"Hey," he says, "she has the expertise, right? She knows art, she knows law enforcement. And arresting you would close the case on it, wouldn't it?"

"You think she could have taken out those French cops?"

"Hell, maybe. Who knows."

"I don't think so, Herk."

"Well, who cares what people think. We'll know the truth soon enough."

A minute later a gang of redhots passes us, brandishing purses and caroling celebrity gossip. When they're gone, trailing a cloud of warring perfume and hair product, Herk nods at the shovel. "Have at it."

I shrug and force the face of the shovel under the gate and start prying.

With one woolen-gloved hand Herk slaps his forehead. With the other he grabs the shovel from me, inserts it through the bars of the gate, laying the metal face upon the magnetic strip in the concrete that—it now occurs to me—detects the presence of a car. Servos whine and the gate creaks open.

"Well," I say defensively, "what do I know about breaking in? I'm not talent."

"Clearly."

We hustle through the garage and, courtesy of Herk's shepherding, away from the elevator, which, I am reminded, will certainly have cameras. Right-o. We take the stairs. When we get to eleven Herk fishes out a mirror from the bag and tells me to use it to look around the door and see if the hallway has any cameras. I don't see any but Herk isn't convinced, so we don our ski masks, and then, very suddenly, we are at Schermer's door. I press my ear to the wood and hear only the AC and the hum of the building itself. Herk extracts something from the bag and starts working the lock.

"Fuck!" he says.

"What?"

"It doesn't take Diner's Club." He holds up an age-cracked credit card.

"That's your lock pick?"

"I should have known. No one takes fucking Diner's Club anymore."

"You're an idiot. Why did I ever agree to this?"

"Let me try again." He does, and the brittle card snaps in half.

"Perfect," I say. "Now what?"

"Don't be so negative. I brought my master key." Herk makes a fist the size and shape of a woolly shot put. "Sneeze loud on three, will you?"

I sneeze, the wood around the brass fixture explodes, the door flies open, and then, just like that, we are staring into Schermer's apartment. The AC washes through the openings of the mask like the cool spray of a waterfall, but it doesn't comfort me. There is something frightful, rabbit hole–like, about the gaping doorway. It's a passageway through which I will exit my old life of preventing crime and enter my new life of committing crime.

I find myself reciting in my mind all sorts of words that describe unlawfulness. Infraction, arraign, misdemeanor, felony, penitentiary, shiv, bunk bitch.

To break in, I think. They break in. He breaks in. I broke in.

Oh God. What am I doing?

Herk is already inside. He is singing a tune—AC/DC's "Big Balls," I realize—and he turns around, pats me chummily on the genitals, nods me into the room.

And before I know it, I'm in.

Schermer's apartment has self-important faux-Federal appointments that aspire to create the veneer of aristocracy. The leitmotif is cordovan and dollar green and polished, Endusty surfaces. The bookshelf floating in the middle of the room makes it look like he bought everything ever published by Taschen, just to cover all the bases, and the window treatments look as if they have been lifted from the set of *Wall Street*. It is a room that wants very badly to have "comma Esquire" after it. Aside from being a reassuring testimony to the axiom that money does not purchase taste, however, it does not immediately offer anything useful.

"To burgle," I say out loud. "They burgle, he burgles, I burgled."

"Focus, Starks," Herk hisses at me from the bedroom. "We've only got an hour."

I try. I peel off the mask and affix it rakishly to the head of a Cupid statue, push my face flush against an air vent, and breathe deeply. It is refreshing but doesn't do much else. There is nothing incriminating in the living room, the kitchen, or the entryway. His datebook doesn't reveal any appointments with Azar; there is no suggestive "RB"[53] jotted anywhere. I am beginning to succumb to discouragement when I hear from the other room a very upbeat "Bingo!"

"You got something?"

Herk enters the room carrying a cardboard box and wearing, outside of his homeless getup, a matching set of frilly, mauve ladies' undergarments. He puts the box over his head, like a woman carrying a jug of water from the river, and gives me some grotesque Cuban motion.

"Schermer's got a girlfriend?" I say, amazed.

"I think Schermer *is* the girlfriend."

Herk unshoulders the burlap bag and throws it on the sofa, freeing up his hands, then shakes the box for me, sifting back and forth as if panning for gold, revealing hundreds of lavishly airbrushed tableaux of young boys engaged in erotic contortions with excited adult men. At the bottom of the box is a dildo so enlarged, and so curved, that it cannot possibly have any real-world application. It is the flawless and glossy taupe of Silly Putty, except for the head, which is an alarming, veined violet. Herk puts it to his hip then unsheathes it as if it were a scimitar and drops speedily to one knee in a dramatic, hood-ornament posture.

If we hadn't been laughing we would have heard the footsteps sooner. As it happens, though, I don't shush Herk or push him into the kitchen or duck behind the bookcase until Schermer is practically at his door.

"What the fuck?" signals his discovery of the disabled lock.

To convict, I think. They convict, he convicts, I am convicted.

In the reflection of a picture's glass I can see Schermer stalk-

53 Or "PC."

ing down the entryway.[54] He inserts a hand into the coat closet and it reappears grasping a massive shotgun.

This more or less eliminates all verbs from my head except for "to die," which presses against my skull with formidable energy.

"Whoever you are," says Schermer, "I know you know what this sound means." In the picture I see his hand jerk up and down, making the unmistakable and terrifying sound of a shotgun chambering: *chick-CHICK!* "This is a Remington 870. At fifty feet an 870 will knock you head over heels. At ten feet it will blow your head clean off. If you want to live, come out now with your hands up."

From the kitchen Herk is waving at me like mad and making a clasping gesture, up and down, in front of his face. Then I get it: the ski mask. I crane around but Cupid is in the corner twenty feet away. I cast about for a weapon of some sort but outside of coasters and crystal candleholders there is nothing within reach. The footsteps get closer. A drop of sweat falling from my brow to the floor sounds, to me, as loud as a snare drum. It occurs to me that this may be a metaphor of some sort: Otto Starks, betrayed by his conscience.

Maybe killed by his conscience.

Then the footsteps retreat. Schermer's reflection turns his back to me and enters the bedroom. Herk makes avid shooing gestures at me, urging me to the mask, and I make a madcap, tiptoe dash to the Cupid and run back behind the bookshelf, for which I at first congratulate myself. But Herk isn't celebrating. In fact, during my daring expedition across the room and back I see Herk waving me off like a baseball manager. He wants me to do something else. But I can't think on more than one thing when I'm tempting death, and it isn't until I return to my hiding spot behind the bookcase that I notice Herk pointing wildly

54 Also visible is the glossiness of his mouth; what *is* that stuff?

at the sofa. I pull the ski mask on and shrug at him. What does he want me to do this time? Stuff my shirt with pillows?

Then his hand assumes the shape of a gun.

The Glock is in the bag, he's telling me. The bag is on the sofa. The sofa is thirty feet away from Herk. It is five feet away from me.

Vigorously I shake my head, but then, with the *chick-CHICK!* of the shotgun echoing in my ears, I nod. I make a tentative half-step out from behind the bookcase then chicken out and go back. I brave another few steps, my fingertip tickling the polished leather of the sofa, then I high-step back again. I go back out and am bending fully extended over the sofa, within inches of the bag, when I hear footsteps and bolt behind the bookcase again.

"I don't want to kill anybody tonight, but I will," Schermer says, sounding like he means it. "I heard you. There aren't many more places you can be. Come out now and I'll let you live."

Herk is mouthing something urgent at me. He has the dildo in his hand and is making fervent clubbing movements with it. I wave him off. No, I mouth back. Hell no.

Hell yes, he says, conking the dildo at his head to demonstrate its exemplarity as a bludgeon.

I try to communicate that my reluctance is not just predicated on cowardice but on the fact that I am not renowned for the refinement or alacrity of my motor skills, and that there may be a risk-reward factor that should be considered before he throws at me what is at best an improvised cudgel that would, at any rate, be outclassed by even a much smaller firearm than the head-vaporizing 870.[55]

But Herk is not deterred. He points at Schermer, illustrating that his attention is focused elsewhere momentarily and,

55 Or a knife. Or a blackjack. Or, probably, a rolled-up newspaper.

while previewing for me his gentle underarm swing, pantomimes one...two...three...

And then the dildo is airborne. As it rotates, spins, and tumbles through the air in a nightmarish, Kubrickian slow motion,
the memory of all the things that have ever been tossed to me
and dropped—car keys, brewskies, small items of fruit—flashes
before my eyes. It is not any kind of positive visualization and,
consequently, when the dildo encounters my palm, flattened
by terror, slicked with sweat, it squirts like a greased water bal-
loon out of my grasp and clatters to the wooden floor.

The hard wooden floor. The polished hard wooden floor.
The gleaming polished hard wooden floor. Probably the last
floor, wooden or otherwise, I will ever see. For an instant it
produces in me powerful feelings of love for the floor.

Don't kill me yet, I think, I'm not done looking at this beautiful floor.

The dildo rattles on the transcendent floor, frisking between
my ankles like a contrite puppy. Instinctively I bend over to
pick it up and then: bang. I am showered in splinters and
the glossy confetti made from the shotgunned pages of the
Taschen collection. The fantastic hole in the bookcase is where
only nanoseconds ago, it seems, my head was located.

This time I don't delay. I leap out from behind the bookcase, dildo aloft, swinging it from the scrotum like a war hammer, and charge at Schermer, who, falling backwards, again
discharges the shotgun. There is an explosion that seems both
deafening and impossibly quiet and then, nearly simultaneously, I am aware of a violent wind scorching my face. I wonder
if I am now headless, but then I realize that it is the dildo who
is headless. The blast has missed me entirely but has vaporized
the entire business end of the dildo.

But I still have balls.

I vault onto Schermer and start flailing at his head with a fist reinforced, brass knuckle–style, with the contents of a plastic scrotum. My level of output, I have to think, is equal to that produced in defense of Charlie that day in front of the Frick—I am, after all, highly motivated; I passionately want to injure Schermer in a lasting way—but my results are much poorer. Not only do I fail to render him unconscious or make him cry out girlishly but I am unable to prevent him from gaining a position of superior leverage over me. I'm not pinned, but I am sustaining heavy damage on my skull. Luckily he can't get at my face, but he's all over my cranium. For some reason, it doesn't hurt yet. My head is ringing but my brain merely makes a note of the damage and files the pain away for future consultation.

One sensation that I do process is Schermer's hands around my neck and a sudden reduction in oxygen reaching my brain. Through the dildo dust fogging my vision I can·just make out my last hope: the bag is only a few feet away. I throw a hard elbow that connects with something sharp, presumably teeth, then dive on the bag and extricate the gun. I am unable to issue any orders or thrust it anywhere uncomfortable or humiliating, however, before Schermer tackles me and secures my gun-toting hand in a firm grasp.

We stagger together into the bedroom, where we smash various items of furniture without resolving the issue of gun ownership. I find it forced perilously close to my head, then Schermer discovers that it's nearly trained on him, and it seesaws like this for what seems like a very long time before there's another terrifying crack and my face is burned with cordite.

For a moment we both stop, stunned. I stare at Schermer. He stares at me. We both stare at the hole in the ceiling and the ballet of plaster dust floating down upon us. I stare again at Schermer and apprehend, too late to do anything except observe, that he has taken advantage of our intermission to throw a well-placed haymaker that connects above my ear. This time it hurts. It also sends me grapevining across the room and into a shelf that disgorges its contents onto my head as I slump to the floor.

For a moment I am occupied mainly with savoring the painful cacophony in my skull and the steel-wool taste of bloody ski mask in my mouth, but then I realize that one of the items scattered around me is a plate-sized piece of wood. I pick it up and see that its convexities are embellished with cloth, raffia, and cowrie shells. This seems relevant for some reason, but I can't figure why right away, and at any rate it's not as pressing as the barrel of the gun that is now leveled at my head, smelling of oil and burned metal and death.

"Say goodbye, fucker," Schermer says.

Then it clicks.

"The K'plua," I say.

"What?"

He cocks his head quizzically at me holding the mask and then, from somewhere behind him, something flashes like a fish in water and Schermer goes down hard. Herk smiles at me.

The K'plua's mouth is doing something, too, but I wouldn't say it's smiling. I know that it is just a wood carving and therefore not prone to buccinator plasticity, but it now appears as a split and ruptured-looking rictus—a terrible Ugolino gurn. The day of its theft it seemed plenty mad but now it looks absolutely ecstatic with outrage—disapproving, yes, certainly, but also judgelike and vengeance-ready.

I have really let it down.

Sportsmanship and the tenets of fair play require that I check to see if Schermer's all right, or at least alive, but instead

I take advantage of the situation and approach the unconscious body of my longtime foe coolly, with a Steve McQueen
swagger, and punch him in the head as hard as I can.

The moment isn't as triumphant as I would like, though.
Even to my ears, when I cry out "And a-one!" it sounds stupid and childish. I forget to say, "That's for the dog biscuits in
the locker, motherfucker!" as I had fantasized about doing for
so long. And there's something a little unfulfilling about smit-
ing a nemesis who doesn't move. It's like punching a stuffed
animal. Additionally, at the moment of impact, Schermer,
already knocked out, makes no noises of distress and I do:
something painful happens in my thumb and I let out a star-
tled yelp.

"Jesus," Herk says. "What did you do? Hit him with your
thumb inside your fist?"

I shrug.

"Who taught you how to punch?"

"Jessica," I say. "Cardio-kick. Tuesdays/Thursdays at seven."

"Should have fucking known. Is it broken?"

"I don't know. It still wiggles." I demonstrate this for Herk.

"It wiggles. Fantastic. I'm so relieved. Now grab that gun
and let's get out of here."

"The K'plua," I say, pointing.

"I see it. The cops will see it, too. I'd rather they don't see us.
Let's go."

"We were right!" I say joyously. "Schermer's the mang!"

"Congratulations us. Now let's *go*."

We sprint down the hall and into the stairway, two frightened figures in rancid clothing, one covered in blood and
skin-toned dildo dust, the other in a matching set of mauve
bra and panties, but by the time we get to the street, which is

soon swarming with cruisers and awash in red and blue lights, everything is stuffed into the burlap bag and we, more or less, are once again the same people we were two hours ago.

Except that I now have a chance.

I High-Beam the Dream

Given the considerable guilt I have charbroiling inside me over my night of breaking and entering/assault and battery/ attempted murder, combined with the superelectric thrill that things might be working out for me, I don't have a prayer of getting any rest tonight, so I do the only thing I can think of.

I go down to the boatyard to ogle my boat and wait for the news to break.

Amid the city's hungover stillness, the East River streamering between the gritty tumbleweed litter of Queens and the smutty glitter of nighttime Manhattan, I sit there and high-beam my sailboat. I have never laid eyes on it before. Since I still owe Deke—and since he still has the title—I never felt like I deserved to see it. Until today, the prospect of looking at it seemed like a heartbreaking reminder of failure and loss, like uttering the name of a stillborn child. I just couldn't bear it. But today is different. Today I've been staring at it for hours now—the sun is finally starting to turn the horizon a polluted iodine color and the heat is beginning to smother the gravel-filled lot of the boatyard—and so far I feel nothing but joy.

For about the five hundredth time I crack my Web phone and check to see if anything on Schermer has come over the net and, for the five hundredth time, it hasn't, so I just kick back and stare through the chain link at my boat. I'm having a haptic fit; I desperately want to touch it, but—last night notwithstanding—I am an obeyer of laws, an upholder of laws, and I still feel a crippling taboo about off-limit areas, so I force myself to be content with a visual.

In the brochure's digital workup the boat looked plenty cool but in person it is even sleeker and more hydrodynamic. The lines are graceful but masculine, the keel has a natural, porpoiselike curve, and the mast looks impossibly high, as if it would never clear the Verrazano. There are other boats in the yard, all buttressed by metal stilts—it looks like a hospital full of patients in extreme traction—but the numbers don't make my boat seem ordinary.

Deke may still have the title, but it finally feels like it's mine.

Correction: mine and Charlie's.

Ours. That's a big word.

I say it out loud a few times: "Ours."

But I experience an additional, complicated feeling, too, a feeling that if it weren't so fresh might be wistfulness but which instead is only pain: it was merely two years ago that I conferred to the East River, not even a half mile south, the last installment of the last remains of Pinkerton. Despite my best efforts, the memory comes to me. The boxes of varying size messengered every day for a week, the incomprehensible contents, the notes whose only message was the scratchy, inexpert drawing of that hat with the knife through it. It starts poisoning the elation of looking at my future, so again I check the Internet and, finally, there it is on the *New York Times* Web site.

The good news couldn't be any better if I had written the piece myself.

The report confirms the discovery of the K'plua in Schermer's apartment and the arrest and charges. The DA affirms that the evidence makes an incontrovertible connection between Schermer and the Rat Burglar, and he is hopeful that very soon the arrest will lead to the apprehension of the Rat Burglar himself. The only pictures on the *Times* site are of Schermer exiting a cruiser with his hands cuffed at his waist and his head down, but on WhoIsTheRatBurglar.com there are close-up shots that indicate that the cops assuaged their longtime frustration with the thief by engaging in some extracurricular activity on Schermer's person. The color of his cheeks is a crazy peppermint—an improbable mass of bright red and screaming white—and his face is now a pulpy Rorschach of what had once been an array of features in the usual arrangement. Now they are all debatables, open to conjecture, a critical adventure. "That's the nose. No, that is. I assume you're being facetious; that is clearly a nostril...."

They have beaten the Blistex right out of him.

It's hard to look at, and I can't help feeling a pinch of sorrow for Schermer.

The only other part of the report that isn't custom-made for my delectation is, I finally see, the concluding paragraph in which Detective Nunes's only comment on the Schermer–Rat Burglar connection is "We're still waiting on forensics."

Unfavorable, I suppose, but so what. Only yesterday my woes were like the plotlines of a Russian novel and now things are—dare I say it?—going my way.

Perhaps crime committed in the service of justice really does pay.

Again I inhale powerfully and savor the trash-torn riverscape. The water smells of diesel, decomposing organics, and waterlogged plastics; the boatyard has an overwhelming odor of fresh composite, marine oil, and sailcloth, and underneath it all the city summertime morning air—already chewed and spat out by millions of people—is trying and failing to offer something fresh.

But it doesn't matter. To me it smells fantastic. To me it smells like life.

When I crack open the velvet box the creaky hinge doesn't sound coffinlike and when I spread the words out over the dead, despoiled air—"Do you know what that sound is?"—I do not feel the mortality crush.

I feel hope.

What the Covet Girl Tells Me

Charlie misses our boat night. The next day she is also out of touch. Ditto the day after that—Monday, when my locker is devoid of insulting Schermeresque pranks and when, gloriously, Po-Mo apologizes on behalf of the board, pats me on the back, and formally assigns me to the Nakamura job as floater—even though I have left about nineteen messages. This is weird not only because normally Charlie's cell is clamped to her ear like a lamprey but because in each message I explained, rationalized, apologized, and groveled in every way known to modern man.

The fight was bad. The accusations against the Rat Burglar—and the accusing erection—didn't help. The strike to her jaw was terrible. I know that.

But I've never known Charlie to give the silent treatment. It feels all wrong. Apparently, though, the twentieth time is the charm. I am in the middle of leaving a message telling her that I recovered that prospect I thought I lost to the Yankees when my call waiting buzzes and I see her name on my screen for the first time in days. Just the sight of those letters in that arrangement—C-H-A-R-L-I-E—seems like a tremendous relief. My screen has missed them.

I switch over. We talk. It's all right, I guess, but something is off. The meter in our conversation is halting and broken. We're a little too polite. It's like we are a couple of students in a first-year foreign language class, unsure of the vocabulary and enunciating everything with too much care. Getting it wrong by getting it too right—robots of formality.

"I'm sorry about your jaw."

"That's all right. It was an accident."

"How does it feel?"

"Fine."

"That prospect didn't sign with the Yankees. I got him back."

Tonelessly: "That's great."

"Thanks."

"You're welcome."

"Do you want to come over tonight and celebrate?"

Insert a pause. Not a long one, but an incriminating one: to this pod-person Charlie the question is not rhetorical. It does not elicit an immediate yes. It requires thought, thought that produces a sentence of hurried syllables that tries to cover up the awkwardness but only emphasizes it.

The ring box pinches uncomfortably in my pocket.

"That sounds great. Sure. What time?"

It's excruciating, and when I get off the phone instead of being excited or love-charged, I have an ominous out-of-the-frying-pan-into-the-fire feeling.

But I push it aside. I tell myself I don't care.

For now I am a man of action and tonight, whether every-thing is perfect or not, I'm popping the question.

When Charlie shows up she has a fragrance I've never detected on her before that is at once acidic and yogurty, stinging and curdled. It's not atmospheric, that's for sure. It's not something she picked up from the environment. It's biological. It's either anxiety or fear. Maybe both.

Even worse: she is still talking to me as if I'm a difficult mai-tre d' and every smile she gives me is efficient and careful, the kind of smile you give to someone you have just met and on whom you are trying to make the right impression.

Or from whom you are trying to hide.

Is it wrong of me to feel an exultant, stomach-clearing relief· when she tells me about her father?

He was in an accident, Charlie says. On the Pacific Coast Highway near Hurricane Point. It wasn't that bad, and he's basically O.K., but he lost a finger and the backseat contained a certain number of empty beer cans and, she says, boxes and boxes of balloons. Hundreds, thousands of balloons; he had been drinking and driving and inflating. His *finger*, she says. She finds this hard to articulate; she gasps it out. To me, though, it sounds like no big deal to lose one digit in a highway-speed smashup—to me it sounds like an opportunity to thank lucky stars—and I have to work fast to alter my relieved-face into one of sympathetic worry.

"No one else was hurt," she says. "But he's been put into some kind of therapeutic seclusion at a psychiatric hospital out there. I've gotten all this information from the police and from his intake person at the hospital, Miss Sharon, and Miss Sharon won't let me see him or talk to him or anything. It's been like this since Thursday, and it's just been making me crazy."

Thursday, I think. The day after I lost the K'plua. Ever since then I've been so wrapped up in my own problems I didn't stop to think that Charlie might have had some of her own.

"His fin-ger," she says again, stricken, her tongue snagging on the syllables.

Mentally I tally Charlie's recent events: unkind Rat Burglar argument; hostile hard-on and smack in the face underscoring death threats against RB; theft of thesis by underhanded academic; unapologetic send-off into the night, braless; father's accident and loss of digit. All in all, not a propitious set of circumstances under which to propose, but if I don't do it now I don't know if I'll ever have the guts again. Besides, in a way that I hope is not sicko, seeing Charlie all kaleidoscoped with sadness like this makes me love her even more. It makes me want to protect her.

That's part of the job description of a personal pulse, isn't it?

With both arms I reach out, lasso Charlie, and pull her to me, her face slicking my neck with saltwater, her hair hot and fragrant as a rain-soaked garden. But it is an unsuccessful embrace. I have been demoted somehow—to some degree my access has been denied—and the embrace is out of proportion with the current level of intimacy. It has the unhappy feeling of door-to-door salesmanship, the uncertain plummet of solicitation, and Charlie shrinks minutely from it as if the victim of an overhug by someone she has just met. Or someone she does not trust.

Still, it does not stop me from saying, probably too brightly,

"Hey, I forgot something at the store! Do you want to go for a ride with me?"

In the car I try to cope with Charlie's sadness with a certain negative capability, and, as far as is possible, I try not to let it poison my excitement.[56] It might not be the most opportune moment of all time, but, I tell myself, it still has to be right. Even the radio seems to encourage me; when I fire up the Reliant the radio is playing that annoying Rat Burglar song by the Hard Twenties—"Steal *Me*"—but when I change the channel the first thing I hear is that ubiquitous commercial for Covet perfume. It's right at the end of the spot, when the woman from the billboards and TV, the one in the sexy red dress that echoes the contours of the bottle, says in that sultry backroom voice, "You know you want it. What will you do to get it?"[57]

I think: you're right, sultry-voiced vixen in the sexy backless dress.

I do want it. And now I am going to take it. I am going to make Charlie mine.

Originally I had planned on pulling over on a leafy, Frost-like, Connecticutian country lane, but now I can't help myself.

56 Which, when the woman you love is sniffling next to you in your car and has a face jotted with mascara stains, courtesy of her wounded father, and a kidney-shaped bruise on her jaw, courtesy of your own hand, isn't far.

57 The voice sounds intimate and direct. The Covet girl is talking to *me*. She has been observing my progress and, like a Greek goddess about to give her imprimatur to a mortal daring to attain some impossible love, is urging me to action. Part of me knows that this voices-in-your-head phenomenon is frequently associated with various types of schizophrenia, but I'm not paying much attention to that part.

I barely make it down Clinton and right onto Lafayette when I blurt it out.

"You hear that?" I say, my nerves making me emit a noise almost like a giggle.

"Hear what?" Charlie says, studying the ramified cracks of the windshield.

"That noise."

"What noise?" she says, looking dead ahead.

"Sort of a crunching sound?"

Eyes front, soldierly, she cocks her head as if listening for something inaudible.

"Maybe it's more of a grinding. Maybe the axioregulator bushings misaligning."

"I don't hear anything."

If I weren't so disoriented by Charlie's uncharacteristic fearlessness at my car's polyglot noisemaking—and her first-ever refusal to participate in one of our oldest rituals—I would laugh, for it's clear I am not making it up. The noises of distress that the Reliant is making are so clear that they are discernible not only as vibrations in your inner ear but as vibrations journeying through the car seats and deep into the tissue of your body.

The car is literally humming with ailment.

"That," I clarify.

"The radio?"

"No, the noise that is making the gauges rattle around," I say as the engine gags brutally. "The noise that sounds like a flock of California condors getting sucked into a jet engine."

"The what?"

The car shudders, groans, spits something metallic onto the asphalt below us.

"That," I say again.

"I think it's just warming up."

"Warming up?" I say in a tone of voice that may fall somewhere on the anger spectrum. "Do you know what car you're in?"[58]

A lifetime of honing the wrong instincts impels me to step on the brakes and yank the car to the curb. Before I know what I'm doing I have popped the hood and extracted the ring box from the engine bay. Beads of perspiration rappel down my back, forming freshets. I can feel each one coursing down its route, splitting and rejoining, making me an idiotically grinning delta of sweat. I am also suffering from a momentary fugue of anti–déjà vu: nothing is identifiably like anything else. I walk this street all the time, I shop all these stores, yet suddenly I cannot name them. For reassurance I peer around the hood and look at Charlie. Through the cracked glass her features are split and Cubist-like, nearly frightening, her expression a glossary on anxiety and confusion.

Something in me tells me to stop.

Something else tells me to go go go.

I feel light-headed, as if I've just noshed on a gift basket of Pavulon and Nix. I open the box. The ring is impossibly brilliant and seems to embody a purity I can never hope to attain. I close the box. I run a fingernail over the surface, making characters of unknown meanings in the velvet. It feels good: complicit and rare. Almost erotic. I wonder why I've never snuggled this box. That would feel great. A homeless Asian guy attired in a smock of canvas and discolored paper maps hobbles past, smiling in a way that makes his face go bruised and

58 Smooth, Starks. Way to set the mood.

troughed like a dried apricot. Again I open the box. The ring is still there.

Platinum-banded shine: check.

Otherworldly sparkliness: check.

Inexplicable feeling of mortal dread: check.

I start staggering around the car to Charlie's door, gargling some spit so I can speak.

How Memory Harvesting Can Save Your Life

In orientation Janus has a training segment for all new pulses to help them resist torture and/or to maintain clarity under chemical duress. Sensory transposition, they call it. During the "preenactments"[59] you are instructed to perform a "mnemonic dramatization," a strategy that basically boils down to "if you have bamboo shoots shoved under your fingernails/barbed wire up your urethral meatus/ten milligrams of Nix sizzling in your brainpan, you should try to think pleasant thoughts." In order to do that, however, you need to perform "memory harvesting" so that you can create a bank of vivid positive experiences to which you can retreat while enduring whatever pain you've got coming your way.

For me, sensory transposition is useless as a technique for enduring physical torture, but it's perfect for making a triple-shift solo gig—or your whole life—seem less lonely, and I am

59 Another, better, more candid term might be "educational torture sessions."

in the habit of keeping a vigilant lookout for as many Charlie memories as I can harvest.

The carbonation and pomegranates in her mouth.

The Coco Rico pop-tops.

The image of her falling off of her bike. The consequent boomerang bend in her nose.

Her gracefulness when naked.

The childlike look on her face at the moment of orgasm.

Rubbing my jaw after I've gritted my teeth all night.

Her inexplicable love of my handwriting.

And, now, this moment.

I want to make sure I have what happens next available to me forever, so for a long moment, before I am able to speak, I just look at Charlie and do my best to deposit this moment, everything about it, in my memory bank for all the desolate hours I have left in my life.

I want, in other words, to freeze-frame perfection. I want to stop-time pure love.

The Sound of Our Future Together

But I do not get perfection. I do not get pure love.

When Charlie steps out of the car and faces me she is as beautiful as ever. She is standing sideways in a nervous, defensive posture, a kind of fighting-stance contrapposto, her face half turned from me aerodynamically, her pelvis slanting away in the slender silhouette of a bird in flight. Her hair is kiting behind her in the hot nighttime air and her cheekbones are awash in the blaze of cheap light from the storefronts. She is holding her breath in a way that makes the cords on her neck flex and the concavities of her collarbones deepen. And when I say the words I've waited so long to say—"Do you know what that sound is?"—I detect the pneumatic hitch of emotion in her voice and water makes her brown eyes turn slick and black as wet coffee grounds.

But they are not the imminent tears of joy, and the aspirations that only I can hear are not caused by the sudden apprehension of momentousness. They are something very different.

"What?" Charlie says, barely audible.

"Do you know what that sound is?"

I am overwhelmed by the feeling that the ring box I'm hiding behind my back is a live grenade. I want to throw it as far away as possible; I want to fall on it; I want to hand it off to someone who knows what to do with it.

I feel faint. The world around me shudders and dilates. Objects go melted-clocky.

"Do you know what that sound is?" I say in a voice that sounds as if someone has been using my tongue to streetsweep Flatbush Avenue.

As I start bending down onto one knee, Charlie's left foot takes a step backwards. Then her right. Her lips twitch with words that won't come and her eyes explode with water like a busted fire hydrant. Then she is spinning on her heels and running down the pavement away from me. I make a few Reliant-like noises, a few Reliant-like spasms, as I watch her sprint past

the crippled buildings and thresh between the clots of unrec-
ognizable people. I watch her get smaller and smaller until I
see her disappear down the stairs into the Clinton/Washing-
ton G stop like a boat slipping beneath the waves.

I pop open the box. The ring is still sparkling. It doesn't
know any better.

"Do you know what that sound is?" I say to it. My voice
is weak and hollow and has the faraway acoustic property of
enbottlement. I shake the ring box but it produces no noise
whatsoever. I shake it a second time and get only silence. "That
is the sound of our future together."

Bullet by Bullet

Down at the Snug things are quiet. Tracey isn't working and
none of the mimes I know are there. Not even Alpha. Herk
doesn't answer his phone. I start dialing Po-Mo but then realize he is not actually my friend and hang up. I search my pockets for a dose of Nix but, luckily, come up empty. For the ten
thousandth time I wish my family were still alive. For the ten
thousandth time I wish I were someone else. On a hunch I take
a cab through the hardscrabble backroads of Queens to the firing range, where I find Herk, who, with one hand, pinwheels
a sinister, matte-black handgun in the manner of a wild west
showman and, with the other, pulls me into the kind of hug
I wish I had received from Charlie: unpremeditated, unresis-
tant, honest.

He is glad to see me.

"Unfuckingbelievable," he says.

"What?"

"I'm going to have to buy you a whole new underwear wardrobe, my man."

"What do you mean?"

"Your *huevos,* amigo. Your balls are getting too big for your britches. You're busting out. Never in a million years did I think you'd actually want to learn how to shoot a gun."

"I don't. That's not why I'm here. I was just…in the neighborhood…."

Why is it so hard to talk to another human being? It's almost as hard as silence.

"Oh, come on. You came here for a reason, compadre. And that reason is to learn how to kill the Rat Burglar. You know I'm right."

"I'm not killing anybody. We've been over this."

"You can change the channel with a remote, right? Same thing." Herk gives no indication he has heard anything I've said and starts demonstrating the stance for me. "See? Just point and squeeze. Put the Rat Burglar on mute forever."

"You might not have noticed this but the last time I held a gun it didn't go so well."

"That's because you didn't know how to shoot. But now you're here, and you can learn from the master."

"Thanks no thanks."

"Watch this." With a fat Sharpie Herkimer makes a childlike drawing of a face on a piece of paper. The lines are grotesque, with cursive eyelashes to indicate femaleness and an eroticized, gap-toothed, Wife-of-Bathian mouth.

"Who's that?"

"Mrs. Chudan, my fifth grade teacher. Social studies, she was, always talking shit about textiles. Gave me an F. Said

I had 'rude, crude, and obnoxious school behavior.'" Herk tapes Mrs. Chudan to the target, puts it out to distance, fires off a dozen deafening rounds, then holds down a button and retracts the target.

Mrs. Chudan's face is now perforated with bullet holes that delineate, connect-the-dots style, a nearly perfectly formed capital F.

"Bang! Who's failing now, Chudan?" Herk rips off the target and sticks a finger into the deep casing behind it that houses an oozing pink substance. "And check this shit out. Ballistic gelatin. It mimics human tissue, so you can see what the damage would be in real life. Check out Chudan's mush. It's fucked from here to Cleveland, right?"

My stomach is still reverberating from the gunshots. I am terrified but also awed; the profile of Mrs. Chudan's face through the Plexiglas container is shredded with shrapnel from the spreading hollow-point bullets. She didn't stand a chance.

"Cool shit, right?" Herk sticks a fingerpoint crowned by an icinglike dollop of pink ballistic gelatin into his mouth. "And it tastes great."

"Disgusting."

"Disgusting? No, it's fun! Go on. Smell my fingers. You smell that? That's fun juice, my man. I just fingerfucked fun."

I wave his hand away.

"And now it's your turn."

On another piece of paper Herk draws a picture that appears to be the state of Iowa and changes as he continues working into, possibly, a shabby spermatozoon and then, finally, with the addition of an unmistakable set of feet and ears and "hair," into the semblance of a rat. He zooms the Rat Burglar target out to half distance.

"I don't want to fingerfuck fun, Herk."

"What's up, sweetiehons? You're tired, you're stressed, you've got a headache, and on top of everything you're getting your period?"

A little too casually for comfort, Herk puts down the gun—still loaded—and I tell him about the scene on the sidewalk. I even extract the ring box from my pocket and open it for him. I put it on the surface next to the gun, where the matte-black gun and the open clamshell of the velvety box and the idiotic, nonstop full-volume glare of the ring's refraction make a strange tableau—one that makes me momentarily consider shooting the diamond at point-blank range.

The confession does not elicit from Herk the surprise I had anticipated. In fact, he merely sighs and clenches his teeth, making hard walnuts of muscle contract at his jawline.

"I didn't want to tell you this, Otto. I thought maybe I was wrong or that...I don't know. Sometimes things aren't what they look like. And I could be totally wrong. Maybe it's nothing. Probably it is nothing. What the hell do I know? But...I guess you had better take a look at this."

A hand goes into a pocket and comes out with the digital camera.

"I was out with a Goldfish the other day and fucking around, you know, taking some pics, and then I saw this woman with this guy. I couldn't be sure it was her, you know, from the pictures you've showed me, but I just had this feeling, so I sort of eavesdropped a little bit—sorry, man; I just needed to know, thought you deserved to know—and I heard the guy say the name 'Charlie' and I knew I was right. I sort of drifted away and I don't know if I did the right thing or not, but now that you're telling me about what she did when you tried to say what you were going to say on the sidewalk and everything—"

"Herk, what are you talking about?"

He hands me the camera. On the screen is a picture of Charlie coming out of the door of a building with a guy with a beard and a turban dyed to the same sky-blue color as his shirt.

"Do you know this guy?" Herk asks.

I want this to be nothing. I need this to be nothing. And so I say, very defensively, as if it explained everything, "I can't know all of Charlie's friends."

Herk advances the screen. Now there is a picture of them facing each other at close range.

"So?" I say with a runt laugh. "It's crowded."

Again Herk clicks the button. Now there is a pic of them embracing. I note that her face looks flushed and damp with moisture that common sense suggests is sweat. She looks indisputably happy, ruddy, frisked-over.

"That's just...comradely."

In the next one Charlie is hugging the guy with her face so deeply embedded into his beard it's like it's in a fucking holster. A body of a passerby is blocking them partially, so I can't see the terminus of the Sikh guy's arms—or hands—but the angle of the shoulders, and a lifetime of examining portraiture of entangled lovers, tells me that it can't mean anything good.

The next pic is essentially the same posture. Even with my optics, it's hard to tell what the hell her face is doing inside that beard, but the general disposition of her head and the way that her arms are laced around his torso makes the whole transaction seem very...unbusinesslike. It doesn't help allay my feelings of jealousy that the guy is unusually large, which in my workaday universe isn't unusual at all—in my line of work, everyone is bigger than me—but this guy, with his muscular shoulders birdwinging around Charlie, his hands doing who-knows-what, his beard getting a good nuzzle—it makes me enraged.

Who the fuck is this guy?

Then, with a Holofernes itch in my neck, I realize I have seen him before. I saw him in an Indian restaurant. Dining with Charlie in a picture shown to me by Deke.

Herk's last photo features the couple in much the same position, only now Charlie's face is upturned toward the guy at the same angle, I'm thinking, that it assumed with me that spring day at the Frick. The beard is too thick to tell what her mouth is doing, but you don't need to score 800 on the Amsler Grid visual acuity test to see that it's unsanctioned.

Or to see why she has been acting so strange lately.

The air punches out of my stomach. When I have the strength to look at the photo again I blink at it but it doesn't help. It doesn't change anything. It doesn't make anything disappear.

"Herk," I say, "give me the gun."

Wordlessly, and without looking me in the eye, he does. I empty the clip into the air. None of them hits the target but as each bullet shrieks harmlessly past the Rat Burglar on a taut, sizzling, gray cable and embeds into the surface of the wall, the tears sting a little bit less. The nausea diminishes. I feel just a little bit better, bullet by bullet.

The Effects of Drinking and Dosing

During the week before the Nakamura job I spend a lot of time stumbling around in a haze of confusion. I am a heartbroken mutterer, a starer-through-windows-dumbly, a stunned tear zombie. When I'm not drinking and dosing, I'm at the firing range. When I'm not drinking and dosing or at the firing range I am sitting with my journal, trying to get out some ink. There's nothing I can say that will make anything comprehensible. It is a failure of language itself. Nothing, not one nibstroke, means what I thought it meant. None of the characters look like letters; they look like poorly drawn games of hangman. I try to pronounce the words "Charlie is gone"—I think that's what I wrote—but it doesn't make sense, not one syllable, not one phoneme.

Honesty? Not what I thought it meant.

Trust? Must have it confused with some homophone I didn't know existed.

Loyalty? Not even close. Never knew it.

Love? Bzzz. So sorry. Try again.

After a few false starts, I pry open the door to the freezer and stare down its inhabitants. All the brides and grooms are standing where I left them last, even Chester Wellington III, as if nothing has changed for them. But it has. They still have a certain aura, but it is decaying. They are no longer smug; they are angry and desperate, as if they know they are losing their power. They are no longer the voodoo figures that haunt both freezer and subconscious.

Now they are just the plastic idols of dead gods.

I remove all the cakes, spread them on the table like poker chips, grasp each figure by the chest, where the heart should be, and yank. Hard. They come off easily, though, easier than I thought they would,[60] and it doesn't take long to divorce each cake from its couple. It is exhilarating, but it is also terrifying. In the garbage can it looks like a Holocaust scene, all those bodies piled on each other. And each tier of cake looks tortured, too: from every place where I removed a bride or groom there is now a gaping woundlike hole in the icing.

But it does not stop me from doing what I must do.

I cry into the holes I've made—planting strange seeds to grow a mysterious fruit—and then, as if performing a tribal ritual by which one hopes to assimilate the powers of a vanquished foe, I eat all the cakes. Every one of them. Every last goddamn crumb.

⊱⊰

One night at the Snug as I sway on my stool, percolating with sugar, liquor, and highly contraband toxins, I get flirted with.

---

60 I know it makes no sense in terms of real-world physics, but I had expected difficulty doing this. A kind of sword-in-the-stone safeguard of worthiness seemed to obtain and I always suspected that I wouldn't have what it takes—whatever *it* is—to extract all the figures from the freezer, let alone remove them from their cakes.

Across the bar from me is a woman who gives me the heavily mascaraed eye. She is wearing a Floridian orange halter top and a jean skirt, but just barely. I don't return her look; I concentrate on the bar, its scrum of glasses and empties. The woman isn't discouraged, though. She comes over to my stool, her anemone hair clouding my peripheral, and starts twirling a swizzle stick suggestively. She is, I now see, an ex-Goldfish, a pharmaceutical rep to whom Herk once said, "Do you have any of that new erectile dysfunction drug? What's it called...Boobsinall? Oh yes, I can tell by looking that you've got it. Do you ever. You've got Boobsinall and *all*!"

"Aren't you that movie star?" says the Goldfish.

I focus intently on the menus standing butlerlike on the bar.

"That one from the serial killer movie? You know the one. The really cute killer, so cute you can't believe he actually is the killer but he is the killer and you can't help pulling for him, hoping he'll get away with it, because you wouldn't want all those good looks to go to waste in prison?"

The mixers are stacked upside down and bunched together like a drum set.

"And then you start thinking maybe it wouldn't be so bad if he serial-killed me just as long as he did it with his hands...."

The bottles are all lined up straight, labels facing front, their pourers striving heavenward like openmouthed birds waiting to be fed.

Pick me, each one says.

"You're him, right?"

I shake my head, but in New York a denial of celebrity is often an affirmation, and this only encourages her.

"Can I get an autograph?"

Dimly, I consider dropping some tissolet into her drink.

"We can go into the bathroom and you can sign it anywhere you like."

She tries to brandish her tits at me, moving them side to side while giving them the upper-arm concertina, but succeeds only in making herself look like some kind of expired meat on a stuttering rotisserie. Her ass sags heavily out of the bottom of her skirt like a beer belly.

"Yeah," she says, "you're him. I can tell. You've got that same quiet sexy criminal look. Tell me, is it true that you're going to play the Rat Burglar in the movie? I always thought you would be perfect for him!"

A movie?

A fucking movie?

Such is my disgust that I almost say something so crass, so Schermer-like, that I know I'd never forgive myself. But I don't; I reel it in. My substitute reaction is to make a helpless squeak of distress and bury my head firmly in my arms upon the bar until she leaves.

When I finally look up Alpha is there, curling his index finger as an illustration of my limp-dickedness. I clench my hand—thumb outside my fist, thank you very much—and unleash it on him. I miss but it doesn't matter because I am already on top of him and berserking. I am saved from a probable lawsuit by Tracey, who peels me off the mime and throws me in a cab.

A Bra Tells the Truth

When I get back to my apartment I realize that in a certain light—in fact, in every wavelength and every frequency of the entire visual spectrum—I am even more of a chump than I thought.

As I scour the apartment for the Nix antidote—I inadvisably took twenty milligrams in the cab, and I have no sensation in my toes or fingers and my tongue is dead weight inside my mouth—I discover the bra that Charlie left behind on the night of the argument. It's wadded up between the wall and the mattress, forlorn, like a treasure-hunt prize that someone planted but forgot. At first it inspires nostalgia: this is the first bra I ever removed from Charlie's body.[61] As with all seductive

---

61 She actually changed into this bra for me. It was our first time being alone together and we were on her sofa, like high schoolers, hands going everywhere, grasping crazily as if we had to touch everything to make sure the other person was real. I made a move through the buttons of her shirt and Charlie jumped as if she'd been electrocuted. I thought, Real smooth, Starks. Had to push it, didn't you? But she wasn't repulsing the move; she was embarrassed about her bra. She ran into the bedroom, explaining that she hadn't anticipated anything happening so soon; she had on a bad bra and wanted to put on a good one. (As if at that moment I cared one whit about the aesthetics of any bra.) When she came back out of the bedroom, though, she had stripped down to only this bra and panties and I was so overcome—the orange glow from the nightlight on her brown body; the striations of the long muscles in her legs and the secret, swollen vacuity between them; the fan blowing through her hair and onto her skin in a way

undergarments, this bra tells lies. The lies are stronger than the truth—they are the lies that you want to hear, have been waiting your whole life to hear—but you can never make them out, not quite. It doesn't want you to. It wants you simply to be curious forever.

Tonight, though, this bra finally tells me a truth. A painful one.

The bra looks just as lovely as ever, a miracle of delicate sheer fabric and clever engineering. I press the gossamer material to my face and breathe it in, detecting the usual fruit-and-powder fragrance of Charlie's breasts and the powerful headnotes of the new perfume she was wearing that night. I also detect, faintly but definitely, other notes—cardamom, cloves, cumin, coriander, fenugreek, peppercorn—and, as they register in my olfactory bulb, I experience a vague but powerful jolt of something imploding nearby, a sickening depth-charge feeling.

Those are all ingredients of garam masala.

Garam masala is used in curry.

The dots connect: the Sikh guy eats curry. Curry gets on his hands. Hands transfer curry to bra.

that made her flesh spread with goose bumps—that I had to ask her to stop so I could look. Just *look*. It sounds weird, maybe, but I promise: it wasn't. It was completely sincere, erotic, nearly mystical, kind of Actaeon-spying-Artemis-at-her-bath. It was the most perfect moment of my life, and I didn't want it to end. Charlie didn't say anything, but she intuited what I meant, and what I was feeling, and she stopped dead in her tracks and stood there, stock-still, the only sounds in the universe that fan oscillating and the deafening sound of blood roaring in my ears. I got up from the couch, stripped out of my clothes, and crossed the ten interminable feet between us. There were the heat waves from her body breaking over mine, her fragrances, our gravities, and when I reached around back, my fingertips finding that mechanism—what do you call those things? tenterhooks?—I pinched it open. First try, too: another reason why this is my favorite bra.

I want to vomit. I want to shoot someone. Instead I throw back a cool thirty milligrams of Nix and wait for the hurt.

It comes fast.

When I wake up I don't get it. I don't understand why I have been spooning the pillow so hard that it has disgorged its feathers all over the bedding. It doesn't seem significant that I am grasping a beautiful black bra as if my life depended on it. All I know is that I am physically exhausted and that I have a terrible headache from gritting my teeth. Charlie always rubs my jaw at these moments, and I cast about fruitlessly for her. I call out her name but don't get anything back. I bang the mattress childishly. Nothing. And still I don't get it. But when I finally roll out of bed, it hits me.

Charlie's not here. Charlie's not here because she is somewhere else. With someone else. Doing something else. Something...unspecifiable.

I am splitting. My atoms are separating. I am fissioning with grief.

Gun Therapy

The only time it doesn't hurt is when I am at the firing range. The irony is incomprehensible but it is nonetheless true. The sharp recoil, the smell of cordite and drop ceilings and sizzling gun oil, the bone-cracking vociferation of the blast—it heals me.

Each burst of muzzle fire sounds like a godlike "No!"

No, I will not be called Potap. No, I will not accept my family's death. No, I will not let anybody take what doesn't belong to them. No, I will not lose my career. No, I will not allow Pinky's death to go unavenged. No, I will not let the *Clean Getaway* get away.

No, I will not turn into a miserable, muttering, soul-broken homunculus without Charlie.

If a gun is the final utterer of the final word, if it has the supreme power of absolute negation, if it says No to everything on the other end of its barrel, then the only person with the power of Yes is its wielder. Me.

In this case: Yes, I will pulse the Nakamura job successfully.

Yes, I will get my life back.

Yes, I will kill the Rat Burglar.

In the effort department, I excel. I put in the hours on the range and I have the blisters and exhausted extraocular muscles to prove it. But my early results do not earmark me for prodigy status. The first shot during my first lesson screams way wide of the target. That's not the surprise. The surprise is the shell. Femtoseconds after the shot rockets out of the barrel, the shell discharges out of the breech. Normally its trajectory is perpendicular to the gun's user; under normal circumstances the shell tumbles harmlessly to the side. This time, however, some gremlin of physics causes the shell to eject straight backward, an angle that sends it careening through the scorched air between the smoking gun and the flat prominence on my forehead.

Bull's-eye.

I make all the vocalizations you would expect when one gets shot in the head. I also do the footwork.

"What happened?" Herk says, picking the gun carefully off the floor.

"Fucker!" is all I can manage.

"What was it?"

Vigorously I rub my forehead.

"Fuckfuckfuckfuckfuckithurts."

"What did you do?"

"Fucking thing shot me in the head."

Herk peels my hands away and inspects.

"No, no. It's just the brass. It ejected funny."

"Brass?"

"The shell."

"Fucker is hot."

"You'll live. Relax."

"Is there a mark?"

"Oh yeah. Looks like you've got forehead herpes."

"Fantastic."

"Now let's see you come within ten feet of the target this time."

"Have you ever seen that happen before?" I say, still rubbing.

"Never in my natural life."

"Well, I'm glad I got that statistical anomaly out of the way."

Taking the gun from Herk, I raise the muzzle to the drawing of the Rat Burglar taped over the ballistic gelatin, grit my teeth, and squeeze. The primary charge ignites, the bullet shrieks past the target in a harmless, neighborly way, and the shell shoots out of the breech and, miraculously, right into my forehead.

The pain registers, as does Herk's poorly stifled laugh, and

I double over, rubbing my forehead like mad while telling myself over and over: this is not a metaphor.

>‹

A couple of days later Herk finally congratulates me. I have attained the skill to hit the target with some frequency at ranges under thirty feet and, as if the gun has finally vouchsafed some respect, I am no longer getting hit in the head with the shell. In celebration of my remedial semicompetence Herk produces a folded paper bag, out of which he produces a clean black pistol that appears to be identical to the one with which I've been practicing.

"There she is," he sings regally, "Miss America..."

"What's that?"

"Just a little something I picked up for you. You couldn't get one through proper channels fast enough, obviously, and naturally you can't use mine, so I got you your own. Through a friend of a friend. Don't ask. The numbers have been filed off and it's a virgin, so you can just say that you bought it off the street and it can't be traced to anyone. It's the same make and model as mine, though, so it will be the same as shooting the one you've been learning on. Nice, right?"

It's supposed to be touching, and in a way it is—Herk has gone out of his way for me again—but it also makes the situation very immediate and very real. I know that this has been the case all along, but until this moment it seemed as if someone else—another Otto, a stronger, more confident, less guilt-ridden Otto—was going to be the fingerman. But that's not the case.

It's my gun.

It's my job to kill the Rat Burglar.

I make myself say thanks.

"You got it. Oh, and here's the job sheet."

Herk hands me the details. It's on Janus letterhead with the motto right there in italics, *Ne Cede Malis*, which apparently means "Don't Give in to Adversity," but which I used to think meant "Don't Give in to Badness." I think I best understood the motto when I misunderstood it, though. It seemed like an affirmation that I had chosen the right line of work, that Janus was going to help me become a better person. It would help me recover something. It would make me worthy of love.

Now, as I hold the letterhead in one hand and a gun in the other, I'm not so sure.

Am I giving in to badness?

Or am I asserting myself?

"The MacGuffin is a samurai sword?" I say, mystified. "How is that eight figs?"

"It's a special sword, a vengeance sword. This guy Hioki was some kind of legendary samurai sword maker. A rival raped and killed his wife. Hioki made a special sword. Its only purpose was to rub out the whole family of the guy who killed his wife. Supposedly he forged the sword in his wife's blood. Her name is etched in the blade. The grip is wrapped in her hair. They say you can still see red in the blade, and the hair on the grip never broke." Herk whistles. "Hioki was true to his word, too. Killed every member of that guy's family. Women, children, everything. Forty-four murders. He killed them in duels, cut them down on public streets, stabbed them to death in their beds. Extincted the whole fucking bloodline. Then when they were all dead he hari-karied himself. Now I guess it's got some sort of legend about it. Hioki is like some kind of proverb in Japan for the downside of rage or something."

"So it's got some historical and cultural value, O.K., but it still doesn't make sense. Even the finest examples of samurai swords don't crack seven figs. They aren't exactly rare."

Herk shrugs.

"And why the hell would he pay so much for two pulses on the job?"

"Beats me. But best not to look a gift gig in the mouth, right?"

"I guess."

Next to us a blond woman is firing shots at her target over fifty feet away. Her hair is thick and curly like Charlie's, but a little bit shorter, and she has the same forearm muscles that are so lean they look as if they've been stenciled onto her skin in pencil. She is wearing stylish hip-hugging, low-rider slacks and an expensive-looking blouse that accentuates her narrow, athletic waist. I feel like I'm looking at some kind of doppelgänger, a Charlie from a parallel universe with blond hair and a gun fetish.

"Hey, you O.K.?"

"Herk," I say, "you know about women. Do you think I did something to make this happen? Is it my fault?"

"How could it be your fault?"

"I lied to her. Have been lying to her. From day one. For over a year."

"What do you mean?"

"She thinks I work for the New York Mets, Herk."

"That? Jesus. That's no big deal. That's just regulations. You got no choice there."

"You think?"

"Sure. That's just lying small. What she did, that's lying big."

"I guess so. I just can't help feeling like it's my fault." Looking at the woman, I say, "And also that I had it coming. I mean, she is pretty much out of my league."

"Out of your league? Are you kidding? You're a handsome

dude. You dress really interestingly. And you're great with women. Women really respond to you."

"I'm a handsome dude?" I say. "You think women respond to me?"

"Of course. Blondie blonde over there has been checking you out all this time."

"She has?"

"For someone with your sense of vision, you don't see shit, do you? What about Sylvia from the Snug? That waitress from the Lithuanian place? Mackenzie at work? You think Mackenzie is always coming over to your locker for saline shots because she leaves hers at home ten times a month?"

I wonder if he's right. Maybe I have been spending too much time in dark rooms.

"And blondie blonde here. She's great, right? Looks good and smells good, too. I walked past her a few times before you got here just to get a good whiff, and sure enough, let me tell you, amigo, the girl is pH balanced."

Herk nudges me. The woman has taken off her ear protection and has noticed me noticing her.

"My friend was just admiring your form," Herk says.

"Is that right?" she says, hand on sculpted hip.

"Yes," Herk says for me.

"And what's his opinion?"

Herk nudges me again. He is doing the talking but she is looking at me.

"Um," I say, "I guess...I'd need to see a little more?"

She raises the pistol to the target, giving me her best profile, and then, smiling out of the corner of her mouth, she makes firing bullets into a piece of paper full of concentric circles look sexy. As her body vibrates with each recoil, I do as Herk suggested: I inhale her. It should be wonderful—she smells like a beautiful woman—but instead of being aroused, however, it only makes me sadder. It makes me homesick for Charlie's odors.

When the woman turns to me and purses her lips and play-fully blows the smoke out of the muzzle I wave at my face as if it is the cordite that's making my eyes water.

WWPD: What Would Pinkerton Do?

The day before the Nakamura job I take the F train and walk to my old street—Orchard between Delancey and Rivington. The "Bargain District." It hasn't changed. Maybe it shouldn't have, not in just one year, but in New York when you move away from a street, a neighborhood that was really yours, that place always seems to die from your absence. During your tenancy there the streets were alive, the asphalt and metal and glass were sentient. The birds knew you and whether to bother with begging for crumbs as you stood on the corner with your bagel. Even the people you didn't know, you knew. But when you come back, all is changed, changed utterly; its terrible beauty is dead.

Without you, it has become just a place.

At first Orchard Street looks the same. The racks of single-stitched sweatshop guayaberras for $7.99. The leather and shearling and fur outlets, none of which sell leather or shearling or fur. The shop windows full of cosmetic, Kevlar-less vests. The daughters of tourists in their sherbet-colored minis getting eyefucked by vendedores. The suburban kids in Ramones concert tees, tribal accouterments, and black matchstick jeans, hoping to absorb some grit and ethnicity, maybe a new obscenity in a foreign language they can bring back to school like a pet that does tricks.

But something is wrong. I came here for some kind of reassurance. I wanted my Lower East Side to say to me, "Don't worry, Otto. I know who you are. You had a life before Charlie, and you'll have one again."

It doesn't, though. It doesn't say anything. It has no clarity for me anymore.

So I check to make sure the plastic container of Thai chicken hasn't opened in my bag, reshoulder it, and then head to the East River to observe the same prejob ritual that's been holding me together for the last year.

Pinkerton didn't like dog treats. He refused Greenies and Jumbones and Choo-Hooves. He'd sniff a Pig Snooter—perhaps because, in a Nietzschean way, it sniffed back—but he never ate one. He only wanted human food. Correction: he only wanted the food he saw me eat. Normally, even the blandest human food gives dogs the shits, but my usual menu—soaked, I'm sure you can guess, in exotic hot sauces that feature on their labels all manner of medical warnings and legal disclaimers—was all he ever wanted.

Now, every day before a gig, I come here, past Cherry Street to Corlears Hook, and sit in this spot, the place where I made Pinky's watery grave, and make an offering of his favorite dish.

The ritual helps a little. The act of tossing each bite into the water, remembering the way his powerful jaws could clean a spoon so gently, is comforting. So are the noises around me: the grind and whine of the traffic, the voices tumbling out of windows overhead, the arias of struggle, the sonic riot of want.

The noises of the living.

Half an hour later the chicken is all gone but I don't feel any different. I take the brochure of my boat and stare at it. Then I stare at the Janus letterhead. *Ne Cede Malis*, it reminds me. I think about the gun.

Nothing is clear.

"I don't know," I say to the water. "Am I doing the right thing?"

A garbage barge cruises by, shrouded in warring gulls.

"Should I shoot him? Will that make anything different?"

In some ways, the gun looks like an answer to my problems. In another way, it looks like a gun. I'm having a hard time differentiating heartbreak, rage, vengeance, and loneliness.

"So which is it, Pink?" I say to the churning, garbage-choked water. "Do I shoot him?"

"That's a felony, Starks." I whip around and there she is, the grim *frileuse*, her shoulders bunched up and her chin pinned to her chest as if the hot wind is cold, an umbrella hanging off her arm. "You wouldn't want to add to your sentence, would you?"

"Afternoon, Detective," I say. "Nice day for a stalk."

Nunes makes a terse flexion with her mouth. It's a hard smile, a precast smile, one that has probably been there since 1975, unmoving, beating the elements at their own game.

"We've missed you at the station. I expected you to come give a statement."

"I had some personal things come up."

There is something unreadable about Nunes's eyes. They are

the same expressionless eyes found on those superpredatory subbenthic fish. Eyes that know dinner when they see it.

"Shouldn't you be questioning the Rat Burglar's accomplice, Detective? Shouldn't you be using your ways of making him talk?"

"Schermer's already talked."

"Then why are you bothering me? You want to bust me for littering? You can't. This is food. You want to book me for fish-feeding, go ahead."

"Schermer said he isn't an accomplice."

"So did I."

"But I believe Schermer."

With one hand—with nearly Rat Burglarian dexterity—Nunes rolls a cigarette.

"But the news said that after Schermer was attacked by the Rat Burglar—"

"Assailant."

"What?"

"Assailant. Schermer was attacked by an unknown assailant. Not necessarily the Rat Burglar."

"Hunh," I say, my stomach contracting. "Well, you have any leads?"

"Schermer's description puts him at six-two, one-ninety, Caucasian."

"I'm five-ten, one-sixty-five."

"You probably know that most victims of assault exaggerate the size of their assailants by ten to fifteen percent. That puts the assailant at your size."

Nunes continues looking at me with those eyes.

"No identifying characteristics?" I say. "Police sketch?"

"Unfortunately he was wearing a ski mask."

"Shucky darn."

"But Schermer said he was able to strike him in the head a few times. Say, your ear looks a little red. What did you do to it?"

Self-preservation advises that I say something respectful, or at least plausible, but instead I say, "New aftershave. Girls can't resist."

Nunes looks off into the distance, giving me a break from that stare, and I realize that I have been holding my breath.

"What about the evidence? I thought that they had a dispute or something and after the shots were fired the Rat Burglar—assailant—fled the scene and left behind some kind of evidence on the"—I nearly say K'plua—"evidence."

"Evidence on the evidence?"

"You know what I mean. Isn't there some pretty solid evidence?"

"Oh yes."

"Great. What is it?"

"Latents."

"What does that mean?"

"Latent prints, Starks. At the scene. And on an item stolen by the Rat Burglar."

"Prints on a stolen artwork? Isn't that fairly conclusive proof of guilt?"

"It sure is."

"Then what's the problem?"

"Two things. One, the latents don't implicate Schermer."

Suddenly the pride I've been feeling about my discovery in Schermer's apartment is replaced by consternation: those are my prints on the K'plua. I picked it up; I didn't think twice about it. Why would I? I don't think like a criminal because I'm not a criminal.

Except I am.

And now I start sweating like a criminal. I sweat additionally when I realize that my prints are on file at Janus. It's not a governmental agency—she can't access the prints instantaneously—but I know Po-Mo has already shown her some of my file. Would he give her these? Would he require a warrant? And what about the Department of Defense gig I worked that time? Did I send them copies of my prints or not? Are my prints already on AFIS because of that job?

When I realize I can't remember—and consequently don't know if I should continue to bluff or to come totally clean—my sympathetic nervous system redlines. I sweat, my pupils dilate, my throat starts to constrict.

"Hunh," I say with a pubescent squeak. "Not Schermer's prints. Weird."

"Not really."

"What's the other problem?"

"The item discovered at the scene is made of wood and raffia."

She is looking at me closely, as if trying to ascertain if the surprise I register is genuine.

"Oh. The K'plua? Well, Janus will be so relieved. Owners, too."

Nunes exhales a plume of dirty smoke. The air is so heavy with moisture and sickness—it is soupy, an oxygen-and-carbon-monoxide chowder—that the smoke doesn't rise. It just idles there at altitude next to Nunes's head like a polluted thought-bubble, communicating the worst, until the dead river wind pushes it sideways.

"So the problem is that you don't like raffia?"

"Raffia won't test for prints," she says. "And miraculously, when the mask was grabbed, each digit, including the thumb, touched only the raffia."

I try to disguise my massive exhalation of relief as a cough.

When I recover, I say, "You can't get the prints from that? Are there other prints anywhere?"

"There are prints on some surfaces and on the fragment of a sex toy but they are all complicated by pressure distortion and oil and some unknown chemicals."

"What chemicals?" I say, wondering how many other suspects are going to have very rare and very contraband toxins in their sweat.

"Don't know yet. Lab's working on it, though. Should be any time now."

"Well," I say, trying to sound innocent, "not having prints sure is a problem."

"No, that's not the problem. I didn't say we couldn't get prints. I said some materials won't test. Lots don't. Lots do, though. Window screens, most living plants, human skin. Hell, a spray of ninhydrin can bring up Confucius's prints on a fortune cookie. Did you know that? It seems like something you would know, given your expertise in chemicals."

I shake my head.

"I'm asking because the manner in which the mask was grasped—allowing the fingertips to touch only the part that will not hold prints—suggests familiarity with the process of fingerprinting. And I can't think of anybody who would know these chemicals better than you."

There is nothing I want more than to come clean. I want to tell her that the placement of the prints isn't due to expertise or design but only to dumb luck. I want to tell her the whole story, that I'm on her side. That I want the Rat Burglar even more than she does. But I've lied to Nunes nonstop, I've omitted my involvement with Deke, I've broken and entered, I've assaulted an unconscious person, and tomorrow I'm going to try to shoot someone else. Tomorrow I might be a killer.

I can't tell her anything. I'm in too deep.

"I don't know anything about nin..."

"Ninhydrin. How about silver nitrate?"

"Nope."

"Both of them test wood, and they both revealed very good prints. Unfortunately, they are palm prints."

"Palm prints don't indicate identity? That's the problem?"

"That's not the problem either, Starks, but you're getting warmer. Palm prints provide a very high index of accuracy. They are as unique as fingerprints, in fact, and we have very clear samples from the hypothenar zone and the fourth palmar zone. What that means to you is that there are many more points of similarity than we'll need to make an indisputable match." Nunes draws on that cigarette. She is watching me closely for my reaction. The riverfront around me is bright—I know my pupils are dilating in fear—and reflexively I squint and try to keep my face calm.

"And for conviction," she says.

"Detective," I say, "I still don't see the problem."

"The problem, Starks, is that Janus doesn't record palm prints. Neither, funny enough, does the Department of Defense."

"No one has a record of palm prints?" I say. "That *is* funny."

"I've been laughing about it all day. Mind if I take yours?"

"Laughter?"

"Palm prints."

"Yes."

"But if you're innocent, Starks, then we can eliminate you as a suspect. Why would you mind if I take them?"

"I'm saving them for my wedding night. I want to have something special to give."

"I can get a court order."

Even though I have no idea if I'm right—I know I am just

talking cop-show—I can't help saying, "Not without probable cause. And simply not liking my aftershave doesn't constitute probable cause."

"I could arrest you."

"I doubt it. Not after all those false arrests made by Fritzy. I can't imagine the DA is too eager to have the media get wind of any improprieties from the police yet again, do you?"

Nunes doesn't smile. Neither do I, but her unsmile is stronger than mine.

"All right, Starks. We'll play it this way. But my offer's off the table. It's just a matter of time until you screw up—if you haven't already—and when you do, you'll end up in the same ward with Frankie Nickels. No clemency. That's a promise."

Nunes turns around, umbrella swinging at her side, then stops and says, over her shoulder, "And by the way, where were you late last Friday night?"

Again something in me advises passionately against the sentence I have loaded in the chamber; again I ignore it.

"I was begging for spare change with the homeless."

Nunes kills the cigarette with her heel. I know how it feels.

The Nakamura Job

The only problem with the dummy is the wig. Everything else is perfect. He's my size; he bends easily into a sitting position; his skin tone matches mine precisely. He doesn't teeter or show signs of wanting to fall out of the chair. Even just idling there in the shadows he seems to have a brooding kinetic readiness.

Yes, he's a little stiff but that only enhances the authenticity. His unblinking, motionless, Beefeatery rectitude is pure Otto Starks. And when we put a Janus cap on backwards, the brim sloping down his neck, the wig is good enough.

Again I run over my checklist. I've got a new button with GPS.[62] My hiding place behind the crates of lesser MacGuffins is undetectable from most angles but has a clear sightline to the Nakamura sword and the dummy. In order to entice the Rat Burglar into the room I have eschewed many of the normal safeguards—no movie butter on the floor this time—and have placed my body double in a position where it is easy to attack him from behind. To the bottom of my shoes I've taped thick sponges. It looks stupid but if I'm going to sneak up on the Rat Burglar sneaking up on me, I need to be silent.

"You ready for this?" Herk says.

"Sure."

"Gun fully loaded?"

"Yep."

"Safety off?"

"Yep."

"Remember the grip? Remember the stance?"

"Jesus. Yes."

"How's the finger?"

I wiggle it to demonstrate its full functionality.

"Balls?"

"Huge." When Herk doesn't look convinced, I say, "Honest. I'm ready. I'm going to, um, take his ass down." When I say

---

62 One click of this sucker and the site-dedicated four-man team of Janus's armed special retention force will rush to within three feet of the GPS button in under ninety seconds. The slowpoke cops usually follow after another ten minutes, God bless them.

this last sentence it comes out ridiculous—it's obviously a stretcher—and I sound like a bad actor uttering a bad line in a made-for-TV mafia movie. It does not inspire confidence.

"All right. Don't take any chances. No head shots. Aim right for the middle of his back. That thing is loaded with Speer Gold Dot jacketed hollow-points," he says. "One-shot stoppers. It's like setting off a grenade inside the soft tissues of the body. It doesn't matter what you hit, it's going to destroy everything in the neighborhood."

"The back?" I say. "Shoot him in the back?"

"Don't get squeamish on me, Otto."

"You never said—"

"This guy isn't an amateur. Do you remember what he did to those French cops?"

"Yeah, but—"

"Do you think you are more qualified than they are to sub-due him?"

"No, but—"

"Do you think he is going to let you take him in like a little fucking piggy going to fucking market?"

"Maybe if I could just—"

"You couldn't, dumbass. You're going to get one shot at this. Literally. And you have to put it in his back. If he turns around and has a chance to make some move, he will. And Vegas won't be betting on you, you know what I mean? Not even the long odds. Got it?"

"O.K.," I say sheepishly. "Sure. In the back. Right."

"You sure?"

"Yeah."

"Right. O.K."

After an angry interval, Herk says, "Am I going to regret switching positions with you?"

"No, no. Go on. Float. I've got the room. I've got the gun. I'll get the Rat Burglar. Just like we talked about. No problem." I make some bang-bang gestures as reassurance. He doesn't look convinced, but he slaps me on the back, manufactures a wink for my benefit, and heads off to fill my floater rounds.

When he's gone I hunker down into my hiding place and wait. My jaw aches and I keep wishing that Charlie were here to rub it. Then I feel guilty for being enough of a sucker to miss her. Then I feel guilty about feeling guilty and I pop a handful of synthesized *Amanita phalloides* to sting myself out of it, but it doesn't work. There's probably not enough sting in the whole bottle for that.

I try to do some non-Charlie memory harvesting but the only thing I can think of is Nunes and Schermer. Something has been bothering me since the conversation I had with Nunes by the river. If Schermer is not the mang—if he's not up to anything more sinister than his usual assholery—then who fixed the scores on the comps? And if Schermer is the mang, why would he try to get me off the Nakamura job in the first place? On one hand, it makes sense that he would want me off the job because I'm the most accomplished pulse at Janus, but on the other hand I do seem to be the favorite target, don't I? Why would the Rat Burglar spend the last year dosing me with nonlethals only to push me off a job now?

Or is it all just happenstance?

Was Schermer snickering in the parking lot a coincidence?

My presence on the Nakamura job itself is confusing. If Schermer is cleared of any charges, why didn't he get reinstated on this gig? Why didn't Po-Mo pull me from the job? And why hasn't he asked me to make good on my promise to resign?

Hasn't Nunes told him that I'm still her prom date?

Shouldn't she be very interested in keeping me far away from all MacGuffins?

Yes she should. Unless she's the Rat Burglar, that is, and this is part of some set-up.

But what are the chances of that?

Perhaps there is no mang at all. Maybe the Rat Burglar just happens to want the MacGuffins that I happen to be pulsing. It's possible—isn't it?—that the reason I scored second on the comps is just because I performed poorly.

But if there is no mang, how does the Rat Burglar always know what tox to use?

And what the hell was the K'plua doing in Schermer's apartment?

It doesn't scan. None of it does.

I upend the container over my mouth and suck down the rest of the death caps. Sure enough, it doesn't hurt enough to make much of a difference. The inextinguishable force of habit makes me reach down to pet Pinkerton, and when my hand comes up empty my heart nosedives so hard I almost hit the floor.

Of course. Pink isn't here anymore. Neither is Charlie. It's just me, the Nakamura sword, the gun, and the specter of death.

With the button in one hand and the gun clasped firmly in the other, I train my sights on the room in front of me and fight myself calm. I make myself mindful of respiration, heart rate, even the salinity of my eyes, pushing my awareness down into that deep, doughy, ultrafocused ataraxia of mine. This is a one-week hold, and I need to be prepared for the long haul. It could be hours or days before he appears. It could be the last minute of the last day. It could be never.

But it isn't.

The Rat Burglar doesn't drill up through the floor. The power doesn't suddenly cut off. A rope doesn't descend mysteriously from the ceiling. No mechanized puck slides into the room and releases toxins into the air. He doesn't appear from within the panels of the podium supporting the Nakamura sword. It isn't the air shaft again. It's much worse.

He just opens the door and walks right in.

The entrance is just his style—audacious, unexpected—but this time something is different. His posture isn't arrogant. His movements are halting and tentative, his steps ponderous and reverie-slow. He doesn't scan the room and, consequently, does not detect the gun trained on him. He cannot take his eyes off of the mannequin—I've seen the same spellbound stasis in people viewing holy artifacts at the Museo Sacro—and when he reaches for the dart gun in its holster, he misses it twice before finding the grip.

I click the button. Now I have ninety seconds to shoot him.

The Rat Burglar raises the dart gun to the dummy, but instead of shooting at range, as is advisable, he starts creeping up behind it, risking detection with every step. One crack of an ankle bone, one squeak of shoe rubber, and he's busted. He knows my audiometry; why would he risk it? It makes no sense. But it affords me the best chance I'll get.

With my guts tied painfully in a Spanish bowline, I sponge across the floor toward the thief who has stolen everything from me. Unfortunately, when I train my sights on the Rat Burglar I realize it's a lot harder to squeeze a trigger while viewing a human being on the other end of the barrel than it is a cube of ballistic gelatin decorated with the facsimile of a rodent. My arm shakes wildly. I have as much of a chance of hitting the Nakamura sword as I do the thief. I'm going to need to get much closer.

The sponges exhale under my shoes as I creep forward, but only I can hear it. At twenty feet I am still too far away to be confident in my marksmanship. Ditto fifteen. Ditto ten. I sponge forward until I am five breathtaking feet away. The Rat Burglar's gun is aimed at the mannequin's back. My gun is aimed at the Rat Buglar's back. For a long moment we stand like this, suspended in time, guns wavering in space.

At this range, and at this angle, I detect two things. One, the syringe is a fatty. At least one hundred milligrams. And two, its odor signature is sperm whale feces and hamster vomit.

Motherfucker is going to juice me with over a hundred milligrams of Nix.

Then the Rat Burglar does something astonishing. His arm sags as if the dart gun is impossibly heavy. His head hangs. He reholsters the gun and pulls out a Cincinnati cord, wrapping the rubber tube twice around each hand. For totally inexplicable reasons, he wants to do this the old-fashioned way. He wants to choke me out.

The Rat Burglar's arms are shaking. So are mine. We look like a tandem team executing a subpar field sobriety test.

He takes a step toward "me." Behind him, I flex my arms until the barrel wavers mainly in the area between his shoulder blades. My vision goes fuzzy, then ultraclear. Bile and water tide in my mouth. Even though I have rehearsed dozens of tough-guy things to say at this moment, I cannot utter anything. Instead I just chamber a round and let the gun speak for me.

"Stop or die," the gun says in imperative gun language.

The Rat Burglar freezes at the sound, slumps in defeat, turns around.

"This is a third-generation Sankt-Moeller button with GPS," I tell him, holding it up. "I already pressed it. The building is already in silent shutdown. The response team is on its way. They'll be here in under a minute. You've got nowhere to go. So just be cool, and—"

Then the Rat Burglar is moving. He bobs under my aim, dips a shoulder, spins, and suddenly a leg is sickling through the air at an improbable angle toward the gun. Color and shadow flash before my eyes. Part of me thinks of the four French policemen. Another part realizes suddenly, and with formidable desperation, that I have been laboring under a significant misapprehension regarding my relationship with the gun: I am not a killer. I don't want to shoot anybody. Not in his personal person. And not to kill. Not dead for all time.

A related epiphany: I don't even want the gun to be a gun. I want it to be a time machine. I want it to shoot me back in time to before the Rat Burglar. To when I first met Charlie. The day at the Frick, maybe. The moment when I first unhooked that bra. I'd settle for two weeks ago or the night of the botched proposal.

Any time when it still seemed possible that Charlie could love me.

This comes to me in a neural flash, an instantaneous electro-chemical burst, and before I fully process my choices—shoot or retreat—I am already yanking my hand away. As I pull it away from the accelerating foot, whiplike, over my head, I can't help admiring my speed. I am fast. Very fast. But not fast enough.

><

It's hard to tell what happens first: the fearsome, godlike crack; the gun jumping in my hand like an angry animal; the blood exploding from the Rat Burglar; his body hitting the concrete.

It's only been a split second, but he looks dead already. His muscles are absolutely soft and unresponsive and his body is crumpled, his limbs all jacked up at crazy, Keith Haring angles.

"Shit," I say. "I'm sorry. I didn't mean it. Don't die. Please don't die."

For the first time I realize how woefully unprepared pulses are for any emergency situations that require something more than clicking a button. I can sit around in a chair for seventy-two hours without the teensiest reduction in attention or sensory acuity, sure; I can detect nearly any sign of intrusion, no doubt; I can take heavy shots of almost any toxin on earth. That I can do straight. That I can do butch. In that particular freakish, sedentary, do-nothing discipline, my kung fu is strong. But what about anything else? Anything normal? I don't know how to fight; I can't shoot straight; I know next to nothing about providing medical aid. What use am I?

My first instinct is to prod the body with my foot. No volitional movement. I wring my hands and perform a spastic, tippy-toe jig of panic. No improvement is manifest. In exchange for saving the Rat Burglar's life I offer to cut a deal with God on any terms he deems reasonable, including but not limited to swearing never to think anything bad ever again/never to do anything bad ever again/never to ask for anything else ever again, but the only response is an expanding puddle of blood on the concrete.

The term "apply pressure" comes to me, but putting down the gun doesn't seem advisable. Neither does letting him die. Fuck.

What did I do?

What am I going to do?

When I kneel down in the hot slicker of blood, when I put the gun on the ground so I can use both hands, when I cross myself three times despite not being religious in any way whatsoever, the Rat Burglar is unresponsive. All indicators are that he is deeply unconscious. But when I try to take his ski mask off to use as a bandage, his body jolts to life. With his good arm he lashes out and spear-hands my throat. There is a gagging pain in my neck and a blinding clap of sheet lightning in front of my eyes, but I can maintain just enough clarity to see his bad arm struggle toward the gun. He gets a handle on it but isn't strong enough to lift it, and before he gets a chance to switch hands I hit him with everything I've got.

"And a-one!"

It's not much of a punch. It has no technique or art. It looks more like a sidearm pitch or an improvised swim stroke, but it has accuracy going for it. It hits the guy right in the bullet hole.

He emits a piercing, womanish screech and the gun skitters across the floor and under some crates. This constitutes a serious demotion of my prospects, as I am now forced into a gunless physical contest with the Rat Burglar. When he springs to his feet, I try to end things early by throwing a hard, terse cross at the middle of the mask. But he steps inside the punch, crisp and clever and quick, and delivers a stiff palm heel to my solar plexus. All the air—more air than I ever knew I had—punches out of my abdomen and I double over, sucking wind.

He tries to sprint past me toward the door—toward freedom—but I scramble on top of him like a vervet. It seems at first that due to the disability of one arm the odds may have been evened, but they have not. We exchange positions of advantage enough times for me to feel as if I have a good shot at delaying him until the cops arrive, but then several painful and demeaning things happen rapidly to my face, at the conclusion of which my nose flattens, its cavities collapse, and I am scarfing down injudicious amounts of metallic-tasting liquid.

Again he breaks for the door and, even though I am discharging blood prodigiously and handicapped by running on sponges, I again give chase and ensnare him. We knot and unknot and knot and unknot. He's not as strong as Schermer but he's much faster. His movements are efficient and disciplined, bird-quick. When we separate again, the Rat Burglar, hunchbacked in agony, circles right in inebriated, limping steps. I try to shake my head clear, gasp for oxygen, and circle left. It is evident that I don't stand much chance going toe-to-toe. Chaotic lawlessness, flailing, and, possibly, groin shots seem to be the order of the day. So I decide to bum-rush the guy, a decision that seems wise until the moment when I lunge forward only to observe an uppercut launch straight up and into my chin. My head snaps backwards, after which there seems to be a short interval of timelessness and void, and then I madcow violently across the room.

Before I fall over he is on top of me. A forearm presses sharply into my carotid. Turning my head sideways I find the biceps, get a mouthful, and bite down as hard as I can. The arm flashes away and I spin around, throwing an accidental elbow that lands squarely in the Rat Burglar's mush. Red liquid sprays out of the nose opening in the ski mask. Now I will be able, at minimum, to say, "Yeah, but you should have seen the other guy."

Flushing with pride, I cock back a fist, but before I can even cry out "And a-two!" something pulps my kidney and I hunch over sideways. Next thing I know I am on the ground again with my neck collared by his legs and I'm breathing heavy shoe leather.

This time the chokehold is on snug and certain. I can't move my head one inch. I can barely move my eyeballs. A shinbone cuts sharply against my larynx and a tube of darkness constricts around my vision. I try to gag but no air comes in and no air goes out. Twinkling lights appear before me, dance merrily, and sizzle against my eyelids. Being a connoisseur of unconsciousness, I know this heralds an unfavorable outcome.

The only thing I can see is the tuft of the hypo in the dart gun. It looks very red.

My options are few.

Corralling the remainder of my motor control, I stretch out a feeble hand to the Rat Burglar and administer a few impotent swats. I try to smite his balls but don't have the angle. Then I perceive a patch of warm liquid on his clothes. Blood. Following the trail, I blindly claw upward on the arm until I detect a radiant, fecund wetness. I make two fingers go hard and straight and then, as I feel my body going faint and starry and buoyant, I ramrod the open wound.

The Rat Burglar shrieks and the chokehold releases lickety-split.

When we separate something clatters to rest at my feet. It's the dart gun. Amazed, I pick it up.

One hundred milligrams of Nix.

It's too good to be true.

Sucking down a luxuriant mouthful of oxygen, I straighten up in a way meant to convey authority and say, "All right, pal, let's try that again...."

I don't mean it as an invitation. In fact, I mean it as a threat whose object is to dissuade him from trying again, but alas, the Rat Burglar seems immune to irony. He takes it literally. As I stand there, endeavoring to lord it over him, a leg pistons toward my hand. It comes from another unpredictable angle—where do these kicks come from?—and there is the same blur of color and shadow. This time, though, I don't yank my hand away.

This time I fire.

As I pull the trigger I feel a sharp pain in my wrist and shortly thereafter something else knocks me powerfully backwards. My sternum registers a shattering pain and my skull makes a concretinous crack on the floor. The only consolation is that I heard the dart gun go off. It made a noise remarkably like Charlie's pop-tops.

Pfffft.

When I pry myself up on one elbow, I see the Rat Burglar is bent over, absolutely frozen. He is staring at me, immobilized with the same intensity with which he spied on the mannequin. That's some fast-acting Nix.

"Not so quick after all, are you, tough guy?"

The spectacle of the Nixed Rat Burglar is obscured by something hot and sticky in my eyes. I wipe at it and my hand comes away covered in red syrup. All of a sudden I want dearly to vomit. Sleeping also presents itself as an appealing option. But I'm not done gloating yet. I try to writhe myself upright but cannot. My neck and shoulders are awash in warm liquid. I can feel it seeping down my spine and into my trousers. The Rat Burglar moves toward me, his gloved hands outstretched.

It is then that I realize, with distress, that his body is tuftless.

Mine is not.

My leg is sporting a red-tufted dart. It is planted midthigh, firm and proud and erect as a conqueror's flag.

My senses detonate. My nose and mouth flood with the nauseating odor of Nix. My tongue has turned into a furry yam and the nerves in my extremities are flayed and burning with an unbearable heat. I try to pry out the dart but my hands won't move. All over, my skin feels as if it's swarming with stinging insects. My visual field ruptures and beads with shifting, luminous channels. I can hear the sound of huffing and puffing and footsteps sprinting down the hall, but it all seems distant and small, as if the mouse response team were scampering to a crime scene in their mouse boots, tiny keys jangling.

"Rethponth team ah heah, ath-hole," I tell him.

The pain from the Nix vies for brain recognition with the skull fracture. My inhibited nervous system dimly perceives that the puddle from my head has expanded on the concrete to engulf my back and hips. It feels as if I'm wrapped in a wet, blood-warm, amniotic cape.

Finally the concussion wins. My eyelids succumb to gravity and I surrender to the undertow. As I'm pulled down I am grateful that my last vision isn't the Rat Burglar's mask but Charlie's beautiful face, lips parted, expectant and alive, her eyes full of love.

The Treachery of Images

At first my viewfinder finds no view. There are only noises to indicate whereabouts: juddering plastic wheels on industrialized surfaces, the self-important clicking of ballpoint pens, the stentorian burr of powerful machinery drawing an immense electrical charge far below my unergonomic gurney, and, underneath it all, the constant beeper-bleat and sneaker-squeak obbligato of the late-shift hospital.

My sensation starts to return, too. I feel not just paralyzed but peristalsied; there is a livid body-heat to it, a grublike feeling of inertia and filth. I don't feel as if I am lying under sheets; I feel as if I'm buried in mud. Or steaming mulch. But at least I feel. Correction: at least I feel in most provinces. I do a roll call of body parts. I squeeze fingers, curl toes, flex limbs and abs and facial muscles. Everything sounds off except my left leg. Opening my eyes doesn't reveal much except a voltaic charge and sheen of pulsating ultramarine light. Nowhere is my leg manifest. I may have to accept that it has been amputated.

As I'm reconciling myself to the idea of a life of pegleggery, my consciousness incandesces between what all cues inform me is the usual reality and another, vibrating, ulcerated one. In both worlds, one sentiment lifebuoys unsinkably: forfeiting one leg in exchange for the apprehension of the Rat Burglar is a very worthwhile, very equitable trade.

Over the next *x* number of hours I experience an interminable catalogue of segued hallucinations. The quiddity of myself and my many hopes dissolve into the sheets and then re-form in the fueled visions of Charlie bending over me; of an ownerless leg gamboling around the Janus locker room, trying to find me; of my *Clean Getaway*, pilotless, stalled out somewhere in the doldrumsy Atlantic, idle as a painted fucking ship upon a painted fucking ocean.

Through the diaphanous, slugsilver webbing laid over my vision I also see people. Their features are anamorphic and disturbing, jack-o'-lanterny. Outside my door there is a matching set of cops standing sentry in a discouraging, immovable *repoussoir*. Next to me, gurneyside, is a looming Detective Nunes, the tissue of her neck hard and pebbled like sharkskin. Her mouth moves but I can't interpret the noises. Her voice has a faraway, semimystical, didgeridoo drone. It is, no doubt, meaningful—the expression is as grim as a Schmidt-Rottluff—but the meaning is lost in my logjammed brain.

Behind her is another image. Sitting on the bench outside of my room's window, hanging on to an aged mop, is a guy who appears to be roughly the size of a tugboat. Underneath his orderly whites he is wearing a powder blue shirt that matches precisely his pleated turban. I've seen him before but can't quite place him. He smiles at me covertly and gives me a crabbed, secret wave, as if we're in study hall and he has something totally important to say, dude, but doesn't want to get busted.

I reprimand my subconscious and submit a requisition for better visions. I squeeze shut my eyes—either real ones or dream ones—and tell it, Charlie, for God's sake. Pretty please, give me Charlie.

When I scrape together enough consciousness to open my eyes, I again see Detective Nunes. How do I know it's the corporeal Nunes and not the wraith? The odor of menthol and pencil shavings, the drop in air pressure, the fact that she is shaking me rudely.

"I know you're awake, Starks. Do yourself a favor and get up." Nunes bends over me with hieratic menace. She is the biggest thing in the room, with the strongest gravity. She has the larger-than-life presence, the absolute centrality—the outraged divinity, even—of a truly pissed-off Christ in a Byzantine mosaic. Not answering snappily does nothing to appease her.

"It doesn't matter that we don't have the videotape we planted on the Nakamura job," she says. "We don't need it. We have you on a traffic cam at Eighty-sixth and Lex on the night of the break-in at Schermer's, carrying the shovel. We have the shovel from the parking garage. You're done, Starks. You're hog-tied. Your only chance at a sentence recommendation is to tell us where the Rat Burglar is. And where the Nakamura sword is. Every minute counts, Starks. So start talking."

I try to voice my outrage and confusion—what tape of the Nakamura job? what traffic cam? and what the hell do you mean, the Rat Burglar got away with the Nakamura sword?—but my mouth is glued shut with dried spittle, and my facial muscles are mostly unresponsive. When I move my mouth it only sneers uselessly, an expression I hope is obscured by the breathing mask on my face. Taking the only defensive action of which I am capable, I close my eyes and try to think thoughts unrelated to hard time.

She again shakes me ungently. "Starks, get up, damn it."

An angry female voice comes to my rescue. Deciding that ostrichism is the better part of valor, I keep my eyes closed.

"Doctor, you don't understand—"

"Step away from my patient immediately, please."

"Otto Starks has—"

"I said you could wait for Mr. Starks outside of his room. Outside. When he's stabilized and alert and oriented, you can speak to him. Not before."

"I have a warrant for his arrest, Doctor."

"Unless that warrant says you can kill him, you're just going to have to wait."

I can almost hear Nunes's jaw muscles popping.

"When can he be moved?"

"I don't know."

"He was awake just a moment ago."

"I doubt that, Detective. He hasn't had any muscle movement since admission."

"Otto Starks is an accomplice to the Rat Burglar. Every minute that I can't talk to him the Rat Burglar gets farther away."

"Who's the Rat Burglar?"

"Put it this way. Otto Starks has helped steal over thirty million dollars' worth of art. And he's the only one who can bring in the thief."

"I don't know anything about a Rat Burglar, and I don't know much about police interrogations, but my guess is that a dead subject won't do you much good."

"Doctor Zandipour—"

"I also doubt that the kind of answers Mr. Starks could give you right now would be very useful. If you were to ask him two plus two he'd very likely tell you 'spaceship.' "

"I have very simple questions to ask him."

"They're just going to have to wait. Even if he were A and O, which he isn't, he couldn't do much talking. His lungs are busy with the respirator right now."

A gristly moment of silence ensues.

"Are his hands busy with anything?"

For the first time the doctor seems uncertain. She pauses, says, "No...," and I hear her teeth click shut.

"Then you won't mind if I print him."

Something cool presses against my palms and fingertips. I hardly breathe.

"And I think I'll restrain him, Doctor. For his own safety, of course." I feel plastic zip-strips encircle my wrists, binding them to the railing.

"That's hardly necessary, Detective. This man has suffered a serious concussion. He has also been injected with one hundred milligrams of nixolophan. Do you know what that means? In this case, that means he might not be coherent for some time. He might have memory loss. He may never speak. He might not even breathe unassisted ever again."

I crack open my eyes, grateful not only for my optics but for my mother's long lashes, and see Nunes clap a piece of paper to my chart. She is giving the doctor an unambiguous diecast look.

"I'll leave the warrant here." Nunes tosses the clipboard onto my groin. I don't emit an incriminating groan, but it's close. "When he's awake I want to know about it. If I hear from either one of these officers here that you wait even ten seconds to call me, I'm considering that obstruction. Do you know what that means? In this case, Doctor, that means jail time."

⇒⇐

Again I am awakened by shaking, but this time it feels good—gentle, solicitous, it eases me out of it. The odor accompanying the action isn't of the precinct, either; it has a full headnote of sandalwood and bamboo over something else, something Hesperidean that I can't quite place: Covet.

"Wake up," says the doctor. "We don't have much time." Standing before me is a tall, slim woman with the complexion and pointed canthus of someone from East Asia. Her lab coat has a name tag that says Dr. Nair Zandipour. When she takes off the mask I open my eyes, cough-clear my throat, and speak.

"Don't I need that respirator, Doc?"

"You were never on a respirator. You are breathing just fine."

"But I heard you say—"

"How do you feel?"

I want to tell her that I feel like...no, the truth is that the pain of Nix is unsimileable. I don't feel like anything else. If I had to offer something, I'd say it feels as if all the iron in my blood has rusted. But it's more than that. There's also a paradoxical numbness, a hacksaw pain in my head, and an excruciating, allover chemical burn.

"Bad."

"I can open up the drip a little but you're already on a pretty heavy dose."

She dials up the IV and I do my best to act relieved.

"Do you know where you are?"

"Hospital. Not sure where."

"Do you know what day it is? And your name?"

I tell her.

"I'm going to tell you three words right now and in a couple of minutes I want you to repeat them to me, O.K.? Cowboy, marshmallow, sailboat."

"What about the guards?"

"They've discovered Nurse Annibal. I don't know if she's two-minute cute or ten-minute cute, so we've got to be fast."

"Fast for what?"

She pricks my right big toe with a needle. "Can you feel this?"

"Ouch. Yes."

She pricks something else. Its contact registers, but it's not painful. The startling thing is that it seems to be registering in...

"Yes," I say, looking down. "Oh my God! My leg! I still have my leg!"

"Of course you do. Can you feel this, too?"

"Sort of. It doesn't hurt, but I know it's there."

"Move your toes for me." I do. "Congratulations, Mr. Starks."

When I stop crying, I say, "I think I've been hallucinating. Is that normal?"

"You have quite a concussion."

"I imagined Nunes was here. Was that true?" She nods. "And you? This is real, too? I still have my leg? How do I know?"

Dr. Zandipour pinches me. The pinch may or may not have some flirt in it.

"Why are you helping me?"

"Name six months for me, going backwards from March."

"March, February, January, December, November, October."

"Good."

"You could get in trouble, you know."

"You're an interesting case, Mr. Starks. There is so much going on here I've never seen before. You took one hundred milligrams of nixolophan and not only survived it but seem to have suffered only partial nerve damage. Can you explain that?"

"Lucky?"

"I don't think so."

"I drink a lot of milk?"

"I think this might have more to do with it." She lifts the sheet and shows me my leg—my beautiful, extant leg—and around the needle mark is a black circle drawn in Sharpie with the caption *100mg Nix*.

"What the..."

"Someone at the scene administered some antitoxin before we got there."

"Must have been Herk," I say to myself.

"Nine-one-one also received an anonymous call from a

samaritan giving them the details. We were able to prep the ambulance with antitoxin—not exactly the sort of thing an EMT usually carries—and we rerouted to this facility, which is probably the only reason you might ever walk again."

"I might walk? But I thought—"

"Quiet," she says, nodding over her shoulder at the cops flirting with Nurse Annibal. "Can you feel this?"

"Yes," I say, thrilled that the needle in my thigh hurts even a little bit. "Doc, why are you covering for me? Didn't you hear that I'm the accomplice of a notorious thief?"

"The Polecat isn't a thief," she says.

"What?"

"You of all people know what he has done for Iraq."

"I'm not his accomplice. I don't know anything." She looks at me dubiously. It occurs to me that I may be getting favorable treatment from Dr. Zandipour precisely because she does think that. I take a different tack. "Let's pretend for a second that I don't know anything that he has done in Iraq. Tell me."

"The same thing he has done for the art of just about every other country on earth that doesn't attend the G-8 summits."

"What's that?"

But she doesn't tell me. She just swats me playfully, as if I had authored a witticism.

For the first time in my life I'm grateful to be in the presence of a Rat Burglar nut. Even though she doesn't really seem like a nut. She seems like a smart, beautiful, great-smelling woman. One who may be flirting with me because she thinks I'm associated with the Rat Burglar.

One who is helping deceive the cops because of that association.

"So you're helping me because you think I work for..."

"I don't owe any loyalty to the art police. My first and only responsibility is to the health of my patients. Now, can you repeat those three words for me?"

"Cowboy," I say. "Um..."

"Are you certain?"

"I think so. Cowboy, and then, ah..."

"It's important that you're certain of your answers because if you cannot correctly repeat those three items then I cannot consider you alert and oriented. Under those circumstances I could not approve any questioning. So concentrate on your answers."

"Oh," I say, getting it. "Fire truck...giraffe...soda pop."

Even though I don't utter the correct third word, I think it, and "sailboat" brings me painfully back to real life. I have no *Clean Getaway*, no career, no Charlie. Even if I manage to hobble out of the hospital somehow, I'll be a fugitive. I have no family to hide me. I'm too broke to start a new life in some Central American country. I have plenty to run away from, but nothing to run to.

What's the point?

Then I remember the point: Deke.

If I don't give him a sizable chunk of change real soon he is going to do something awful to Charlie. And it will be my fault. Herk would kill me if he could hear this, but: I still love her. I can't help it. And no matter what she's done, and with whom, I can't let anything happen to her. I don't know how I'll find the money, but I know I won't find it in a jail cell.

"Doc, I've got to get out of here," I say. "Like pronto."

"I can't remove the restraints. I cannot do anything to abet your escape." As she says this she leans over me to punch some buttons on a machine and the scenic area beneath the neck of her shirt opens over my face, giving me a noseful of Covet.

Her contortion also nuzzles one of my restrained hands inside a pocket in her lab coat, where it encounters a cell phone. "Unfortunately, I cannot be confident in your neurological function and so I cannot at present approve any questioning or removal from hospital care. Given the urgency of the police investigation, however, I will have to return shortly to examine you again. I'd say you have an hour."

Before she turns in a graceful whirl of lab coat and long hair and Hesperidean mystery, I get another pinch in an area that leaves little doubt about its flirtation. Frantically I start keying in a text message to Herk, the scent-memory of Covet still blooming in my nose.

Herk to the Rescue

It's unclear, even to me, what Herk will do to spring me. He's too big to execute any kind of sneakiness, and as witnessed by the Schermer break-in, he's as much of a criminal mastermind as I am. Maybe he'll sic an entire school of Goldfish on the cops. Maybe he'll flex his biceps and make them faint. Maybe he'll just loom.

But he doesn't. He shows up in the reflection from the window of my door, dim and glossy like a figure from a rain-slicked Arntzenius, steamrolling down the hall dressed in scrubs and holding a doctorish clipboard. At first it looks like he is going to perform some kind of con, but when one of the cops holds up a hand to deny him entry and says, "Only Dr. Zandi—" Herk, barely breaking stride, jabs the metallic edge of the clipboard violently into his throat. The cop goes down like a fainting goat. The other one reaches for his gun but doesn't get it. Herk has already hit him in the face with a hard, sinking hook. His shoulder is in it, and the guy's head snaps back onto the metal doorjamb and he, too, slumps to the floor.

This all transpires so quickly I don't have time to say anything until Herk drags the cops into the room and dumps the bodies behind the gurney, out of sight.

"What the fuck?" I manage.

One of the cops is groaning and making a dreamy sign language with his hands. Herk—who still has not looked at me or spoken a word—wraps a forearm around the guy's neck and squeezes until his face goes as red-black and engorged as a raspberry's drupelets. After some muffled snarfing of air and spittle, the cop goes horribly silent. Herk lets him drop.

It's got to be another hallucination. I blink and shake it out but Herk is still there, and so is the cop-mound.

"Are they dead?" I say.

A fist addresses itself violently to my skull. It takes my Nixed brain a beat to comprehend, but then I understand that it couldn't be the cops, or me, or a new entrant in the room. The process of elimination tells me it's Herkimer's fist.

The hit hurts plenty, but it wasn't meant to hurt. It was meant to shut me up. It does that. It does something else, too. It makes me cry. "What are you doing?" I want to say, but instead a fat gumball of saline beads up in my eye and rolls down my cheek.

Against orders, my nose emits a miserable, gurgling sniffle.

Herk is annoyed. He is muttering under his breath. He should have done this himself in the first fucking place, he says. Fuck the setup. Fuck the Polecat. Dead's as good as jail.

It's still as if I'm not in the room.

He breaks out some zip-strips, sees that my wrists are already bound, swears, shoves them back in his pocket, and pulls out a large hypodermic needle.

It smells of sperm whale feces and hamster vomit.

"Herk…"

This time it's backhanded, open-fisted, a bitchslap that makes tear pellets spray around the room. Then, still not looking at me, Herk peels off a section of duct tape and seals it over my mouth.

"There. That's much better. I should have done that a long time ago."

With his banana-finger Herk flicks the hypo, squirts out the leader, then grabs a wad of hair and forces my head backwards, chin-high. I try to grab at him but my hands, zip-stripped, can only perform a useless, lobsterlike scrabble. I thrash my legs. I champ and spit against the sticky tape. I jerk and jive against the restraints. I discharge sweat and tears at him.

None of it matters.

With my chin upturned, my head jacked back into the wall, I cannot see anything except ceiling tiles. I feel a terrible pro-tonostalgia for my toes. I want to watch them wiggle one more time, one last beautiful time, but I can't see them. Then there is a painful bee sting in my neck and I feel the needle inside my jugular. Nausea and dread rise up in my gorge and push against the tape.

I think: What are you doing, Herk? Why?

I think: Don't. I need to pay off Deke.

No one else can save Charlie.

My vision is all ceiling tile, so I can't see it, but I hear it. And I feel it. Before the toxic liquid plunges into my bloodstream there is a gonglike ringing, a gurney-trembling collision, and the grip on my scalp releases. When I look down I see the truly astonishing: Herkimer wavering on his feet, his eyes clicking up and down like the spinners of a slot machine. He reaches dopily into his pocket but before he can extract anything he is again hit in the head by the fire extinguisher. When he falls onto the unconscious cops with a padded, mattresslike whomp, the guy in the turban strips the tape off my mouth.

I just stare at Herkimer.

"My name is Jagjeet Singh," the guy says. "I am here to help you. You must do exactly as I say. Do you understand?"

My mouth opens wide but the horror noises are not audible. Maybe dogs can hear them.

"Nod if you understand."

I am still trying and failing to scream. It hurts; it's like having dry heaves in the lungs.

"Otto Starks, nod if you understand."

Mouth open, dry heaving, I nod.

"Good."

He reaches into Herkimer's pocket and produces a cruel, curved knife. He uses it to cut me free from my many tubes. Bending down, he puts his fingers on the cops' necks. Then he puts the blade up to Herk's throat. Now I can speak.

"No," I croak. "Don't."

"If I don't he will come after us."

"No he won't. He's my friend." I say this in spite of the flagrant evidence to the contrary. I say it because I need it to be true.

I can't lose Herk, too. I couldn't survive it.

"He will find us and kill us."

"No. He's my friend."

"He is not."

"There's a reason for what he was doing. I know it."

I'm crying again.

"This man is not your friend."

He grabs Herkimer's arm by the wrist and pulls back the sleeve, revealing a tattoo that features a knife piercing, like Cupid's arrow, the unskillfully executed, nearly childlike image of a hat. I think: I've seen that image before. On a file at Janus, on a Crimies card, on a note I received in a box containing the remains of Pinkerton.

I think: it can't be. I think: please no. Then I think nothing at all.

The Truth About Herkimer

I don't care that the cops chase us avidly. I don't care that I am still strapped into my gurney and pinballing around the back of the ambulance in an injurious way as it careens dangerously around unknown streets. I don't care when we ram something ahead of us and I pitchpole onto the diamond plating of the ambulance floor, my face grating away. After the collision, when the guy in the turban throws open the doors, cuts me out of the zip-strips, hoists me on his shoulder like a side of beef, runs me down several blocks, through one residential building, into another, out the back door, and, finally, into a cabbie garage, at which time he dumps me into the footwell of a cab and pulls leisurely into traffic past bewildered cops looking everywhere, I don't care. Even ten blocks later, when I recognize on him the same scent of garam masala that was on Charlie's bra and my heart spasms—still, I do not care.

Herkimer is Jimmy the Hat.

"I know," says my driver-cum-rescuer-cum-cuckoldmaker.

"Who are you?" I say. "What do you want with me?"

"My name is Jagjeet Singh."

"You stole Charlie from me."

I punch the plastic divider. It doesn't break. My hand might have.

"I did not."

"Bullshit. Let me out."

Even though we're going thirty and surrounded by thronging cabs, I try to bail out. The doors won't open.

"Special cab," he says, almost apologetically.

"Pull over and let me out."

"We have to get out of this neighborhood first."

I slump back into the seat, defeated.

"Herkimer," I say, still stunned. "It can't be true. That would mean...all those dead pulses. The guy in Seattle. And...Pinkerton."

"I know."

"How do you know? Who the hell are you?"

"Let's just say that I know what trouble you're in. And that I'm here to help you."

"Why should I trust you?"

"You're alive, aren't you?"

I grunt.

"So...Herk is the mang," I mutter.

"Yes."

"He isn't fucking Taoist."

"No."

"He didn't believe shit about receptors. Fucking Spam. Goddamn Golden Elixir of Life. He wasn't spiritually opposed to someone seeing his naked arms. He was hiding his tattoo."

"Yes."

"That's why he freaked at Alpha that night at the Snug. He almost revealed it."

My body is still draped in severed rubber hoses. I look like a marionette who has been cut down and extinguished, a tortured Švankmajer puppet.

"And when we broke into Schermer's. The K'plua..."

"Planted. To incriminate you."

"He was wearing gloves."

"Of course. No prints in the apartment."

"And he didn't get recorded by the traffic cam. There never was any Goldfish at the intersection, he just wanted my hat to cover his face. And the gun. He wanted me to kill Schermer."

"If it worked out that way."

"And the shooting range and everything. Why did he teach me to shoot? Why would he switch places with me on the Nakamura job?"

"He wanted you to shoot the Rat Burglar."

"Then why would he fix the comps so I didn't get the job?"

"He didn't."

"You mean I really was outscored by Schermer?"

Jagjeet shrugs. "Once you were off the Nakamura job he had to get you back on it. Breaking into the apartment and planting the K'plua would get Schermer arrested and you back on the job. Your fingerprints showing up later would seal Nunes's case against you."

"Why would he want me to kill the Rat Burglar?"

"He wanted you in prison for being a mang. Murder was a backup plan."

"Murder," I say, just to hear the word.

"The gun he gave you will be traced to a murder committed in Miami last June."

"I had a job in Miami last June."

"Of course. It's part of the setup."

The windows of the cab are calcined with solidified dirt and hardened grease. It makes the world I glimpse through them an oily netherworld of crime and deceit. I know it always has been, but I thought I was fighting against it. Now I see I am just a part of it.

"He was never trying to help me. He didn't care. I told him everything. He wasn't..." I sniffle shamefully. "He was the only friend I had."

"I'm sorry," Jagjeet says.

There's nothing in the backseat to touch or cling to except the seat belt. I pull it out, wrap it around my arms, and nuzzle the buckle passionately with my face. I drizzle on it. I whisper to it. I hug that seat belt for all I'm worth.

A few minutes later I say, "Why set me up? Why not just kill me?"

"Azar's strict orders."

"And the Nix?"

"Azar's orders."

"But why, though? Why me?"

"It's complicated."

"Pull over. Pull the fucking cab over. Let me out."

He heads down some cobblestoned West Village side street. He pulls behind a van, throws it in park, regards me with a look that is at once pharaoh-stern and tender—he is trying to determine my risk as a runner; he also seems to feel sorry for me—and opens the door.

Scraping my numb leg behind me, I pull myself out of the cab. The afternoon Manhattan fever of hydrocarbons and trash pushes heavily on me.

"Explain it," I say.

"Two years ago you put away Frankie Nickels and Tony 'Kong' Mavrogordo."

"I know that."

"Frankie Nickels is Azar's cousin."

"What?"

"Azar has had it in for you ever since."

"Cousin...," I say, amazed that I didn't know this. That Janus didn't.

"Azar didn't want to kill you. He wanted revenge. He wanted to do to you what you did to his cousin. He wanted you—"

"Disgraced," I say, understanding. "In jail. Paralyzed."

"Yes."

"And there was so much Nix because Herk knew I was vulnerable to it."

"Sort of."

"You've got to tell me. How do you know all this?"

"I work for Azar, too."

"Then why did you save me? Won't he kill you?"

"That's the complicated part."

I wither at him. "More complicated than you stealing Charlie from me?"

"I didn't steal Charlie."

"I saw the pictures."

"You saw what Azar wanted you to see. To make you angry enough to kill."

"The photos were doctored?"

"I don't know what you saw, but I swear to you I am Charlie's friend only."

"Really?"

Hope ignites in my stomach but I clench against it. I don't trust it.

"Otto Starks, she loves you. She needs you. I can take you to her."

Is he chicaning? I almost don't care. At this point, anything could be true.

Why not love?

Against my best efforts, my heart dives and loops like a stunt kite. Gushing like an idiot, I say, "O.K. Let's go! I don't want to waste any time!"

"Otto…"

"Come on. It's going to take an hour to get to her apartment from here."

"It's not going to take an hour."

"Ozone Park? Oh yes it will. Trust me."

Jagjeet looks direly pained by my assertion.

"No it won't," he says gently. "We're already there."

"What? She lives in a dumpy little—"

"Otto, brace yourself for a shock."

The Polecat

Jagjeet opens the door and the truth swarms over me. Cling-ing to the door frame for support, I stare into the wonderland of shock and hurt. Panning left in the apartment, the familiar: a stack of scholarly books whose titles I recognize, her utilitar-ian tote, identifiable shoes. Panning right, the alien: a coffee table littered with arcane-looking tools and electronics, a can-ister of face paint, black RealFeel gloves, scattered hypodermic needles and vials of toxins—the paraphernalia of talent. There is an olfactory component to the horror as well. On the air are the usual Charlie odors but also the sour, glandular tang of live animal—a ferrety smell that is not ferret.

Sure enough, the Polecat is a woman. My woman.

A bubbling sack of poison bursts open in my stomach. I vomit discreetly over the threshold. Jagjeet looks down on me, his face velvety and bunched with pathos. He is sorry for me. Of course, given the power of my discernment about people, perhaps he's mocking me. Either way, the grief and heartbreak and betrayal manifest themselves in a novel way. I haul off and deck Jagjeet in the face as hard as I can. I don't cry out "And a-one" and I don't miss, but he doesn't make a noise or move to block it. He just takes it. As if he deserves it. Or as if he wants to give me something, and this is the only thing he has. Blood worms out of one of his nostrils and he just keeps looking at me with those I'm Sorry eyes, saying nothing.

Snooping through the rest of the apartment is no less vertiginous and no less painful. I find notebooks with detailed records of all manner of Starksiana: my toxin resistances, dosages, vulnerabilities, on-job manner, schedule, locations, provenances of the works I pulse. Everything. On the coffee table is a case of very faintly colored blue contacts—tricky—and in the closet I discover a set of foam body-contoured padding, the man-suit that Charlie wore under her clothes to disguise the narrowness of her waist, the curve in her pelvis, her breasts. There is a second bedroom[63] whose only furnishing is a cage with a polecat whose fur is so patchy it looks as if he's suffered the depredations of chemo: the oft-scissored source of Charlie's calling card, I real-

---

63 It unbalances me to think of the patrician implications of this term as it applies to Charlie; to have a "second bedroom" seems all wrong for the struggling assistant professor of art history I thought I knew and loved.

ize. A plaque bolted to the wires says "Otto." Jagjeet shrugs as if to say, "Who can possibly plumb the mysterious workings of a woman's mind?" I put a finger through the bars and he puts his wet, twitching, calico-and-pink nose on it, sniffs, comes to some kind of mammalian determination, and licks me.

The kitchen is weirdly stocked with dozens of bags of potato chips,[64] but the living room is just a living room, and the bedroom, thank God, is just a bedroom. On the table are three pictures—one, a shot of me and Pinkerton at the Tompkins Square dog run that I didn't know she had; two, a faded, perfectly square, eighties-era Polaroid of a beautiful woman with her dark hair up in a red kerchief, holding a baby who is clutching at her necklace; and three, a picture of adult-Charlie standing beside a gray-haired man with a manicured beard. There is something donnish yet mischievous about him. Sad, too. He is smiling, but it's too tight, tympanic—it's trying hard to cover something. His arm is around Charlie, who is wearing a blue and white dress with sandals. It's somewhere outdoors and there is a lake and green mountains behind them. Maybe it's just the vernal scene, but Charlie seems much younger. Maybe it's the dress, or the fact that her hair is straightened, or—then I get it: her nose. It does not have its boomerang bend. It hasn't yet been broken. It didn't happen when she was twelve. She wasn't riding her bicycle along the wall. She hadn't been trying to wave at a boy.

Even that was a lie.

64 This is worrisome not only because it's a startling visual spectacle—I have never seen so many bags of chips outside of a D'Agostino aisle—but because I never knew she even had a passing fancy for chips. I've never seen her eat potato chip number one. Maybe it's dumb, but it makes me feel tremendously betrayed: I have been loving *who*? Apparently I don't know. Have never known.

Again I lash out at Jagjeet. This time he grabs the punch in his catcher-mitt hand. One freebie, it seems, is all I get.

"Tell me everything," I say when he releases me. "Start at the beginning."

"There isn't time. When Jimmy the Hat wakes up he will come after us, and he'll think to come here. I needed to show you this so you would believe me, but now we need to go," he says. "Charlie needs our help right now."

"She what?"

"She needs our help."

"In case you didn't notice, Charlie is the Rat Burglar. And she has taken everything from me. Everything."

"She's in trouble."

"She ruined my career."

"She needs you."

"I'll probably go to jail because of her."

"She helped keep you out of jail."

"She tried to fucking paralyze me!"

"No, she didn't."

"She lied to me just like Herkimer. Jimmy. Whoever the hell he is."

"You lied to her, too."

"Not like this."

"Otto, we can argue later. But she's in bad trouble now—right now—and I can't help her alone."

"Have you been following this conversation? Charlie ruined my life. Why should I help her?" The words sting; immediately I regret them.

Jagjeet beetles his brow, looks out the window anxiously, then pulls a DVD out of his pocket and inserts it in the player on the dresser.

"What's this?" I say.

"Security recording. Last night," he says. "Watch."

On the screen everything happens all over again: the Rat Burglar taking out the Cincinnati cord, the gunshot, the attempt at resuscitation, the horrible, womanish scream when I punch the wound, the hectic fight. As I watch, I realize that my hand is opening and closing, feeling the phantom weight of the gun. Its textured grip. Its sharp recoil. I doubt I'll ever get that feeling of death out of my hand.

"I don't get it," I say. "The Rat Burglar always disables the cameras. How did this recording happen?"

"The camera wasn't part of the system. It was a discrete unit operating on its own power. A home video camera. Hidden. Installed by Nunes with the cooperation of Janus. Charlie almost didn't catch it."

"Nunes knew it would happen," I say, marveling. "That's why I wasn't pulled off the job. She wanted her proof. How did you get it?"

"Look here," Jagjeet says, ignoring my question. "The choke-hold she is putting on. It is a blood choke, not an air choke. It is completely safe. She is trying not to hurt you. But it gives you enough time to find the wound. It was a mistake for her to do it, but she was trying to take it easy on you."

"She wasn't taking it easy when she hit me in the mouth."

"Can you open your mouth?"

"Yeah."

"Do you have all your teeth?"

"Yeah."

"She was taking it easy."

"What about the damn Nix, then? What about that?"

"Just watch."

The rest of the fight unfolds exactly as I remember it. Things transpire as quickly on-screen as they did in real life. The Rat

Burglar—Charlie, I mean: *Charlie*—kicks the dart gun out of my hand; I shoot myself; a second kick sends me James Browning sideways, after which I fall and crack my head on the concrete. The crisp sound is clear even with the poor audio of the portable video unit, and the dart is so firmly embedded in my thigh, protruding with such erect majesty, that it looks like a permanent fixture of my leg, a red-tufted prosthetic.

Then Charlie is on me. She yanks out the dart, skitters it furiously across the room. She pulls off her mask—incriminating herself on video for all time, I realize—and presses it firmly to my head with one hand, stanching the flow of blood. With the other she pulls out a vial of whitish liquid and, while weeping onto my unmoving face, administers the antitoxin.

"Forgive me forgive me forgive me," she's saying.

At the last moment, Charlie pulls her mask back on, and then the response team rushes in, guns drawn. For one second, they stare, stunned to be, finally, in the presence of the Rat Burglar, but then they descend on her. Charlie clings to me, desperately trying to deliver the second dose of the antitoxin.

"Step away!" one yells, gun drawn. "Step away with your hands up!"

But Charlie won't. Neither will she defend herself. Both hands administer to me. One of the guys pistol-whips her in the back of the head and Charlie goes limp. Another kicks her in the ribs just to make sure. She doesn't respond. The men then enjoy a moment of celebration—they have just apprehended the Rat Burglar; they're all going to get laid—and as they congratulate each other I see behind them Jagjeet streaking into the room, a blackjack in each hand.

A flurry of startling activity ensues and several harrowing but nonlethal-looking blows precipitate the men onto the floor. Jagjeet rouses Charlie, who groggily tries to resume dispensing antitoxin, but sirens are already screaming outside the building.

"Cops," Jagjeet says. "We have to go."

"No. He needs at least three more shots. At thirty-second intervals."

"We're leaving," he says. "Get the sword."

But Charlie ignores the sword. She cuts my pant leg off, circles the puncture wound, writes *100 mg Nix*. Then she grabs a radio from one of the downed men and, assuming a comically masculine voice, makes the report to 911 as she casts about the room, looking for something. She finds it, her eyes locking with mine. She beelines for the camera, her face getting bigger and bigger until the only thing I can see is her watery eyes.

It clicks off.

"She risked her life to save you," Jagjeet says.

"I need a minute alone with this," I say.

"Jimmy could show up any second."

"I need to look at this alone. Just give me one minute of privacy with it. You can stand right outside the door. And then we can go. Please?"

Jagjeet looks wary, peers out the window again for any sign of Jimmy the Hat, nods reluctantly. When he closes the door behind him I rewind to the moment when she takes off her mask. I can't believe it. I see it but it doesn't compute. Play, rewind, play, rewind: it doesn't change. It's always Charlie's face.

I burrow my head into a pillow and make a keening, locust-like sound of misery. Then I scrape myself together, open the window, step out onto the fire escape, descend to the pavement, and, as fast as possible, I gimp down the street.

Do I or Don't I?

Giddy with heartbreak, barefoot, attired in a hospital gown that is prone to flapping open, my head wrapped in blood-stained gauze, and reduced to a deranged limp, I despair of getting a cab. But I do. On the first corner. At first it looks like bad news—"Hey psychokiller," he calls out, "hey shooter, get in"—but when he asks for an autograph made out to his daughter I realize he thinks I'm that actor. With a grandiose, ringleader gesture he informs me that it will be his pleasure to chauffeur me anywhere I like.

"You do any grisly murders lately?" he says. "You shoot anyone? Eh, killer?"

I make a whimpering noise and bang my head against the window in remorse.

"That's amazing," he says. "God, I love it. You guys never turn it off, do you?"

Outside my apartment there is a homeless guy squatting in his cart, shrieking at an imaginary friend on an imaginary cell phone. All he's got are ghost friends. Poltergeist lovers. Take away the outfit, the besmirchment, and the poor dental hygiene, I think, and that's me.

Inside the apartment I don't feel much better. Someone has redecorated in the style of late Visigoth. The fridge has disgorged its contents onto the floor, the sofa and mattress and Pinkerton's doggy bed have all been disemboweled, my books are shucked of their jackets and scattered about like victims of genocide. In short, everything that is breakable or cleavable or pierceable has been broken and cleaved and pierced. Even Charlie's bra has been lacerated.

I wade through what was once my life. When I tread on something crunchy I look down and see that I have stomped on Chester Wellington III and his bride. I do not feel colossal, however. I feel like the Ür-dupe. I let Chester get to me for no reason. With merciless clarity, with exquisite shame, I see now just how precious and moronic my proposal was. "That is the sound of our future together." If it seemed possibly sentimental before, it now makes me cringe with shame.

And it was all for nothing. There never was going to be any future.

The odd thing about the ransacking is that all my valuables, quote unquote, are still present. Nothing is missing. This might make the point of the destruction ambiguous, but an enormous graffito on the wall makes the message of the violence, and the identity of its author, irrefutable: in black spray-painted numbers above the sofa is the disheartening, nearly incredible six-figure amount of money that I still owe Deke.[65]

Weird, I think. I still have like two weeks before payday.

What's his beef?

When I click on the TV I see his beef. On Patriot TV the familiar machine-gun report indicating a new segment fires away, rat-atat-tat. Then Doreen is on the screen, BREAKING NEWS

---

[65] By the transitive power of art I realize that Deke has authored a convincing metaphor: the evisceration and breakage so richly evoked in my apartment provides a visual analogue for what awaits my body. Deke looked for satisfaction in the entrails of the sofa to no avail; the next logical place to look for satisfaction is the entrails of the sofa owner.

posted under her gobbling visage. Hovering above her shoulders, like angel-devil figures, appear two images. On the left is the familiar rat icon, and, on the right, my Janus ID picture with a caption that says WANTED.

"Rat Burglar accomplice Otto Starks, formerly of the Manhattan specialized security firm Janus, is a fugitive from justice," she says. "At two fifteen p.m. today Otto Starks escaped from his guarded room at an undisclosed CDC facility. Severely injured in the escape were two police officers..."

I click it off.

No wonder Deke is pissed. Now he knows I'm a pulse. And, he thinks, I'm also the accomplice to the Rat Burglar, and liable to bring the cops to his doorstep.

The idea of waiting around for Deke to do to me what he did to my upholsterables isn't attractive. Neither is being apprehended by the police, who—you would think—should be staking out my apartment right now.

I wish I had friends I could flee to. I wish I had a family. I wish I could call up the K'plua and ask him what to do. He'd know. If I were Amish I could take one of those buggies to a distant village and they would hide me from nasty cops and robbers. Maybe even from my own past. That's exactly what I need, I realize. A whole new life. An obliteration of all my memory harvesting. At first I don't take it seriously. At first I'm just horsing around with the idea while I contemplate the manifold dooms awaiting me, but then—

Lightbulb: I can do this. This could actually work.

All I have to do is wrangle up every item of value I have, pawn them, and get a bus ticket. I'll call my dealer and cash in all my toxins for a bonanza of heavy-duty memory suppressants. Yeah, that's what I'll do. I'll get a bus ticket to Dutch Pennsylvania and the motherlode of ipurfan. On the bus I'll write up a note that says my name is Jonas and I lost my wife and children in a terrible barn-raising accident in Illinois. You lost everything, the note will say, and it sure is sad, but you came out here to start a new life. It won't say anything about talent or muscle or moneymen. It won't say a word about betrayal or deceit or falsehood.

You have always been loved, it will say.

Now go love someone else.

Next I'll scarf down all the ipurfan.

And then: blotto.

I vault off the ravaged sofa and start frisking the apartment for anything portable that I can sell—my CD player, an old Sankt-Moeller button, the ring in its velvety box. When I am bent over the sofa searching for stray containers of toxins a pair of hands picks me up by the neck with little regard for the forces of mass or gravity, thrusts me face-first on the area rug, and then I'm grazing on thick green shag.

A pair of pliers exerts cruel genitalian pressure.

My attempt to verbalize is useless—the pain is literally breathtaking—but it probably doesn't make a difference. I know what's coming. Before it comes, however, a piece of paper is slapped onto the floor by my head. It's the title to the *Clean Getaway*.

"You die either way," he says succinctly. "But sign it over to me and I won't kill your girl." A pen drops onto the title. "There is no discussion. You have three seconds."

This seems like a good plan. Dying seems an expeditious alternative to living with my memories. If I can't be an amnesiac Amish guy, I think, I might as well be dead. But when I pause momentarily while searching for the correct line to sign on—these things are confusing—and Deke gives my nuts a hurry-up squeeze, I blink in agony and then see only one thing: Chester Wellingon III. He is lying on his side, nearly face-to-face with me. The sight of him witnessing my imminent offing while giving me that smug I'm So Married and You Never Will Be look makes me inflame with rage.

"Chester Wellington," I say, the syllables parsed with loathing.

"What?"

"Fucking English fuck."

"Sign it, Starks."

"Your girl didn't lie, did she?"

"What?"

"That's the only reason you're married, fuckplug. You're not any better than me."

"Who are you talking to?"

"Die, Chester Wellington!"

I reach for Chester. Deke reaches for something in his jacket. I get mine first. Grabbing the snotty figurine I scythe it into Deke's face. I poleax the guy. He falls backwards, a gun tumbling out of his grip. He groans and clutches his face, blood seeping between his fingers. Still in a trance of rage and terror I pick up the gun and, standing astride Deke, shaking, I aim the muzzle squarely at his forehead, giving him the full glare of the barrel, its mouth of absolute darkness.

Its God-hole.

Killing Deke, I realize, could solve a lot of my problems. Finally I would have a clean getaway. Not the one I wanted—I'm broke and crippled and utterly alone—but a clean getaway all the same. I can take all the money Deke has on him now, cash in the title to the boat, and go to Pennsylvania. I would never have to worry about him finding me. Or finding Charlie.

I could be an amnesiac Amish guy with means, and I'd still have no memory of any of it. Shooting Deke could make all this happen.

I don't shoot Deke.

The World I Know Nothing About

The grisogonol I inject into Deke's bloodstream makes his body go limp and peaceful, but I still stand guard over him while his consciousness sips out. When I'm confident that his breathing and heart rate are stabilized, I change out of the hospital gown and into some clothes that escaped most of the scissoring. In the bathroom I wash my head under the faucet and look at my face in the mirror. My eyes are gouged and unknowing, the whites clotted and red. The reflection looks like someone else. I unwrap the gauze from my head and splash my face with cold water but I don't like it any better.

With the ring, the title, and the GPS button in one pocket and $1,300 of Deke's money making a bricklike bulge in another, I head down to Waverly and fire up the Reliant. Then I cut it off, write a note that says FREE, stick it under a windshield wiper with the keys, and start heading to the Clinton / Washington G stop. I am contemplating a list of Amishy surnames for myself when a cab pulls up next to me.

"You'll never make it on your own."

"Go away, Jagjeet."

"There's an APB on you."

"I don't see any cops around here."

"You will. Right now they are all over your address on Orchard. They'll figure out their mistake soon enough."

My file—it still lists my Lower East Side address. He is right; Nunes will realize this quickly.

I keep limping toward the G.

"There are cops in the subway, too, you know."

"They don't know what I look like."

"Everyone knows what you look like."

"I'll keep my head down."

"Can you keep your limp down, too?"

That stops me. I look around wishfully, as if there might be a solution to everything double-parked on Lafayette. There isn't.

"Get in," he says. "You've got nowhere else to go." He's right. Even if he weren't he could induce me into the cab by force. And besides, what am I going to do? Pogo my way to freedom? I get in.

"You don't understand what's happening," he says as we cruise past Classon.

"She's a goddamn thief. What else is there?"

"She's not a thief," he says. "Not the way you think."

"The hell she isn't."

"Otto, since the invasion, there has been widespread looting of museums in Iraq."

"Why is everyone talking to me about Iraq?"

"It's probably the most extensive looting since the Nazis cleaned out Europe. There is no computerized inventory system, you know, so it's hard to get an exact total, but we're talking maybe one hundred thousand items." He stops to let that make an impact. It does. "The works are smuggled out and sold in first-world art markets. Mostly England and America. The entire country's heritage—the history of the cradle of civilization—is being stolen. The only comparable thing in this country I can think of would be if someone stole the Declaration of Independence or the Liberty Bell. If those items were nine thousand years old, that is."

"The Liberty Bell is too big to steal."

"Not if you have an army."

"What does that mean?"

"Otto, in World War Two it was the German army. This time it's American."

"Impossible," I say. "There's got to be some sort of resolution or something."

"There is one. UN Resolution 1483. It specifically protects Iraqi art."

"Well, there you go. See?"

"You don't know much about the world you work in, do you?"

"What do you mean?"

"That resolution is window dressing. It's enforced as often as jaywalking. And it didn't stop them from loading up the *Saqueador*."

"The what?"

"*Saqueador*. It's a Portuguese freighter. It's loaded with stolen Iraqi art in US diplomatic containers, so they're unsearchable. Unseizable. There's maybe twenty thousand works. A huge, huge portion of Mesopotamia's cultural artifacts. It's basically a floating museum of stolen history." He clears his throat. "It was bound for a US port but never made it. No one knows where it is, but it's out there somewhere. And everyone wants it. The difference is the DOD wants to sell its contents to the highest bidder and Charlie wants to return them."

"I haven't heard anything about this on the news."

"Why would you?"

I hunker down in my seat, hoping for a skepticism that doesn't come.

"I don't honestly care about Iraqi art right now. I've got more immediate problems. I owe Deke hundreds of thousands of dollars that I don't have. I am a fugitive. I can barely move my damn leg. And I just found out that the woman I love is actually—surprise surprise—the thief who is responsible for it all, so pardon me if I don't give one single flying philharmonic fuck about Iraqi art."

Jagjeet ignores this. He continues telling me the story I don't want to hear.

"For a long time we worked together for another guy, Giardinelli. He'd let us sell to whoever we liked. It was no problem for Charlie to return works to where they belonged."

"What a relief."

"But then Azar killed Giardinelli and wiped out his organization. Azar was the only game in town. She couldn't get jobs without him."

"Bullshit. She could be a tither."

"And sell back to the insurance companies? Who return works to their 'owners'? You're missing the whole point of her work, Otto." I scowl uselessly at him. "If she wanted to be able to return these stolen works to their original countries, she had to sign up with Azar. I told her not to—I told her to retire—but she didn't listen to me."

"This is crap already. No way does Azar let her sell to those countries. They're always the lowest bidder, right?"

"He made her do other jobs. Non-Polecat jobs. She was basically working two full-time jobs with two different identities."

"And somehow she still found time to teach, to set me up for imprisonment, and to poison the hell out of me. Remarkable woman."

"She spent the last year finding ways *not* to poison you. Why do you think she used the Kolokol-9? The oxonone? They're nonlethals. And the pachylax? It's not even a toxin. It only incapacitated you. She was trying to keep you safe."

"She found out about my vulnerability to Nix. And used it."

"No she didn't. She kept reporting to Azar that you had no weaknesses—including Nix—but then Jimmy found your journal in your locker. Azar ordered her to use the Nix on the Inanna vases, but she didn't. Nor the K'plua. She just couldn't."

"Very noble."

"After the K'plua she went to Azar. She leveled with him. She said they'd had a good partnership. She had restored many works and she had earned him a lot of money, but now she wanted out. She begged him. She told him she loved you and couldn't do it.

"Azar said, 'Is there nothing I can do to change your mind?' She said no, she had made up her mind. And he said O.K."

"That doesn't sound like Azar."

"No it doesn't. But it's what he said. And you should have seen her. Otto, I've never seen anyone so happy. She couldn't stop smiling. She kept hugging people. But the next day she got a package. Inside was her father's finger and a note that said 'Are you sure I can't do anything to change your mind?'"

"Oh God," I say, comprehending. "It wasn't a car accident...."

"No. Azar had her father. Charlie had a choice: do the job on you or turn her father over to Jimmy. She could Nix you and set you up for jail or she could let her father be tortured and killed by Jimmy the Hat."

"I don't get it. Why would Azar have wanted me to kill her, then?"

"Charlie did that to herself. Once he realized you were really in love he saw a way to go one up on what you did to Frankie

Nickels. Not only would he get you disgraced, in jail, and paralyzed, but it would be at the hands of the woman you love. And if things worked out, you would also—"

"Kill her."

"But she couldn't do it. She couldn't use the Nix. She tried to choke you out."

"It still hurt," I say defensively.

"After she called 911 about the Nix she made me wait outside the facility. She knew they'd take you to some special CDC unit. She went after her father—alone—but made me follow you. To protect you, Otto."

"Are you her servant or something?"

"I've known the Izzos my entire life. Charlie Senior brought my family to this country. He supported us. I owe him everything. So when Charlie decided to enter the business I swore to protect her. So I became her muscle. I'd die for her father; I'd die for her."

"Then why didn't you stop her when she went after her father alone?"

"I didn't know. She didn't tell me she was going."

"Why the hell would she go alone?"

Jagjeet sighs. "Charlie is great talent. Probably the greatest I've ever seen. But it wasn't enough. She wanted to be muscle. Her father wanted a boy. He always did. He never let her forget it. It killed Charlie, and if she couldn't be a boy, she said, she could at least be as strong as one. When she was thirteen she asked me to start training her, and I did. I've been training her ever since. And she's good. Very, very good. But Jimmy the Hat..." His voice pulls with despair. "I should have known she'd go after her father. I should have known that. It's my fault."

"She got caught?"

"She can handle some cops, but Jimmy the Hat? She wasn't ready for that. Not at her best. And she wasn't at her best. She was injured. She didn't have any tech support. She didn't stand a chance."

"If she didn't tell you she was going, how do you know she got caught?"

Wiping at his eye, he hands me his cell phone. On the screen is a picture of Charlie in her underwear, gagged, her wrists and ankles duct-taped to a metal chair. Her head is hanging down, her beautiful hair curtained over her face. The picture is grainy but I can see the marks on her body. I also see Herkimer next to her, leering at the camera, a blade in his hand.

"What's he going to do to her?" I say.

"What do you think?"

I can't bring myself to say the words.

"Unless I bring you in," Jagjeet says, "he's going to do exactly what you think."

I squeeze shut my eyes. Against the image, against the truth, against everything.

"You should have let me kill him," Jagjeet says.

"So now what? You're going to turn me over to Azar?"

"I would if Charlie wanted. But she does not want to live without you."

"So what do you need me for?"

We've been going in circles around the neighborhood. Jagjeet pulls the cab over, not far from where I failed to propose to Charlie, slides the Plexiglas window open and stares at me as if I'm thick.

"I'm just muscle. I don't know anything about alarm systems or electronics or surveillance or anything. I need your expertise to help get her out."

"Me?"

"You're a pulse. You know all about security."

"Not really. Not in a useful way."

"What?"

"I don't know anything about alarm systems or electronics or anything. Nothing. Nada. I can't pick a lock. I tried to break into Schermer's apartment and I couldn't get past the garage door."

"But you're a pulse."

"Right. I keep people out. That doesn't mean I can get in."

When I punched him at Charlie's he hardly moved a muscle but he recoils from this news as if struck in the head with a shovel. His expression swallows itself, then gags. The lights go out in his eyes, but seconds later they flash back on like searchlights.

"I know who can help," he says, throwing the car in gear. "I know where to go."

"You still haven't given me a reason to help her."

Cutting up Throop, he again he looks at me in the mirror like I'm stupid.

"Because you love her."

He thinks I can't argue with this. He's right. I hate Charlie but I love her, and I have nothing to live for except keeping her safe. If I can save Charlie, I will. If I can die while saving her, even better.

Kong's Price

In the Foxhole the windows and walls are upholstered in red velvet curtains that are pocked with cigarette burns and the ceiling is covered in whipped cream–like foam soundproofing. Grating, undanceable German techno throbs out of speakers bolted above the stage. An off-duty girl in a full-sex Tron outfit lets a guy buy her a twenty-dollar Pepsi in an eight-ounce can. Another one in a defunct schoolmarm-dominatrix outfit and Wendy O. Williams hair is chumming the floor with worn cleavage and cheap, petroleous drugstore perfume. Onstage, surrounded by men on stools with dead faces, a fat stripper jiggles for the crowd. She leans over a guy, giving him a nuzzle, then slips and tumbles off the stage. The guy, recoiling in horror, rolls out of the way. On the floor, her dollars spilling on the wet carpet, the stripper flushes with shame. While she's down, the men throw things at her. One makes a piglike noise and truffles in her ass. She makes a move to the back room—she wants out of this—but the floor boss orders her back onstage. She climbs back up, her naked body muddy with beer and peanut dust, and finishes her song as the men laugh and toss coins.

That's the kind of place it is.

That's where we meet Tony "Kong" Mavrogordo.

Kong considers the Foxhole his place. You can tell by how he sits at his table. His posture has a low-rent, in situ majesty, an outpost-against-time quality. When he is not abasing himself at his Geek Squad gig, apparently he is playing mafia don of table 12 at the shittiest skin club on the shittiest block in Queens, and the shittiest thing of all is that this criminal, this ex–tech mastermind, is the only person who can help us.

In fairness, he isn't tickled to see me, either.

"Starks?" he says to Jagjeet, nearly spitting out his lost-and-found cigarette. "You bring me Otto Starks? In here?"

Kong's appearance lives up to his sobriquet in more ways than the speediness of his anger. Sprouting from his shirt cuffs, his tightly cinched collar, the gaps between buttons are dense patches of coarse, black, gorilla-like hair. His body is carpeted in it; his beard begins under his eyes and only barely spares his nose; there are tufts of dark hair protruding from his aural canal and attached to his pinna, making his ear look like a bristling Venus flytrap. He is not the Wolfman, exactly, but he could cover for him on a sick day.

Naturally, instead of hands he has two curved metallic pincers. He is so distressed to see me that he makes impassioned gestures of outrage with them. The maneuver is disconcerting. In order to open and close the pincers in disgust it's necessary for him to shrug both shoulders—they operate on a wire connected to that area, it seems—and so the eerie clawlike gestures of scissoring metal are underscored by an incongruous penguin dance.

I'm far from laughing, though. For one thing, this is Kong's turf, and I know he'd like to kill me. But for another, I see in Kong someone who probably craves sitting alone in dark rooms as much as I do.

I also see a guy whose life has been destroyed by Jimmy the Hat.

"Please just listen," Jagjeet says.

"I got nothing I want to hear that involves this guy. If he was holding a ten-foot check with Ed McMahon's signature on it in the blood of Swedish virgins, I wouldn't want to hear it from this guy."

I say, "Mr. Mavrogordo—"

"Is this guy talking?" he says to Jagjeet, amazed. "Is he verbalizing at my table? Guy comes over to my fucking table, words coming out of his fucking mouth?"

I say, "I'm sorry, but—"

"Shut this guy up," Kong says to Jagjeet, not looking at me.

I say, "Charlie is—"

"Shut this guy the fuck up."

Stupidly, I say, "Jimmy the Hat has—"

"If this guy says one more word I'm going to stab him in the eye with this hook. You got that, Jeet?"

So far this is not going swimmingly. But as Kong raves against me Jagjeet is able to convey to him that Jimmy the Hat has Charlie. That pulls him up short.

"Charlie?" he says.

Jagjeet nods. "If I don't bring Otto to him then he's going to torture and kill her."

"So what's the problem? Bring him Starks. What's the fucking holdup?"

"Charlie would never forgive me."

Kong struggles with this briefly, but not long enough.

"I like that girl, but: not my problem."

"It's *Charlie*," Jagjeet tells him.

"Not my problem."

"Remember Istanbul? You owe her."

"Not. My. Problem. Not like this." He nods at me. "Not for the guy did this to me." Kong pulls off one of his pincers and shows Jagjeet his wound. The skin is striated and puckered like the end of a hot dog and its color is a tender, nearly translucent, inhuman pink. A pink like the nose of a newborn mouse.

"Otto didn't do that to you," Jagjeet says gently. "Jimmy did."

"Don't tell me who fucking did it! I was there, asshole! And I'm not helping."

Jagjeet flips open his cell and shows him the picture.

"You know what he'll do to her, Tony. We can't get in without you."

Kong tries not to look at the picture, but he just keeps on looking. He has a hard time with it. So do I.

"Look, Jeet," he says with surrender in his voice, "even if I wanted to, what can I do? You're not talent. You two don't have the first fucking clue. Breaking into Azar's isn't like robbing ye olde gift shoppe. I can get you past the primary systems, but then what are you two bumblefucks going to do? Do either one of you know anything about the capacitive loads of bus network topology? Or the schedule of cellular telephony report patterns? Or how to accommodate a Neiderer-grade multiple-impedance relay?"

"With your help we can do it."

Again Jagjeet pushes the picture of Charlie toward him.

"A hundred to one," Kong says, riveted to the picture. "At best."

He says, "You can't pick a lock and this guy can't even walk."

He says, "Hamburger. That it? You want to be ground fucking chuck?"

He says, "Besides, she's probably already dead. I'm sorry, but it's true: dead."

Then, still unable to take his eyes off the picture, he finally says, "Fuck. All right. I'm going to regret this. But it's going to cost. You know what I want." He makes a meaningful pincer slash across his throat.

"O.K.," Jagjeet says. "I'll try."

"O.K. what?" I say, confused about what deal has been struck. "What's O.K.?"

"Jimmy," Jagjeet says. "He wants me to kill Jimmy the Hat for him."

"No," I say. "No one's killing anyone."

I say this because it is the only part of myself that I have left. I am a liar, a criminal, a man without friends or family, a failure at work and life and love, all true. But I am not a killer.

Kong says, "Then forget it."

"What about money?" I say. "I can pay you."

"Yeah?" he says to Jagjeet. "How much can this guy pay me?"

I empty my pockets on the table and spread out all my remaining possessions.

"I've got thirteen hundred dollars in twenties. I've got some pills. The street value of this stuff is got to be close to a grand. This is a Sankt-Moeller button. It's only second generation but it's still got GPS and everything. Not sure what you'd use it for but it's kind of cool. When you press the button it alerts Janus and the cops to your location and it's got this really cool light that blinks like this and—"

"Guy's funny. I don't know if I want to laugh at him or shoot him."

While Jagjeet pleads with Kong I feel something curdle in my stomach. I can't help thinking about her. She just pops in there. Like this: when Charlie was in my bed it had its own ecosystem. It had her heat, her fragrance, the dewy thickness of sleep. That animal warmth that was also a promise. It swore that I would never be alone again, but now the heat is gone and the scent is fading from the sheets. That's how the promise breaks: the fragrance fades to nothing. I'll never be able to sleep in that bed again. Not that I'm going to get the chance.

Prison sheets probably smell like bleach and fear and crippling male loneliness.

"What about this?" I say, and slap down the title to the *Clean Getaway*.

"What's that?" Kong asks Jagjeet.

"It's the title to a boat," I say. " A Najad 55. I'll sign it over to you."

"A fifty-five what?"

"Sailboat. An oceangoing sloop."

"How much it worth?"

I want to tell him: only my whole life.

Instead I give it to him in dollars.

"Wait, how much?"

I tell him again. Now, for the first time, he looks at me.

"Say again?"

I do.

"This is a boat we're talking about, here, right?"

Again I assure him of the value of the boat.

"If you're fucking with me—"

"I'm telling you the truth. It's all my savings. It's all I have."

Then I take a chance.

"No more Geek Squad," I say. "You'll never have to say the word 'reboot' again. No one will be able to make you do anything you don't want to do. You'll be untouchable. It can be your own clean getaway." I let him think on that for a second.

Then I make a Hancock gesture. "If you help us, it's yours," I say. "All yours."

There is a harrowing metaphorical symmetry to this offer—only by forsaking my own clean getaway can I secure Charlie's—and I teeter in my chair with sadness. Kong's breath is a nauseating broth of bad meat and well gin. The title sits flat on the table, alive, sentient, aware of its power of permanence and despair. An article of surrender. My body feels both weightless and immensely heavy.

"Well?" I ask, making another circular motion with the pen. "Do I sign it over?"

For the second time, Kong looks me in the eye. A cocktail waitress does a plaintive babushka waddle over to our table and asks if we have everything we need. No one says anything. In my nostrils is the stench of stale albumin, the fetalike odor of unwashed genitalia. I feel very alone.

Finally, Kong nods at the title and says, "M-A-V-R-O..."

Bathroom Talk

I limp into the bathroom and bang my forehead into the mirror for clarity. None comes. I squeeze my eyes shut until my face hurts. Nothing. When I open my eyes it's still just me. Otto Starks, knee-deep in crime. Bereft of everyone he thought he loved. Then I get an idea. It's a bad idea—in fact, it's excruciating—but it's the only one I've got. I lock the bathroom door, enclose myself in a stall, throw back a few succinylcholine chloride for courage, and call Nunes. My tongue still feels like a piece of burned toast and my voice comes out in radio static, but I still speak the words.

"I want to make a deal."

"Where are you?"

"I want two things. Immunity for myself and—"

"The time for that has passed, Starks. The best thing you can do is turn yourself in."

"I can give you what you want."

"Too late."

"I can bring you the Rat Burglar. Tonight."

"What?"

"And Jimmy the Hat," I say. "And Azar. That interest you?"

There is a long pause on the line. Nunes's respiration seizes up. So does mine, but for different reasons. The deal I'm seeking is justified, I keep telling myself. It isn't evil. Charlie took everything from you. Now you're going to save her life. Is it so wrong to save your own?

And don't thieves belong in jail in the first place?

Is that so evil of me?

Passionately, I tell myself it isn't. I tell myself again. If I can repeat it another 62,398 times I might believe it.

"How?" she says finally.

I don't really have an answer to this. Instead I just say, "Do we have a deal?"

"It's too late for you, Starks. You didn't talk when you had the chance. You assaulted four members of the Janus response team. Two officers were critically injured in your escape from the CDC unit. Any way you look at it, you're getting a long jolt."

"You know I didn't assault anybody."

"No I don't. You've lied to me from day one."

"All right. Fine. I give up. I confess. I'm the mang. You got me. But right now I'm saying I'll bring you the Rat Burglar. And Jimmy the Hat and Azar. Think of the shot of credibility it would bring the department. Think of the art you'll save by putting away the Rat Burglar. Think of the lives you'll save by picking up Jimmy the Hat. Think of the headlines you'll grab by downing Azar's whole operation. Hell, you'll be a hero, Nunes."

"Why now?" she says warily. "What made you change your mind?"

"The Rat Burglar...betrayed me. I want my life back."

"You'll never get it back, Starks."

"Call it revenge, then. Call it whatever you like. Do I get immunity?"

She chews on this, but not for too long. "What's the second thing?"

"The Rat Burglar doesn't go in the mainline," I say, swallowing down the wet sobs in my throat. "I want protective custody for the whole sentence. Nowhere near any of Azar's people. Not at any time."

"The Rat Burglar burned you. Why help him?"

"It doesn't matter. Do we have a deal? Yes or no?"

"Don't get fancy, Starks. You're not smart enough for tricks."

"No tricks. That's what I want."

"Whatever you're trying to pull, it won't work."

"In ten seconds I'm hanging up. You'll never hear from me again."

Thieves belong in jail, I keep telling myself. Pulses don't. I'm not evil. I'm not betraying love.

And anyway: you can't betray a love that never existed.

Right?

"Starks," she says, mystified, "are you...crying?"

"Five seconds," I say. "Yes or no?"

There is another long, portentous silence. In the background I can hear the tumult and whine of the precinct, the sounds of importunity and denial, all the voices wretched, enraged, agonized, stuporous. How many lives are being unalterably ruined in that room right now? My lungs produce a wet, bronchospastic wheezing song of grief.

"O.K., Starks. I'll talk to the judge."

"Good."

"But dead doesn't do me any good. I want them alive—all of them—or the deal's off."

"Fine. I've got a Sankt-Moeller with GPS. SoL signal 1176.441 megahertz. Write it down: 1176.441 megahertz."

"Got it," she says. "When?"

"Soon. Be ready. And I'd bring a lot of backup."

"So you'll just..."

"The GPS on the button is good to within three feet. I'll click it when I have her."

"Her?"

I clap the cell shut and let my tear-cyclone blow into the toilet water.

Good Start

The interior of Kong's van is like the command center of a spaceship from a 1970s-era sci-fi flick—all screens and lights and intermittent beepings—and it is handsomely equipped with gear and guns. Kong outfits Jagjeet and me with minerlike head-mounted cameras, earpieces, and an array of thief tools that look like unpatentable surgical implements. There are various cutters, clamps, tubes, something that I assume is a probe of some sort.

"I told you," I say when Jagjeet opens a gun case. "No one's killing anybody."

"The guys inside Azar's are going to have guns," Kong points out.

I pull a dart gun off the rack. "Then we'll use these."

"You have to load a new dart every time you want to shoot," Kong says. "You'll have ten rounds in you before you get to fire a second shot."

"Then we'd better not miss."

"What if there are more than two guys?"

"Then we'd better not get caught."

"There are only five darts."

"This is what we're using."

Kong expresses his disbelief with a zagging gesture of his pincers but Jagjeet just shrugs companionably—he doesn't seem to mind the prospect of death too much—and holsters a dart gun on each hip.

It's a quiet ride. Kong pilots the van with his hooks. Jagjeet inspects his gear with the scrupulous intensity of a watchmaker. There is an uncanny precision to his movements, a kind of efficient gentleness. A delicateness, even. He has a sharklike attitude: slow, smooth, Zen-like, absolutely cool, interested in nothing, but always there is that suggestion of immense speed. It reminds me of Herk.

I keep staring out the window, my heart withering into something tiny and tuberous and dumb. It doesn't understand anything. It never did.

Before long we're in a part of Queens that I don't know. The streetscape is blasted, postapocalyptic. It smells of diesel and rust and concrete powder and scrubgrass. Emanating from the street is the semivolcanic odor of hot, crumbling asphalt. We pass a scaffolding peeling away from an abandoned project, strip malls with busted-out windows, storefronts offering goods and services you would never want—the Wig-n-Watch, the U-Paint-It, Benny's Stool Store. Everywhere you look there are the petrified chain-link-and-iron remains of industrial slag, the detritus of discontinued construction. It's hard to imagine anything being built here in the first place. There are some people here and there but they don't care about anything. Even the kids crowding around window AC units and licking the trickles of condensation aren't putting much into it. They look inanimate and posed, like puppet children abandoned after a show.

Kong pulls the van into an alley.

"O.K.," he says, pecking heronlike at the keyboard. "Here's the schematic." When no schematic appears despite further typing, he curses, kicks the tower and swats a bulbous '80s-era screen. Amber light flares across the monitor and then we're staring at a diagram of hallways and rooms. "All right. This facility is where Azar stores his stuff before resale. Anything of value, he keeps it here. You can bet Charlie is in there somewhere. That's the good news. The bad news is that it's heavily guarded, it's got a solid security system, and Charlie isn't tagged so we can't be sure what room she's in. We'll enter from the north door here because best guess is Charlie is going to be in one of these rooms here."

"What makes you think that?" I say.

"These are the rooms that have bolted-down chairs and sluice grates. If Jimmy is going to torture anyone he'll do it in there," he says. I nearly double over at this, but Kong doesn't notice. "Now, I can blackout for you but I can't piggyback."

"Um, what?"

"The cameras will still be recording but their screens won't show it. That's the good news. The bad news is that I can't use the signal for us to see anything. So you'll be walking blind."

"How come?"

"I'm not exactly on Azar's payroll anymore, asshole. I don't get the top-notch tech. This is all we got." Again Kong strikes a screen. The picture wavers, then stabilizes. He points out our path through the labyrinthine corridors of Azar's facility. It's a long way to go, and because he can't view us through the video signal he's going to have to talk us through it.

He proceeds to give us a quick talent primer—the most important part of which is to do exactly what he says at all times, no matter how counterintuitive it sounds—does a last sound check on our earpieces, and looks us over critically like an angry den mother.

"All right," he says. "You're not going to get any readier. Let's crack and go."

"Do what?" I say, but Jagjeet is already rolling an ankle in his hands. The joint cracks and pops like dry kindling a few times and then goes quiet. He does the same to his wrists.

"Jesus Christ," Kong says. "Get the cracks out. Come *on*. I don't like sitting out here in a chi-mo van waiting to get made. Crack and fucking go, already."

I do, and thirty seconds later I am standing before a riveted metal doorway in an alleyway, staring at a skein of electronics with wire strippers in my hand. In accordance with Kong's detailed instructions, I snip this, strip that, mate those, and then the door retracts sideways into a sleeve, elevator style.

"Holy shit," I say. "It worked."

In the earpiece Kong grunts.

"You don't think that's a good start?"

"Do I think that's a good start? Azar's in there. Jimmy the

Hat is in there. Probably dozens of guys armed with real guns loaded with real bullets are in there. And look at us. We're using tech that runs on hamsters. Jeet's got no gun. I got no hands. You got one leg. We're all going to die. That's what I think." Then he groans, makes a corrective noise in his throat. I've retained the title for the duration of this job—it was the only way I could think of to prevent him from bolting the scene after we got inside—and even though it clearly pains him to be nice to me in any way whatsoever, he doesn't want to discourage me. He needs me to come out of there alive, with the title to my boat.

Correction: *his* boat.

"I mean, good luck, guys," he says at last. "Go team."

Reunited

Jagjeet and I devise a system. He walks ahead of me through the eerily immaculate, Bauhaus hallways, dart guns raised and ready, as I use my senses to detect signs of trouble. I smell, I listen, I hawkeye for shadows. I remove my shoes and, barefoot, feel for vibrations. It works, and after a few undeadly intersections, my Charlie curiosity gets the better of me.

"Charlie didn't break her nose by falling off her bike. How did she do it?"

"No talking," says Kong's voice in my ear. "Keep it quiet."

Jagjeet shrugs. "I did it. Two years ago. During training. It was an accident."

"What sort of training?"

"You know, her training to be muscle. We were sparring. She always has a hard time staying loose. So I was using potato chips and she choked on one and sort of moved into the punch—"

"Potato chips?"

"*Talk*ing, people," says Kong.

"Oh. In fighting, speed is power. Not muscle. If you're nervous you hunch up, you try to muscle it. It makes you slow. And weak. Like a lot of fighters, Charlie carries her tension in her jaw. If I can get her to relax her jaw she will relax her shoulders, relax her legs. So I make her hold potato chips in her mouth when she trains. If they break then she's not relaxed enough, not fast enough. She has to try again. It's just a training tool."

"The chips in her kitchen..." For some reason this feels like a tremendous relief: Charlie was not hiding a secret delectation for potato chips; they were merely a part of her life as talent, as wanna-be muscle. She had to keep them secret.

"Right," says Jagjeet.

"Talking!" screams Kong in my ear.

"Did, um, Charlie ever talk much about me?" I can't help asking. "I mean, did she ever say anything about, I don't know, marrying me or anything?"

"Hey, amateur hour!" Kong shrieks at me. "Shut your fucking mouth!"

"Kong, it's dead quiet. I don't think anyone's here."

"Maybe Azar has people out looking for you," Jagjeet offers.

At max volume Kong informs me that in the circumstance in which I currently find myself, I have no entitlement to any thought whatsoever and that to submit an opinion on anything is foolhardy in the extreme. He also exhorts me to commit an act of self-sodomy.

Two intersections later I aggrieve Kong even worse. He instructs us to go right, but my body pulls inexorably left.

"Sure it isn't left?"

"Go right, douchebag."

"What makes you think left?" Jagjeet asks. "Do you hear something?"

"No."

"Smell something?"

"Go right, now," Kong says.

"I don't think so," I say.

"Then what is it?" Jagjeet says.

"This hallway hurts."

Kong screeches. "It *what?*"

"Kong knows this facility better than anyone," Jagjeet says reasonably.

"He's wrong."

"Are you sure?"

"I can't explain it, but it's this way. I'm going left."

As Kong monopolizes my sense of hearing, Jagjeet and I proceed down the left hallway and, within another fifty feet, I understand the source of my intuition. I drop to my hands and knees and sniff the floor.

"That's it," I say. "Bread crumbs."

"What, Otto?" Jagjeet says.

"What, asshole?" Kong says.

"Covet. On her shoes. Charlie had Covet on her shoes. It's faint but it's there. On the floor. She knew she might not make it so she left a trail. In case we came for her. It's this way."

I pull like a narcotics dog through the halls until the odor leads me to a locked door. I put my hand to it, tenderly, as if searching for a heartbeat. Although Kong is still occupied mainly with aspersing my character, my IQ, my worthiness to suck the same oxygen that is sucked by cockroaches, he pauses long enough to communicate which wires to cut. I cut them. Nothing happens.

"Did I do that right?" I say. "Did you tell me the right wires?"

Kong execrates me at such volume for questioning his expertise that I have to pry out the earpiece and shove it into my pocket. As I do this there is a mechanical whine, an aerosol sound of hydraulics, and the door retracts into the wall.

There she is: the woman I love, the thief I hate.

I churn with mysterious feeling. My senses revolt as if I've lunched on a salad of *Salvia divinorum* and kokosing root. What's real? It's hard to tell. I waver on my feet, stunned and Gullivered, but when I shake my head clean and focus, the details become intelligible. With the exception of being duct-taped to a chair, clad in her underwear with various body parts spreading in the purple-black plumage of bruising—and, of course, with the hole I made in her shoulder, which now unaccountably has an angry red-black sfumato—all other sensory cues tell me she is the same Charlie as ever. Her black hair, rich with the kind of gloss you see only in the surface of certain concert pianos, is still curly and glistening; it sprays around her head when she jolts upright at my entrance. Her eyes when they see me go wide and soft and voracious. Her expression is one of breakneck joy.[66] Standing there in the cool, moteless air of the doorway, I let my eyes soak it up. There are strange odors in the room—something incongruously like ham and cooked beef—but I can't focus on anything but the fragrances of Charlie: Covet and sweat and her essential female self.

---

66 But joy at what? I'm hardly qualified to answer. It could be she's thrilled to see me. It could also be that a dastardly plan is nearing fruition. The truth is unknowable.

My heart suffocates with it.

"Otto!" she cries. Her body flexes toward mine as if she wants to hug me, but all this accomplishes is a poltergeist-like rattling of her chair.

At the sound of her voice I tremble with love and hatred. I perform an allover body spasm like a horse dispersing flies. I make a sprintlike move toward her but then I jerk to a hard stop as if reaching the end of an invisible leash.

No, I tell myself. Quit it. That's not what I'm here for.

"Hey," I say, trying so hard to sound uninjured that I sound ludicrous. It couldn't be any stupider if I had appended "What's up?"

"Your leg!" she cries. "You're O.K.! Oh, God, I was so—" but the rest of the sentence is drowned in tears and choking.

"Forget it," I say coolly. "There isn't time. I'm here to get you out. That's all."

She flinches—she took a bullet with less expression of pain—and although I ache with regret, I force myself to be hard, indurate, unreadable. I don't give anything back. Not one thing. Wordlessly, I start cutting Charlie out of the duct tape, trying hard not to touch her or smell her or look too directly at her skin. If I'm going to go through with this, if I'm going to hit the button and fork her over to Nunes and imprisonment, I need to keep my senses out of it.

When I cut her good arm free she wraps it around my neck and rains kisses on me and nuzzles my neck like her life depends on it. Right now, it does. But mine depends on resolve, so I shrug out of her embrace, pushing her beautiful, bruised mouth away from my neck, her fragrant hair—full of the joy of our history, full of the impossible longing for our future—out of my face.

"Otto—"

Whatever lie she had coming doesn't make it to the airwaves. It is interrupted by the sound of the door sliding open behind us and, shortly thereafter, the staccato chorus of clicks that signifies the rapid cocking of many guns.

Baconmouth

Like everyone else in my universe, Azar is bigger than me, but only in the belt line. He has a squat, slovenly, bullfrog build. In the notch of this flabby throat he has a nickel-sized hole, a tracheostomy. Pushing out of a sleeve is a chronograph the size of a biscuit. It looks like it could tell you the time, the moon phase, the weather in Tokyo, and precisely how much money you don't have in your checking account. It's a fuck-you watch, attached to the fat wrist that's attached to the kill-you hand.

So this is the magus who sends agents into my life to ruin me. To make me love them. And now here I am. Saliva bubbles in the corners of his mouth. He can barely wait.

He hoists himself through the doorway, nearly sideways, and watches with oily pleasure as Herkimer and various gunmen strip off our gear and install us into bolted-down chairs. They give me the loose one, but I don't have long to dwell on the insult before Azar raises a device that looks like an electric razor to his throat and communicates to me in an otherworldly, vibrating voice that, as our prospects have been reduced to nil, there is no reason to hold out on the location of the Nakamura sword.

"The what?" I say.

Herkimer cow-punches me in the side of my head and my vision flushes with light. The robot voice coming out of the Azar's machine reminds me that it's my role to supply answers, not pose questions. Again he suggests that producing the Nakamura sword might net some small measure of mercy.

"I told you a thousand times," Charlie says levelly. "I didn't get it. Janus still has it. He doesn't know anything. Leave him alone."

"You might be telling the truth," Herkimer says. "I don't know. But now that Otto's here I'm going to spend a lot of energy finding out."

Herkimer wheels a table out from behind some crates. Instinctively I know what it's for, but it's not what I expected to see. I had expected a shiny array of unignorable implements, sharpened and hooked—the tools of a demented oral surgeon—but instead there is only a set of two matching curling irons, their unplugged pigtail cords intertwined like a double helix next to a glistening rump of ham. I don't get it, and I don't want to.

Herkimer picks up one of the curling irons and walks playfully around us, capering and grooving as if enjoying a round of musical chairs. Azar, a satisfied spectator, smiles widely, his trach stretching into a pink rictus. It is then that I detect a weak voice emanating, miraculously, from my pants. It is Kong, I suddenly realize, yelling at me from the earpiece. They removed Jagjeet's, but I still have mine in my pocket. I can't quite make out what he is saying, though, mainly because my brain is frantically trying to ascertain what role that curling iron will play in the immediate future of me and my corpus.

Herkimer circles Charlie, stops behind her, lowers his mouth to an intimate, slow-dance distance from her neck, then bunches her hair in his hand and licks her ear. With his pelvis he performs an obscene hula on her, snaking a hand over her bare shoulder and under her bra. He gropes her roughly, leering at me as if we are sharing a locker room confederacy.

"Isn't this great?" he seems to be saying.

From my pocket Kong is still yelling something at me, but I'm not processing. Herkimer is rubbing the curling iron between Charlie's legs, making erotic noises, flicking his tongue like an excited lizard. When I spasm in outrage against my restraints, Herkimer just laughs at me. It gives him pleasure. But when Jagjeet clenches against the handcuffs, Herkimer raises a heel high in the air and brings it down on his rib cage. There is a moist sound of breakage and Jagjeet groans and then goes very still, his breathing very shallow.

"Don't be jealous," Herkimer says to Jagjeet. "I haven't forgotten about you. We're going to have our special time real soon."

I have never felt more vulnerable, more expendable. Coming here was a mistake. When I found out the location of Azar's facility I should have just told Nunes. I'm not qualified for something like this, and now I'm going to pay for it. And so is Jagjeet. And Charlie.

I should have told Nunes everything from the beginning. That's clear to me now.

With an attitude of ooh-la-la titillation Herkimer starts teasing down the hem of Charlie's bra. To his immense satisfaction I again rage against my restraints—the chair gives a little bit—but Charlie just stares ahead dully. She has his saliva cooling on her face, the heat-memory of the curling iron between her legs, his hands on her body, yet she looks as if she is waiting for a bus. I can detect the tension in her eyes—no one else can—but her jaw is as slack as if she were cradling a mouthful of unbroken potato chips.

This is the inner strength, the coolness, that enabled her to lie to me for a year.

Kong is still yelling at me, but I can't make it out over Herkimer.

"Where do I begin?" he is saying. "It's so hard to decide. Jagjeet is probably a waste of time. I know you're only too eager to die for the Izzos. And Charlie, you're a tough little nugget, aren't you? You've already held out on me." He taps the tip of the curling iron against her bullet hole and Charlie gasps in pain.

"No, Charlie," Herkimer continues, "that's not a good use of my time. I think I'll start with you, Starks. You're the softest."

I've missed a lot of what Kong was saying. I need for him to try again. "What?" I yell out loud. "Say again?"

Naturally, Herk thinks I'm talking to him. He reiterates that I'm the softest and then strikes me again for having the temerity to ask a question when it has already been established that that is beyond my purview. The curling iron against my skull makes a hard, abbreviated crack like the sound of stones hitting the concrete bottom of a pool.

Kong repeats his message, which seems to indicate that he is going to attempt some tech wizardry to empty the room. "If I can get them out of there for a few minutes," he yells, "can you get free?"

At the same time, Herkimer says, "Do you know where the Nakamura sword is?"

With my legs I push against the floor to see just how insecure my chair is. With a gusher of adrenaline—and with two fully fuctioning legs—I might be able to break it. With 1.5 legs, who knows? But what choice do I have?

"Yes!" I yell to Kong.

"Goodie," Herk says. "Tell me and I won't do to you what I did to your dog."

"Screw you."

"Do you know what this is?"

He raises the curling iron in front of my face, moving it in a threatening circle.

"Wax on?" I say.

He punches me in the side of the head. It's not as bad as a hammer, but it's close.

"Try again," he says, rotating slowly.

"Wax off?"

"No, don't," Charlie says.

But he does. He punches me in the mouth and I bleed assiduously upon the concrete. The red Rorschach on the floor looks like a pattern of augury telling me who is going to die, and in what manner. But I don't need clairvoyance to tell that. Common sense can handle that on its own.

"Last chance," he says.

I should just say it. When you think in terms of syllables-per-ounces-of-blood-lost, there is really no viable reason that I shouldn't just say "curling iron" and then move forward with the normal assembly of teeth still in my head. But I can't stop thinking about Pink, and when he gestures threateningly in front of my face I hear myself say the words "Paint the fence?"

He smites me again and a curdlike froth starts dribbling out of my mouth.

"He doesn't know anything, Jimmy!" Charlie pleads.

Again I am battering-rammed. My head rings in full Dolby Digital, but I do not whimper; I just smile with whatever mouth I have left. In one respect this is becoming pointless; in another it's a relief. It hurts, but the hurt is real. It isn't fooling;

there is no question about its cause or its intent. It's an honest assault. After the incomprehensible pain of Charlie, it's almost refreshing.

I spit a mouthful of blood at him, flecking his face tribally. "You punch like a mime," I say.

This gets me punched again. It's still painful, and a set of side-by-side photos will reveal clearly who's winning and who's losing in the exchange, but for some reason I feel as if I'm scoring points. He is hitting me without getting hit, true, but I have that one-up feeling of being in an argument with someone who keeps repeating the same insult. He's losing creativity points.

This feeling doesn't last long, however. Herkimer is tired of the script, too. He sighs as if he's a vexed professor tired of trying to appeal to a recalcitrant student. He unclenches his fist, lumbers over to the table, and plugs in one of the curling irons.

"Jimmy, no," Charlie begs.

Herkimer stabs the ham, gouges a hole, and inserts the curling iron into it.

"Where is the Nakamura sword, Otto?"

Again it registers that I should just say it, but instead I say, "Holland?" Then I make a dunce face and say, "Oh, wait. Or is that Denmark? Or Flemland? It's so hard to keep those straight."

Herkimer doesn't strike me this time. He just makes more conductor-like circles with one of the curling irons—the unplugged one—and smiles at me as the room begins to fill with the smoky intimations of cookout.

"You should have heard the noises your dog made." Herkimer yelps and flaps his hands in front of him in a frantic doggy-paddle. "Burned the tongue right out of his head. Only thing left was this little red finger of meat. Flicking around like this. Flick-flick, flick-flick. It was all wet and shriveled up like his red doggy dick."

"Jimmy, please," Charlie says.

He takes the hot iron out of the ham and waves it in front of me. Heat waves ripple against my face. Even that hurts. I mask my terror of it by discharging a spray of water from my eyes. Then he reinserts the hot iron into its hot ham, providing for me an illustration of what I have in store. Next he pries my mouth open, inserts the cold curling iron deeply down my throat, seals it with duct tape, and casts his gaze between the two irons as if approving of a charming double date. I gag against the cold metal, but it's no use. I can't get it out.

From his seat in the corner, Azar emits a ghoulish, aspirated giggle. He loves it.

"He wasn't even conscious," Charlie begs. "He doesn't know anything."

Herkimer is on her in a flash. He vises down on her neck, making her eyes bulge cartoonishly from her head.

"But you know, don't you? You can stop it, Charlie. Just tell me where the Nakamura sword is."

The rump of ham is sizzling now. Fat hisses and spits from the hole.

"I don't know," Charlie repeats desperately. "I didn't get it. Janus still has it."

"You? The Polecat? Didn't get your MacGuffin? I highly doubt that."

Herkimer walks back across the room and plugs in the curling iron that is taped into my mouth. Then he crosses to the table and starts fucking the ham rump with the hot iron. "See that?" he says, releasing the greasy smell of fatty bacon. "It takes about sixty seconds for it to get hot, so I'd say you now have fifty seconds."

Charlie's cool front is gone. She sobs at Herkimer. She tells him that I don't know. That she doesn't know. It could be anywhere. Pink steam rises out of the ham rump. The hole makes cap-gun explosions of burning fat. The iron in my mouth starts getting warm. Azar wheezes in delight.

"Where is it?" Herkimer says.

My breathing is labored and wet and snarfing and nostrilly—cattle-breathing—and my nose floods with the apocrine stench of fear. On my cheeks, prolific tears dilute the blood. The world around me herringbones. Charlie wails that she doesn't know where it is but swears she'll do anything to get it if he will let me go. Herkimer doesn't care.

"Where is it?" he repeats.

It is then—with the furnace-heat of the moment on me, with Herkimer's hands on Charlie's throat, with Charlie sobbing—that I see Azar's joy pull up short. He presses a hand to his ear and speaks into his mouthpiece. He thinks I can't hear, but I can. There has been a breach of security at the south entrance—the farthest point from here—but the cameras can't locate the intruders. Manpower is needed. And with everyone else out in the city, searching for Starks...

Azar produces a throaty sparge of displeasure and signals to his men to come with him. Herkimer, however, is to stay and finish his work.

So much for that plan. It was a good try, Kong.

The iron is unbearably hot. I shake my head violently side to side, but it accomplishes nothing. Then, as the door closes and we are alone with Herkimer, Charlie bolts upright.

"All right," she says, suddenly very businesslike. "Take it out and I'll tell you where it is."

"Tell me first."

"If you hurt Otto I'll never say one word about the sword, Jimmy. You know I won't. Take it out *now*."

Remarkably, he does. For the second time in as many days, duct tape is ripped from my mouth. I move my tongue around the vault of my mouth, making sure it's still there. It is, but it's not happy about it. It feels as if I've been gargling firecrackers.

"Talk," he says.

"It's here," she says, downcast. "In this building."

Herkimer brandishes the curling iron at me angrily.

"I'm not kidding," she says. "It's here. I stashed it when I came for my father."

"Why would you bring it right to Azar?"

She looks at him as if his ignorance defies credulity.

"Because you'd never look for it here."

He thinks about that for a second.

"Where exactly?"

"Room 331. Near the west entrance. Above a ceiling tile by the door."

"Is it rigged?" he asks.

"No."

"Is it *rigged*?" he repeats, again threatening me with the iron.

"No," she says. "No. If you want I can lead you to it. I'll get it down."

Herk tries to raise someone on his mouthpiece. No one answers. Everyone, it seems, is either out searching for me or attending to the distraction that Kong created. An expression flickers over his face that approximates uncertainty. When he looks contemplatively at the door Charlie hazards a glance at me. Her eyes are complicit and full of hope.

"Nice try," he says finally. He doubles up the duct tape on

her arms and legs. Then he makes a second hole in the ham and stabs it with the curling iron.

"There. That's cute. One for each of you. If you're lying to me, Charlie, you're both going to get one. It won't be gentle, like before. And it won't be quick."

The door slides shut with a hydraulic shush, the air in the room radiating with the terrifying smell of burned bacon.

Teamwork

With one operational leg I kick against the floor and the chair rolls off its bolts. Then, on the floor, I arm-wrestle uselessly against the duct tape securing my wrists. Jagjeet suggests I squirm over to him so he can tear me free but I can't propel the chair that far. Charlie avows that I have the strength but I do not. Seeing no other recourse, I kick over the table and when the curling iron falls to the floor I pry it out of the ham with my foot, kick it toward me, and press the tape onto it as hard as I can. There's plenty of sizzling, and plenty of scream-ing, but I burn off enough tape to pull out of it. Then I peel off the other arm and free Charlie. Immediately, she tries to kiss me but I push her off.

"Think you waited long enough to tell Herkimer about the sword?" I say, trying to rub some of the heat out of my mouth.

"I had to. If I had said anything with everyone in the room, Azar would have just sent one of them after it and Jimmy would have killed us."

"You just didn't want to give up your precious sword."

"Otto, no. I'd never..."

Words fail her. Again she attempts that hungry embrace, and again I stiff-arm her.

"Save it," I say.

She stands there in her underwear, heaving and wounded with something more than physical pain. Even now, like this, and after everything that has happened, she is still the most beautiful woman I have ever seen. And it will always be that way. My blood knows it.

Her eyes beg mine for something—softness, possibility, hope—but I don't give it.

"I'm getting you out of here, but that's it."

"But Otto—"

"Get dressed." I throw her clothes at her roughly. She doesn't catch them; they fall around her feet like birds falling dead out of the sky. When she finally takes her injured eyes off me she picks them up, dully, and puts them on. I scoop up the keys from the floor and let Jagjeet out of the cuffs. He gets to his feet slowly, his body moving with a kind of confusion, as if it only partially remembers how to stand. When he gets steady on his feet, Charlie hugs him. I've seen that embrace before. Now it's clear that it's innocent, has always been innocent. I should be relieved but instead I still feel betrayal, and I take the moment—Charlie's eyes locked shut in affection, Jagjeet's beard snugging her—to slip the handcuffs into my back pocket. I have a feeling I'll need them.

"Broken ribs?" Charlie asks Jagjeet.

He shrugs and smiles. For him this is just a worse-than-average day at the office. It gets worse, rapidly, however: when we try to exit the room, the door won't open.

"Can you get it?" I say.

"Sure," Charlie says. "Easy. Just let me see those tools."

"I wasn't talking to you," I inform her. "I was talking to Kong."

"Jimmy locked it from the outside," Kong says. "Let Charlie do it."

"No. She's not doing anything. She can't be trusted."

"Otto," Charlie says, "you don't understand. I only—"

Kong interrupts. "Give her the tools, Otto. There isn't time."

Defensively I clasp the tools to my chest. "Then you better tell me what to do."

In the interstices of outraged profanity, Kong tells me what to do with the wires. During his instruction, Charlie leans over my shoulder, whispering assurances.

"Do you mind?" I say to her. She backs away but her fragrance—a greenhouse odor fighting down the slaughterhouse smell of the room—still distracts me. I try to blow it out of my nostrils but it's no good. There's nothing I can do about it. If I want to breathe, I'm going to breathe in the odors of Charlie.

After several successful operations, Kong says, "You got two wires left, correct?"

"Yep."

"Black and green?"

"Right."

"O.K. Good. Now just cut the green wire and you're done."

"What?"

"Hurry up."

"Did you say the green wire?"

"Yes!" he yells. "Jesus!"

"What are you up to?"

Charlie says, "Nothing, Otto. Trust him. He's—"

"Cut it, cocksuck!"

"Do you think I'm stupid?"

"Everyone who's ever met you thinks you're stupid," Kong says. "Now cut it."

"It's never the green wire," I tell him. "Everybody knows that."

"The building isn't exactly to code, nimrod. Cut the fucking green wire."

Everyone around me is a criminal. No one can be trusted. But I know what I know from all my years as a pulse, and if I have to believe in something, I'll believe in that.

"No," I say. "I'm going black."

In desperate chorus Charlie and Kong and Jagjeet yell "No!" but it's too late.

Snip.

They all gasp and recoil and clench their eyes as if in the presence of a bomb that just ticked down to zero. Then the door retracts into its pocket. Everything is quiet. We lean our heads out the door and scan left and right: all clear. We step through the door, looking down the hall in varying degrees of astonishment, and still: all clear. Charlie stares at me in wonder.

"See?" I say.

As Charlie nods in concession—admiration, even—the door behind us slams shut and an alarm starts shrieking through the halls.

"Not one word," I say to Charlie, upholding a finger.

"I didn't say anything!"

Jagjeet and I pull left; Charlie pulls right.

"This way," she says.

"No," I say, "it's this way."

"We have to go this way."

"I just came this way. I know what I'm talking about."

It's a bad time for one of our battles of wills, but there it is.

"Otto," she says as the alarm wails, "my father's still here."

My heart pinches. To me, he has always been in some remote Californian village; I have always been working up the guts to ask him for permission to marry his daughter. Now he is in the same building with me; now I am going to put his daughter in jail.

It's not the way I envisioned meeting him.

"Mr. Izzo?" Jagjeet says urgently, lovingly. "Where?"

Before Charlie can answer there is a burst of gunfire and a spray of drywall confetti rains down on us. Jagjeet shoves us around the corner but can't join us before an explosion of white powder above his head forces him to dive behind the other corner.

We are in the hallway that leads to Kong. He is in the one that leads to Mr. Izzo.

My ears burn with the sound of feet sprinting toward us.

"Where?" he yells over the din of the bells and gunfire.

"Room 207, north wing!" Charlie yells back.

Jagjeet is off in a bolt. Charlie takes me by the hand and drags me down the hallway with the sound of sprinting footsteps coming after us. With the alarm squealing it's impossible for me to apply my hearing around corners and so we're running without any idea what's ahead. We could easily run into a bullet.

"Kong," I yell into the mouthpiece, "you've got to cut the alarm. I can't hear anything."

"I can't! I can barely keep the cameras off of you!"

"Just do it!"

Then it gets bad. We round a corner that reveals a long, long corridor. We screech to a stop and stare down to the distant corner. Charlie could make it, but I'll never be able to hobble down there before the guys are on us. We both know it. Charlie stares at me, her eyes watering. Then her hand flashes like a mongoose into the holster on my leg, comes out with the dart gun, and in one continuous motion she leans around the corner and fires a dart into the neck of the lead guy. He goes down fast, but two more are coming at us, guns out.

"Dart!" Charlie yells.

I peel one out but drop it. There is no time to load. Charlie picks it up, hurls it like a quarterback, and gets another neck shot and it's *thirrrp*, boom, down. But the third guy is still coming, and there is no more time.

Passionately I wish that we had a real gun.

As Charlie yanks off her belt, I barely process the guy breaking around the corner, her arm swinging, the polished blur of a metal buckle lashing the guy's hand. The gun skitters to the tiles and, somehow, the belt is now looped around his wrist. Charlie slips a punch, wraps it around his wrist a second time, cinching it, and then by some incomprehensible contortion of physics the guy is in the air, pinwheeling for what seems like a very long time until he hits the floor in a crunchy tangle of limbs. Charlie puts a chokehold on him, and it is not gentle. It is not a nudge into sleep, like the choke she used on me, and in a few excruciating seconds he is out.

Part of me is relieved to be alive. Another resents that I now owe Charlie one.

I pick up the gun and swing out the cylinder.

"Two bullets left," I yell over the alarm.

Charlie extends her hand and for a second I almost hand it to her. But then I shake my head no; she can't hurt me with a dart but I don't trust her with a firearm. She can probably take it from me and do anything to me that she likes, true, but I'm not going to make it easy on her.

When we are halfway down another hallway a second

group of guys appears in the intersection. Charlie and I skid to a staggering stop before realizing that their backs are to us. They haven't seen us yet. Charlie reaches for the gun but I swat her hand away and push her into a storage closet. For a minute we do nothing but breathe. After we hear their footsteps as they run by, Charlie reaches for the doorknob and again I swat her hand. She regards me quizzically but I only address Kong. I tell him that we're stuck in a closet and that we're not coming out until he gets that alarm off. Our only chance of getting out of here alive, I tell him, is if I can sense around corners. This time he doesn't swear at me. His only response is the furious clacking of his keyboard. It is not an encouraging sound.

The closet is safe, but it's not comfortable. It's small and Charlie's body is pressed up against mine. There's nowhere to hide from my senses. I feel her hands clutch at my shirt, her mouth moisten my neck. It's also quieter in the closet—the door muffles the worst of the alarm—and, unfortunately, we can now speak normally.

"I'm sorry, Otto. I'm so, so—"

"I'm not talking to you," I remind her.

"Otto, please let me—"

"No."

"I want to explain."

"You stole my MacGuffins. End of story."

"I didn't steal them. I put them back where they belong."

"You're a thief for Azar."

"Well," she says, with a whisper of indignation, "you pulsed for the DOD."

"So?"

"They're a pipeline for looting in other countries."

"I don't give a shit about that."

"You do, too. Your whole life is about what's right, but, Otto—"

"You lied to me."

"You lied to me, too."

"You paralyzed my leg!"

"You shot me!"

The truth takes the fight out of me: I shot Charlie. I could have killed her.

"I didn't mean to," I say finally.

"Oh, Otto. I didn't mean to either."

"I thought you were having an affair."

Charlie's body shakes in an exhilaration of denial. Never never never, she says, clutching at me, pulling me into her body, rapturous, and for a second I almost give in. Before I get too deep under it, though, the earpiece conveys the sound of the van door slamming, and then Kong is screaming.

"Kong?" I say. "Kong? What's going on?"

"It's Jeet," he says. "He's here. And he's got Charlie Senior. He's O.K."

When I tell this to Charlie she gasps and presses her body against mine. For a long minute I let her discharge tears onto my shirt. I hold her. I say some things. I stroke her head. Finally, though—and as gently as I can—I disengage.

"Charlie," I say, "what else have you lied to me about?"

Charlie squirms, the muscles contracting around her spine, then starts talking. Haltingly, she tells me how she really broke her nose, how she cooked those Maltese meals with incomprehensible names to assuage her terrible guilt, how she has been reading my journal all this time, and how she regretted it but also cherished it because it made her feel close to me. She confesses other things that make me feel very stupid. How could I not see it?

Anyone else would have seen it.

A jury would see it, too.

Finally, when I can't take it anymore, I push her off and say, "Just…move over there, will you?"

"Where?"

"Over there."

"There's no room."

Charlie corkscrews her body in a way that maximizes contact with mine.

"Hey," I say, "what are you doing?"

"Nothing."

"Oh yes you are."

"What am I doing?"

"Don't act innocent."

"I *am* innocent."

"No you're not."

"I'm trying to move where you told me to."

"No," I say. "You're *rubbing*."

The word is vibrant with accusation, as if I am denouncing her for trafficking disabled orphans or something.

"Well, I'm sorry, but there's nowhere to go in here."

I am acutely aware of her breasts pressing on me, her radiant body heat.

"Can't you turn around or something?"

She rotates around, frisking against me, until her body jigsaws with mine, her ass articulating with my pelvis.

"That's not any better."

"I can't help it."

"Quit doing that thing with your hips."

"I'm not doing anything!"

"You know exactly what you are doing."

"Don't blame me, Otto. I didn't pick this closet."

"Just turn here," I say while grabbing her shoulders in a very businesslike way, "and like this..." I position her until she is sideways so that nothing irresistible is pressing against me, but it doesn't help much. My pants still feel five sizes too small.

"Happy now?" says Charlie.

"Very." Then, to Kong, I say, "Any progress with that alarm?"

Kong's geysering of obscenity informs me that he is still working on it.

"Stop moving," I say to Charlie.

"You sure you want me to?"

"What do you mean?"

"Something hard in your pocket is stabbing me."

For a moment I feel abashed—it's hard to maintain any credibility in the I-detest-you-and-revile-everything-you-stand-for department while nudging your girl's hip with a boner—but then I feel something more dire: panic. The button is in my pocket. If Charlie discovers it before I have a chance to summon Nunes, she'll know I'm here to take her in. And that would make things extremely complicated.

I should just push the button right now but something—maybe my overwhelmed senses, maybe Charlie telling me the truth, maybe the fact I still owe Charlie for saving my life mere minutes ago—won't let me.

"Car keys," I say.

"I don't think so...."

And then, before I can formulate another denial, I see that Charlie has prestidigitated out of my pocket—and is now holding in her hand—a velvety box.

"Oh my God!" she exclaims. "Otto! You brought it!"

"Stop—"

"It's"—she gasps like a winning beauty pageant contestant—"beautiful!"

"Wait—"

But it's too late. She has already slipped it on her finger and is staring at it intensely. She is wild, galvanized, maenadic with feeling. The acceleration of blood in her jugular pounds over the alarm.

"That's not for you."

Charlie spins, throws her arms around me, and applies her mouth lovingly—uncannily—to the few unbeaten parts of my face. The kisses hurt anyway.

"Stop," I tell her. "You don't understand. It's not for you."

Words have no impact on her. She continues kissing me without remit.

"Listen to me," I say firmly. "I wasn't going to propose. I was going to pawn it."

"What?" she says, stricken.

"Pawn it. To get a start on a new life. Without you."

"Oh no," she says, unlacing her arms from my neck. "You can't mean that."

"Oh yes I do. Now give it."

"No," she says, clutching it, covetous, to her chest. "I won't."

"You going to steal that from me, too, thief?"

"You were going to give it to me! I know it!"

"Like hell."

Even though I know it is unwise—even though I know that any physical contest with Charlie is unlikely to resolve in my favor—I make a grab for the ring. She closes her fist against me and we start going at it. The closet is so confining that it's more of a fussing match than a wrestling match, and eventually one of us hits the door handle and we spill onto the floor at the feet of two guys with guns.

Abruptly, the alarm stops and in my ear I hear Kong say, triumphantly, "I got it!"

A guy with a gun also says, triumphantly, "Hi, Charlie."

This is an inopportune development on many levels, but the most disconcerting aspect of the encounter is the face of the guy with the gun pointed at me.

I recognize it.

A Picture of Loveliness

In fact, I recognize both gunmen. I can't quite place them, though. While they focus on Charlie[67] I struggle to recall how I know them. They aren't the guys from the torture room; they weren't at the Foxhole; I can't place them from any Janus file.

Who are they?

Charlie is talking to one of them, a gravy-complected guy with teeth like someone out of a Ralph Steadman. She begs him not to call us in. She says something about a job in Zurich that constitutes some sort of indebtedness, but it doesn't seem to have much effect on him. He raises the wire in his sleeve to his mouth and

---

67 Even as they relieve me of the revolver, they are really paying attention to Charlie; in the presence of an unarmed, injured Polecat, it seems, a pulse with a pistol does not warrant much concern.

reports our location to Herkimer. Charlie deflates but I just keep staring.

"I know you," I say vaguely. Then the memory starts coalescing, and I get it. I saw this guy one year ago, in front of a Boucher with an empty picture frame in his hand; I saw the other one as a member of a gang of muggers on Seventieth and Fifth, at first accosting Charlie beside a burst of blooming honeysuckle and then, shortly thereafter, on the sidewalk, under my fist.

It doesn't take much to understand this. Not even the way I met Charlie was real. The homeless guy, the muggers: all a ruse to set me up with Charlie. In the closet she said she had confessed everything. She hadn't.

I think: why should I be surprised? She's a liar.

"A picture...," I say to no one, "of loveliness."

Disgust ulcerates my stomach.

The last time I was confronted with these guys it was a setup. I had nothing to lose. This time I do. This time they are not getting paid to feed me lines or to take a flop. This time I have no illusions about my fighting skills. This time they have a pair of guns. Aimed at us, point-blank. Loaded with real bullets.

None of this stops me.

I wish I could say that my action is motivated by conscious choice but it is not. I am animated by an electric hatred; my body is put into motion by pure feeling. And it happens fast. A dazzling bolt of light flashes before my eyes and then my hand clenches and I step forward and hurl it, hard and looping, as if unleashing a fastball, not a fist, directly at Mr. Picture of Loveliness. It is the punch of my life. It scores a direct hit, too, right in the center of his face. The guy hits the ground before he even groans. The other one spins around to put the gun on me but Charlie's foot impacts his rib cage. He crashes into the wall, then sags onto the floor. Charlie stares at me, amazed.

"That's the bravest thing I've ever seen," she says.

My instinct is to impugn her over failing to tell me about this lie, but instead I grab her hand—the ring on her finger burning hot against my skin—and lead her away. Without arguing, without recrimination, without lobbying for the ring back, I lead us through the silent hallways toward freedom. I do this not because the exertion of violence has made me magnanimous, or because being so close to death has given me a new perspective on forgiveness, or because expedition affords us the best chance of escaping Azar's facility alive.

I do it because it distracts Charlie from seeing me reach into my pocket and press the Sankt-Moeller button.

The Forty-fifth Murder

I bloodhound through the hallways. It's not easy—given Charlie's hand in mine, her scent in my nose, and, naturally, the very real prospect of death looming over me—and I have to focus like never before. If for one second I let myself become distracted I lose it all, but when I order silence from Charlie and Kong, and I reach out mightily with my senses, I apprehend everything. I hear every decibel fraction within a hundred yards; my bare feet on the tile are as sensitive to vibration as any long-period seismometer you can name; I detect the cicada-like throb and sizzle of the building's electricity in my fillings, in the tender egg-white tissue of my eyes.

I am aware of everything. I know all.

At least as long as I can concentrate, that is.

It's a good thing, too. Twice I have to duck down another corridor to avoid incoming muscle. Another time I have to signal to Charlie exactly when to fire the dart gun at a guy sneaking around a corner. On a fourth occasion I have to pull her into a closet to stop her from using the last two bullets in the revolver. All in all, I save us from at least ten murder-bent henchmen.[68]

I know that in the strictest sense this constitutes repayment to Charlie for saving my life, but I still cringe with guilt over having pressed the button. As if it can help, I repeat my flimsy mantra: It's not evil. You're not betraying love.

Finally Kong directs us to an intersection with a long hall that terminates in an open door on the other side of which is a trash-clogged alley and, bordering the street beyond, some balding, spavined trees.

Freedom.

Kong urges us to hurry up.

"The system is edging me out," he says. "I can't hold it forever."

I tug Charlie toward the door but she tugs toward the other hallway.

"Otto," she says, "I've got to do one thing first. You get out. I'll meet you."

"What?"

"There's an equipment room this way. If I'm going to get the Nakamura sword back I'm going to need gear. And I can't go to my apartment now."

---

68 If it matters anymore—if anything does—I also probably save the lives of some of those henchmen, too.

Kong says, "This isn't easy, people. Move."

From the exit comes a grinding sound of hydraulic tug-of-war. The door inches out of the pocket and then retracts.

"No way," I say. "We're getting out of here."

"The sword isn't just a sword," she says, almost pleading.

"What does that mean?"

"It's got a microchip hidden in its hilt that has the tracker code of every single cargo box from the *Saqueador*."

For a second I don't know what she's talking about, but then I remember. I also finally understand why Nakamura was willing to pay for a solo and floater—eight-fig treatment for a six-fig item: the sword is a treasure map to art worth hundreds of millions of dollars. All of which is already crated up for your convenience.

"It's a Portuguese freighter carrying twenty thousand pieces of looted Iraqi art and—"

"I know what it is."

"You do? But then you must understand that I have to—"

"I don't care. We're going through that door right now."

I yank on her hand. She yanks back, hard. The specter of physicality crackles in the air between us. Charlie's shoulders tense. My jaw vises together. I am very aware of the handcuffs in my pocket.

And the gun.

"Otto, I love you. I'm sorry I lied to you. It's the worst thing I've ever done. I hate myself for it. I'm going to spend the rest of my life making it up to you. I promise. But I have to do this."

"You're not getting the sword," I say tightly.

Behind her the door is in spasm. It closes halfway, seizes, then opens again.

Kong says, "Hurry up, idiots."

"I know I'm overmatched," Charlie says. "I'm not at my best. But I have to try."

"You're not going to."

"I have to, Otto. Please understand."

"It's over, Charlie."

I hold up the button. The light is blinking.

"I pressed it two minutes ago."

She gives me a look that knifes into my heart. Her eyes goggle in pain at the blinking light. From her mouth comes a gasp that sounds like ripping fabric.

Unbeknownst to my tortured senses, a third party is present. As I am busy encoding forever the terrible vision of Charlie apprehending my betrayal, I do not perceive Herkimer until it is too late. The first I know of his propinquity is the blur of his fist smashing her cheek. Charlie, already doubled over, crumples to her knees. Before I can do anything more than emit a gurgle of shock, a punch precipitates me to the floor.

From the tiles I see Herkimer go at Charlie with a samurai sword. He makes a few feints, a few exploratory thrusts. Even while clutching her injured shoulder she dodges them foxily, intuitively, but it's clear that she is outclassed. She makes quick, dancerlike pivots and evasions, but her speed isn't equal to his hallway-filling girth, his brute strength. She steps inside a thrust and then successfully blocks a hook punch, but the blow still sends her whole body crashing into the wall. She rolls away as Herkimer makes a violent slash at her head. She slips under it, the blade singing through the air, and staggers backward. A cloudburst of severed hair materializes before her, suspended briefly in the air, then drifts like dandelion snow to the ground. Herkimer smiles gleefully and approaches her, the blade of the Nakamura sword swinging lazily side to side. His grip is loose, almost negligent.

He is expert with a knife. He appears no less skilled with a sword.

And Charlie only has one good arm.

He makes a direct thrust at Charlie's stomach but she side-steps it and kicks his knee out from under him. With Herkimer mometarily hobbled, she delivers several stinging blows to his kidney and the side of his head. They don't seem to inconvenience him too much. During the flurry he merely draws back and backhands her casually in the bullet wound. She shrieks and collapses at his feet. He stands astride her cringing body like a colossus and, gripping the Nakamura sword in both hands, brings it over his head. The large muscles in his shoulders contract and then the tip of the sword is streaking toward Charlie.

I unholster the pistol. I don't think. I just squeeze.

The gun has its gun orgasm. I am made blind and deaf by smoke and din. Herkimer wheels around in disbelief as white particles of foam float down over him: a miss. Herk remains imperforate. The drop ceiling, however, is a goner.

I don't have time to fire the second bullet, the last bullet, before he swats the gun out of my hand. Then I am aware of a fist hammering my skull and my head telescoping into my neck. Amid the twinkling argentine floaters that waltz before my vision, I see Charlie spring up; I see her kick the Nakamura sword out of Herkimer's hand; I see it clatter, glittering, to the floor at my feet. But that's the last of my lucidity.

Suddenly I am viewing the scene from very far away, on the coruscating surface of a star millions of light-years away. It now seems all very vague. I'm watching something transpire that should be significant to me but I can't quite parse it out. I see a very large shadow-person set upon a very small shadow-person. The large one wraps a massive arm around the neck of the small one. From the small one comes a sound like water spuming through a clogged drain. A helpless noise. Then something shiny and curved appears in the hand of the large one. This all plays out very slowly. Irrelevantly. Nothing has any meaning. I can hardly see it. Now I'm nearly gone. I'm drifting, quasar-bright, quasar-distant.

Hatred brings me back.

My eyes refocus, my brain reboots, and I see Charlie struggling uselessly against Herkimer. He is behind her, his legs wrapped around her torso, pinioning her, and as one enormous hand grips a wad of hair from her brow another one advances the knife toward her forehead. Charlie fights against Herkimer's knife hand—she is pushing desperately against the wrist as if to bench-press it—but it's a losing battle. She is not strong enough. The blade of the knife lowers inexorably toward her scalp. Tears wash her face. Her eyes lock on mine. Her mouth opens to pronounce words that do not come.

Time stops. When it starts again I am holding the Nakamura sword. It is weightless. The blade tints red. The hair braided around the hilt, sharp and taut as fishing line, cuts into the skin of my palm. I vibrate with the ghosts of the forty-four lives it has taken.

I give it another one.

The Unreachable

I stab Herk in the back. I plunge the sword into the ponderous meat of his trapezius and drive it downward until only the hilt protrudes from his shoulder, awkward and wavering, quiver-like. At first he doesn't respond; his exertion with the knife is unabated. He is still trying to take off her hat. The blade encroaches Charlie's scalp; it contacts Charlie's scalp. A curved red line appears on her skin. His veins engorged, his fist white with grisly effort, Herkimer starts to saw. It all happens so fast that I can only blink in amazement, paralyzed with shock, but then, very slowly, as if finally comprehending a compli-cated theorem, Herkimer gives in to it. He goes soft and full of understanding. The knife slides to the ground. His hand opens and closes hungrily, reaching vaguely backward as if searching for an elusive itch. His mouth expels a few red balloons, a few red streamers, and then he slumps forward onto his face. His hand keeps contracting like a beating heart, questing over his shoulder, trying to reach the unreachable.

I watch him until his hand quits moving.

Ambiguity

There is a horrible, stuttering, sucking sound. It could be his soul departing. It could be me groaning. I can't be sure. The only intelligible thing I know that I say is one single word:

"Murderer."

Exit

It is unclear how I remain standing, but then I perceive being propped up, underarm, by Charlie. She is saying something to me but I have been made aerodynamic by mortality shock and the words just slide over me. Kong is yelling something at me about a door, but that doesn't penetrate either.

I have just killed my best friend.

The fact of it, the totality, is on me like an iron blanket.

Only when Charlie reaches for the Nakamura sword do I snap out of the death trance. Abruptly, I box her out and extract the sword. Its withdrawal requires considerable effort. It is necessary to prop one foot against the body and yank, hard, speedily, as if pull-starting a lawnmower. Charlie holds her hand out to me but I shake my head no. I pull the sword to my side, blade erect, a gesture of ownership that is at once samurai-like and childish. The posture says *"En garde!"* but it also says "No, I won't give it!" She starts to speak but Kong cuts her off.

"I can't hold it!"

On cue, the sirens start wailing. Behind Charlie the door opens halfway and starts juddering between opened and closed. Charlie again gestures for the sword but I hurl it like a javelin far down the other hallway. She swivels her head frantically from the distant sword to the distant doorway, trying to determine if she has enough time for both. She doesn't. She gives me one last look—harried, passionate, inscrutable—and starts sprinting toward the closing door. I grab the gun and hobble after her. Then the door gives up its struggle with itself. It retracts entirely, as if resetting, then starts sliding smoothly closed. Kong, in his usual thugiloquent manner, communicates that he no longer has any control over the system and that it is now time for us to run for all we're worth.

Charlie takes this advice. Her churning stride is leggy and efficient, the product of expertise and training and native ability; it generates a speed that can be described as "quasi-Olympian." My stride is the product of a lifetime of unathleticism combined with the spasticity of a semiparalyzed appendage; it generates a speed that can be characterized, at best, as "potato-sack racer."

She is going to make it.

I am not.

Sure enough, at full speed Charlie streaks through the frame, skids to a stop in the alley, whirls around, and stares at me through the closing aperture. I am halfway there; the opening is much more than halfway gone. The slow guillotine of the closing door slices away my view of Charlie's face. She is outside. I am inside. I've blown it, and the expression on her face shows that she knows it.

But then something unexpected happens. Charlie starts fighting against the insistent thrusting force of the hydraulics. She is mere seconds from freedom, and instead of running she is trying to pry open the door. She shoulders against it; it edges her out. She pushes against it; it does not slow. She tries to wedge her foot at the base; her foot is mashed aside. No contortion, no exertion of leverage, makes any difference. Then, as my glimpse of the outside world is reduced to a narrowing slat of alley I see Charlie's foot kick up against the wall and her fingers wrap around the edge of the inexorably closing door.

The hydraulics, the closing metal: her fingers don't stand a chance.

I start to yell this to her but it's too late. The sound of Charlie grunting with effort changes into cries of terror and pain and then into something incomprehensible, maniacal. I clench my eyes shut against the sight of what I know must come, but when I open them the floor is fingerless. And bloodless. Looking up, I see all digits are present and accounted for, wriggling with the joy of attachment. But the door is not closed. It's stopped at her fingers.

The incomprehensible sound, I realize, is laughter.

I don't waste any time wondering about the physics of hydraulics versus finger bone; I just run to Charlie and in unison we kick and push against the door until it grinds open and we spill onto the concrete together. She lands on top of me and I grab her protectively. It just happens. I wrap her up. Against the outcry of good judgment, common sense, and all instincts of self-preservation, I keep my arms around her. I hold her as if I don't know what's coming.

Sacrifice

Naturally I apprehend it first: police sirens competing with squealing tires competing with pulsating lights. I know I must act before Charlie perceives the racket of the approaching law, too, so I reach around for the handcuffs but can't grab them before Charlie breaks the embrace and sits up, giggling. She is pixilated, charged with the girlish thrill of sharing something important. It is so innocent, so megawatted, that for a moment she has no idea where she is or what is going on—it is irrelevant right now that I have pressed the button, that cops are incoming. It is exactly the reaction I had hoped she would have when I pulled the car over on Lafayette.

That it's happening now absolutely breaks my heart.

"The ring," she says, holding it up like a torch. It's wrecked; it's a bent polygon with a diamond drooping from it like the bloom of a broken-necked flower. "It stopped the door..."

She can't finish. She is busy crying from joy and metaphor. She thinks I am, too.

I tell myself: I've made so many sacrifices. A last one is required of me, and I must make it before Charlie hears the sirens. So when she buries her face in my neck, her arms wrapped around me, the shockwave of love resonating through my body, I extract the handcuffs from my pocket, secure myself in one and then, while Charlie is distracted by ogling the ring, clap the other cuff on her wrist. The sound of it locking is yet another memory that I can never expunge.

Click-*click*.

Her body heaves and jerks as if possessed by supernatural spirits. She stands up, her arm trailing down into mine, our hands touching. She flaps her arm frantically, incomprehending. She flaps it again. The stars overhead glint dully like dirty dimes. Then she hears it. Her head whips around, her ears locating the direction of the sirens. A word embolizes in her throat. Her whole body shrinks. Everything about her diminishes, contracts, frets with disbelief. Her expression is so horrible that I have to look away. I inspect my shoes, the huddle of overturned trash cans at my feet, the flashing blue lights that stroboscope off the glass of storefronts out in the street. I can hear the many engines revving and the tires shredding on the asphalt. Nunes didn't take any chances; it's a cruiser stampede.

There is another click. Charlie steps backwards away from me. An opened cuff dangles like a gaping mouth at my wrist. It was a stupid idea in the first place. They would never hold her. I must have known it would come down to this.

I unholster the gun and point it at Charlie.

"Here we are again," I say.

"Like old times."

She takes a few wary steps backwards and I refocus the gun on her.

"I'm taking you in," I say. "One way or another."

She takes another few delicate steps toward the other end of the alley. This doesn't seem like my reality. It seems like someone else's, a dramatization, a novelty, a faker. I couldn't possibly shoot Charlie. But I must.

"Stop or I'll shoot." I try to say this like I mean business but the oxygen pipes tightly in my throat and I feel the tears cooling my face. "I mean it, Charlie."

Charlie takes another cautious, balletic step backward, then turns and starts sprinting down the alley. I raise the sights to my eyes and try to make my arm firm yet relaxed, just like Herk taught me. It's a clean shot. No obstructions, no tricky angles. I slow down my respiration, put my heart on mute, and make the sacrifice I knew in my gut I would have to make.

I set my stance, steady my aim, fire. For once, I don't miss. I hit my mark, dead.

I murder a trash can.

Otto Starks, Supernova

As I'm waiting for the cops, Kong excoriates my ear. He is unquiet with questions to which he urgently craves answers. Where am I? Where's Charlie? What was that gunshot? What's going on? Where's his goddamn title?

Answers don't do much to cool his temper. He alleges that I had planned this all along, that he was never going to get the title, that I'm a louse, a double-dealer, a miscreant afflicted with underendowment, that my life is no longer worth the excrement of a constipated pelican.

"You got that right," I tell him.

The cops show up, accoutered in assault gear and balaclavas and proboscis-like optics, chitting like insects. Hordes of them Busby Berkeley past me and dissolve into Azar's building; when they're gone Nunes just stands there coolly, hand-rolled cigarette lolling from her mouth, umbrella hanging from her arm like a corpse. I should be panicking, cooking up plausible story lines, inveigling clemency. But I don't have the strength. I am insensate, dead. I feel like a toy from a fairy tale who, after being vivified by some benevolent magic, has again been made unreal.

"Where's Azar?" she says.

"Beats me."

"Where's Jimmy the Hat?"

"Dead."

"And the Rat Burglar?"

With my chin I indicate the wrong end of the alley.

"Clean getaway."

"You lost her?"

I nod as if it doesn't hurt me.

"And she went that way?"

Again I nod and use my chin to indicate the east end of the alley. To a pair of cops behind her, she points west and says, "That way, boys. Quick." I should have known better than to try to outsmart her. Don't I ever learn anything?

"You remember the terms of our deal?" she says.

"Yeah." I show her the empty cuff dangling from the end of my arm. Making a show of it, I put my hands behind my back and manacle my wrists together. "Let me make it easy on you."

She helps me to my feet. I needed the help.

"You've got to go down for this. You know that." She walks me to the cruiser and puts me in. When she does that cop-move and presses my head down and through the door, her touch is gentle, motherly. She almost sounds reluctant when she says it again.

"You know you're going away for a long time, right? Hey, you hear me, Starks?"

I hear the words, all right, but I don't care. They are like light from an extinct star that arrives thousands of years too late to mean anything. It's already done with, I think. That star's got nothing left. Neither do I.

Snitching

At the station they give me some coffee that tastes like cigarettes and attic. During interrogation I am very agreeable. They ask a bunch of leading questions, they pose many accusations, and I don't resist any of it. I say yes to everything. Yes, I was the mang on the Angkor Wat job, I say. Ditto Entemena. Ditto Inanna and the K'plua and any other job you say. Yes, I've been involved with the Rat Burglar from the start. Yes, I used my inside connection with Janus to target vulnerable MacGuffins. Yes, I assaulted George Schermer because I wanted to cut him out of his share. Yes, I murdered Jimmy the Hat for the same reason. You want to book me for larceny, assault, murder? Sure. Why not? I did it all.

I'm the criminal of the century. I deserve everything I have coming to me.

The only thing I don't give them is Charlie's name.

"For the last time," Nunes says, "who is the Polecat?"

"I can't say."

"You mean you won't say."

"Right."

"You admit that you know the identity of the Polecat?"

"Yes."

"But you won't tell us?"

"Correct."

"The Polecat sold you out, Otto. You're here. She's free."

For some reason, Nunes has started using my first name. Almost like we're pals.

"That's true."

"Why are you being such a chump?"

I take a sip of the coffee. It's so bad it reminds me I'm alive.

"That's my way."

"You're not helping yourself," Nunes says.

"Believe me, I know."

"You remember the deal you asked about for the Polecat?"

"Sure."

"About not going in the mainline?"

"Yes."

"Protective custody?"

"I remember."

"Well, I can get that for you, too. But only if you give me a name."

"I'm not giving you her name."

"You know what'll happen if you end up in the same ward as Frankie Nickels?"

"We've been over this before."

"So give me a name."

"No."

"I'm trying to be gentle with you, Otto. I feel like I understand you now. You're a bad guy, but not the kind of bad guy I thought you were. A lot of the other cops in here don't have the delicate sensibility that I have. They aren't as...subtle...with their technique. It would be best for you if you just told me, Otto. I mean that."

"What are they going to do to me?" I say, framing my face demonstratively with my hands. My hair is shaved off where the stitches snake around my skull. My mouth has fewer teeth than it's accustomed to. My face is a red-purple blancmange of beaten tissue. "Ruin my august profile?"

"If you don't—"

"I'll sign any statement you want, Nunes. I'll say I'm the Zodiac Killer. I'll say I killed Biggie. I'll say I killed the electric fucking car if you want me to. I'll say anything. But I'm not saying that."

Nunes clicks off the tape recorder.

"Otto, it's not humanly possible to be this dumb. Why are you doing it?"

I look her in the eye. My face hurts. My mouth hurts. My leg hurts. My heart doesn't know what it feels.

"Detective," I say, "I am far dumber than you could ever understand."

><

I am escorted to a holding cell that smells of mold, sweat, ammonia, sickness, unisex despair. It gets pink outside the window, then bright, then, sometime later, dark again. I don't sleep and I don't close my eyes. That's where memories are. Instead I stare at a brick in the wall. It's a fascinating brick. Some cop comes in and makes a joke about me wanting to marry that brick but he gives up on getting a response. Later he brings in some buddies and they all laugh and point at me, staring away. To them I'm a circus animal, but they're not sure if they want to give me a peanut or a taser.

When it's bright again Nunes shows up with a large manila folder under her arm.

"We received an interesting care package last night from a concerned samaritan. I'd like you to give it a look with us."

She leads me into a room with a TV and presses play on a VCR. On the screen I see the image of myself holding a gun on Charlie as she approaches the mannequin with the Cincinnati cord. The on-screen Otto yanks his hand away but shoots her anyway. He tries to resuscitate her but instead gets his ass kicked over every square inch of the room. Eventually he shoots himself in the leg and then there's Charlie ripping her mask off to stanch the blood and administering antidote while chanting, "Forgive me forgive me forgive me."

"What do you make of that?"

"Nothing," I say. "That's not how it happened."

"Really? Well, who is that person?"

"I don't know. I've never seen that person before."

"I hear that sentence fifty-five times a day, Otto. It's never true."

"The whole tape is obviously a fake. You can fake anything nowadays."

"That's true. Technology is amazing. But how about this one?"

She inserts a new tape and then I'm looking at myself inside Kong's van. "No guns," I'm insisting. "No one's killing anybody."

"Oops," Nunes says. "Let me fast-forward to the good stuff."

Then Jagjeet and I are zipping around the Bauhaus hallways like Keystone Cops; we break into Charlie's room; a curling iron gets shoved down my mouth;[69] Charlie and I run through the hallways; I punch out Mr. Picture of Loveliness;[70] then Herkimer decks Charlie and sends me into a distant orbit. Nunes slows the tape down to watch the fight. They're both so fast it's hard to tell the difference between real time and fast-forward. I miss Herkimer with the gun. I don't miss with the sword.

During the whole thing Charlie's face is clearly in focus.

"This look familiar to you at all?"

"Nope."

"You've never seen that woman before?"

"Negative."

"She's beautiful, though, isn't she? I guess if someone loved her, he might do just about anything to protect her."

"I don't know anything about that."

"So you can't ID her for us?"

"Sorry."

"Well, that's O.K. We've tracked her down. She's a professor right here in Manhattan. Already talked to all her colleagues, her super, her neighbors. Mother's deceased. Can't locate her father yet. But her name's Charlie Izzo."

"Some name."

"Mean anything to you?"

"Not at all," I say over my pounding heart.

I know I shouldn't keep lying in the face of insurmountable evidence. It's foolish. I know that. But the only thing I have left is resistance.

"That's funny," Nunes says. "Because you say 'Charlie' several times on this."

---

69 Nunes: "That looks uncomfortable."

70 Ibid.: "Nice punch. Ballsy."

I shrug.

"You think that could be faked, too?"

"Sure."

"We thought the same thing. So we're putting some boys on it today to determine authenticity. It's not tough. We'll know in a few hours. I'm not really doubtful what the findings will be, are you?"

"Why are you telling me this?"

"I thought maybe you would tell us why the Polecat—I mean, Charlie Izzo—would snitch on herself to exonerate you."

"How do you know this stuff came from her?"

"Because she said so."

Nunes shows me a letter in which Charlie details everything that has happened from day one. She tells all the details of Azar's program, her insinuation into my life, my ignorance of her plan, my insistence that no one get killed, the value of the Nakamura sword vis-à-vis the cargo on the *Saqueador*. She says I was tricked into breaking into Schermer's apartment. She says I assaulted Schermer in self-defense and that I killed Herkimer only to save her life. She specifies all her own thefts. She even advises Nunes how to find Azar. She gives Nunes everything she wanted.

Except me. And, of course, herself.

"I have responsibilities outside of the country right now," the letter says. "And don't bother looking for me. I won't be back."

"So if this all checks out," says Nunes, "I guess we've got to cut you loose."

"You don't seem to mind it."

"I don't think of it as losing a mang; I think of it as gaining a mobster. That info, at least, was solid." Nunes points down the hall through the glass. Sitting hunched on a bench, wrists locked together, his trach hole sneering pinkly at the world, is Azar. My body flinches at the sight.

"Spooked, huh? Well, he's a spooky guy. But your girl's letter gave us everything we needed. We've got him."

"Congratulations."

"So. Where is she, Otto? How can we find her?"

"I wasn't going to tell you anything when I was up for life. Why would I tell you anything now that I'm free?"

"She helped you. I thought you'd want to help her."

"Help her how? By leading you to her?"

"You love her?"

My response is to double over in my chair, moan, and hug my elbows as if trying to squeeze myself into another dimension.

"If you love her you'll try to protect her. It's a lot safer if we can bring her in peacefully. If she puts up a fight, maybe I'm not there, you know what I'm saying? You take a whole bunch of eager-beaver cops, all those guns, all that anger over making them look bad all this time—anything can happen."

"The letter said she's out of the country."

"So you believe that."

I nod.

"Why do you think she's out of the country?"

"I don't think it. I know it."

"How do you know it?"

"I've been wrong about a lot of things lately, Detective Nunes. I've been wrong about pretty much everything you can be wrong about. But not this time. I know this in my stomach. I know it absolutely. Charlie Izzo is long gone. You'll never see her again. Neither will I."

Clean Getaway

A few hours later I'm on the street. It isn't much better. I don't feel liberated. I don't treasure my freedom. Everywhere I go I feel as if I'm pulling a sadness-drogue behind me.

The next day I call up Po-Mo, but he's got nothing for me, not even a letter of recommendation. Not even a phone call on my behalf. On a lark I go see Invigilator and Steadfast but they don't do anything but laugh. I widen the search nationally, then internationally, but nothing comes up even when I offer to pulse for low-rent operations that have never had a pulse anywhere on-site. I offer uni prices, sub-uni prices, to no avail. That night when I see my mug shot on the *Retention Sciences Today* Web site, I realize that my infamy is global.

That was fast.

⇒⇐

I don't bother tidying up my apartment or buying new clothes. I sit, sleep, eat on shredded furniture. I wear clothes cut into streamers. I retrieve Chester Wellington III from the floor, wipe the blood off his hat, and set him up on top of the fridge in a position of honor.

"You win," I tell him.

⇒⇐

I fail to dispose of the bra. It still has a ghost charge of female electricity in it. It still crackles with Charlie. I have to leave it where it lies, slain-looking, and avoid that spot like a blight, a zone of alienation in silk and lace.

>≡<

That night I write Kong a note. Sorry about what happened, I say. I didn't mean for it to happen like that. I didn't tell the cops anything about you. You're clean. I'm including here an expression of apology. It's sincere. It's legit. It's all yours.

I enclose the title to my boat and mail the letter to Kong care of the Foxhole.

>≡<

The "Polecat" story hits hard[71] and for a few weeks everywhere I go I'm followed by meerkatty packs of guys with telephoto lenses. I don't fight them. They want a zoom-close look at grief? They got it. They hound me with questions—everyone wants to hear the story of the sad-sack pulse who loved the thief who stole his whole life—but that I don't give them. I don't talk to them. If I can help it, I don't talk to anyone.

It doesn't prevent the unchecked dissemination of the image of my face, however. Bedizened with bruises and blood, extinguished by sadness, it stares back at me from

---

71 Strangely, there is no mention of the Nakamura sword. No word of recovery or of loss.

TVs in Rope,[72] the windows of PC Richard, even on that little bus-stop screen in front of Neergaard on the B63 line. It
has more hits online than that actor who is supposed to look
like me. Printed in the crumpled and smudgy ink of the *Daily
News* and *Post*, it tumbleweeds in the gutters on DeKalb and
Myrtle.

All of these haunt me, but they aren't as bad as the
nearly omnipresent pictures of Charlie. The media is rife with
feuding camps—some want her punished capitally, some want
her in Congress; some denounce her as the most contempt-
ible thief of the new millennium, others petition to appoint
her as the head of a new watchdog agency for the interna-
tional art community—and everyone from her past is coming forward for their fifteen minutes.[73] A lot of magazines run
that familiar graphic of a jaggedly broken heart, sundered as if
by a bolt of lightning, with a glamour shot of Charlie in one
half and my hangdog mug shot in the other. Someone has put
up a Web site called IAmThePolecat.com that features all sorts
of Charlie miscellany, including but not limited to biographi-
cal details, reprints of her academic papers, both published
and unpublished, theories of her current location, and starred
reviews of her various "restorations." Apparently there is also
quite a large portion dedicated to her multifarious love life,
complete with prurient Photoshopped images that I cannot
describe.

Never before have I so craved a dark, solitary room.

---

72 I can't go to the Snug. It doesn't belong to me anymore.

73 Quackenbush, I am sorry to say, incessantly offers his insights upon me.
Po-Mo, however, has nothing for anyone. He had no recommendation for
me, true, but he also has no comment for anyone else.

✴

I keep thinking, fondly, that Deke will rub me out but it never happens. Finally I start cruising around his neighborhood, hanging out in dark stairways, by the pool table at Alibi, under the Navy Street overpass. One night I finally see a familiar silhouette doing some business under a tree in Fort Greene Park. He's wearing a hoodie and hunched up underneath a low-brimmed hat. When he sees me, he recoils as if just the sight of me has singed his eyeballs. He shoos the guys away and turns from me into the shadows.

"What do you want?" he says from over his shoulder.

"I don't know," I say. "I thought you might want to shoot me?"

"What?"

"Shoot me."

"Shoot you? Are you out of your mind?"

"No."

"What you want me to shoot you for?"

"What the hell do you think for?"

"Nah," he says. "You don't owe me. You're square."

"I am?"

"You know you are. Now get out of here."

"Well, maybe you could shoot me for—I don't know—old times' sake?"

"Haven't you done enough to me? Isn't this enough?" He turns around. His face looks like it's been moonlighting as an anvil and his left arm is in a sling, the fingers red and bloated as raw sausages. Even his voice sounds broken. "You got to come down here and mock me now? That what you want to do?"

"No," I say. "I didn't—"

"Man, I'm not even supposed to be *talking* to you."

He glances furtively around, as if searching for snipers, then starts backing away from me. His steps are delicate and careful, as if he's worried that any noise might beget certain doom.

"And you tell that psycho girl of yours that I didn't do it. I didn't talk to *you*, man. *You* talked to *me*! You tell her that!"

And then he's running.

Two weeks later I find a job. It's at a disconsolate, fumy parking garage in Rahway. No poured concrete parking structure has much in the panache department, but this one is a dump of the first order. It has prisonlike sight lines. It has clearance problems. It has the cheer, and odor, of a Soviet-era urinal. Eight hours a day I sit on a stool that has been made suave by the shifting asses of countless other unies and protect cars that no one would want to steal in the first place.

The job doesn't make me feel more like a human being. I don't feel a gusher of meaning at practicing even an ignoble facsimile of my craft. I am not getting in touch with the former proud pulse inside me. It produces no residue of self. I am still a sparkless, buzzless drone, a 165-pound hunk-of-carbon occupant of the space-time continuum, a drogue-dragger. That's it.

Three days later as I sit in my box staring at keys dangling from the pegboard, I am certain that I smell Charlie. I eject from my stool and run out to the sidewalk but no one is there.

It's just a scent-cloud of Covet. Whoever it was, I just missed her. I still can't quite place that mysterious Hesperidean ingredient, but I have finally deduced the character of Covet. Now I understand it. It is not an up-front perfume. It doesn't zing you with fragrance from across the room. It doesn't precede the woman. It's an aftereffect, a comet trail of female presence. You only really get it when she has already gone past, but when it hits, you know you won't be able to stop thinking about who she is—and where to find her—for the next hour. Or two. Or three.

Or, in my case, the rest of your life.

Further evidence of my dumbness: I keep thinking that maybe Charlie will come back. Against my better judgment, I keep on a sharp, pulse-eyed lookout for any covert signals she might send me. But they never arrive. Do I get a letter addressed in strange handwriting that contains polecat hair and a secret message revealing her location? No. Does she turn up in a bathroom of a restaurant, tell me to act natural, and then smuggle me into a limo with tinted windows? Nope. Is she ever standing behind me, like that day at the Frick, waiting for me to bump into her and whisk me away into her life? No she isn't. She's a ghost.

Sometimes I think maybe she has just been waiting for the right moment. Maybe she needed some time to realize how much she missed me. Needed me. Maybe she needed some Starkslessness to scare her back. Maybe today could be the day.

But it isn't.

It never is.

The knowledge creeps up on me like, well—like a thief. My life isn't getting any better. This is it for me. There is no clean getaway for me except oblivion. The more I think about it the more luxurious it feels. And the more sense it makes. My whole life has been hurtling toward this moment, hasn't it? All that time in cryptlike rooms. Those deadly drugs. My anchoritic seclusion from life.

I cheated death by being at a sleepover when my family was murdered.

And ever since then I have been training for death.

Over the next few days the thought keeps pressing on me. I fantasize about the ways it can go. Being stricken dead by heartache is reasonable, but, incredibly, it doesn't happen. I'm so prone to staggering around it makes sense that I would fall out of a window, but I'm too scared of heights to attempt it. The idea of becoming a luck-pushing vigilante is attractive. I could use my senses for justice in an unwise way until someone offs me. That is plausible, and it has some altruism to it, which is nice, but what would people call me? The Ear? Captain Hypersensitive? No, that's no good. Besides, my heart isn't in it. I'm not a hero. I'm a criminal.

I consider a gun but cannot obtain one.

I try to will myself into the East River but can't. It seems sacrilegious to Pink.

I rub my Swiss Army knife over my wrist a few times but only manage exploratory, cursory strokes. I'm like a novice violinist still afraid of the bow. My effort lacks conviction, and results. All of my attempts do.

It seems I don't want to die. I just don't want to live.

The next best thing is senselessness.

A brief scouring of the apartment reveals a potent little bouquet of toxins. I scrape the most contraindicated ones into a bowl, sit on my julienned couch, and slurp them down. It takes a lot of swallowing and a long time waiting, but eventually, thank God, I go out. When I wake up I have a hangover that's like a grease fire in my brainpan, but, still, I have wasted six hours of my life. Six hours when I didn't have to remember anything. Or smell or touch or hear or see or taste anything. For six hours, all my senses were dead to the world.

Perfect.

This becomes an important part of my routine. If I'm not at the garage, I'm on my eviscerated couch, scarfing down bowls of pills, waiting for nothingness. The paycheck from my stoolie job is laughable, so I have to sell my belongings to keep me in toxins. I run through that money pretty quickly, so soon enough I have to start hustling at bars, having shot-for-shot contests with the local big drinkers. It's no surprise that I crush them all; what is surprising, however, is that one time I let my ego run amok. I have nine hundred dollars on the table against this big guy—apparently he was a competetive strong-man before dedicating his life to the consumption of alco-hol—and, when he finally palms his shot glass in the gesture of *no mas*, I laugh at him, do an aboriginal dance of triumph, and drink all of his remaining shots. He expresses his chagrin at my poor sportsmanship by punching my punch-worn face. It's a lot to go through to keep myself in toxins, and sometimes I'm not even sure it's worth it.

The oblivion never lasts long enough.

It doesn't last forever.

✂

After another week the presence of Chester Wellington III becomes intolerable. He is always giving me that smug groomy look of his. I know he's won, that it's already over, that in fact my failure to take action against my own life and my craven flight from reality via pills are just the icing under his feet, but I can't stand the feeling of him watching over me. He's like an evil K'plua, mocking me, condemning me. I can't take it. I can't take the whole apartment, in fact—the bed, the bra, the fading odor of Charlie.

So I pack up my bag and head for the marina to see my boat.[74]

Miraculously, it's still there. Hanging like a cursed amulet from its gunwale is a red and black sign that says FOR SALE BY OWNER. It makes perfect sense that this is what Kong would do with it—in fact, this is precisely what I recommended Kong do with it—but when I see it I still wince.

Fleet as a one-legged Polecat, I scale the fence and scurry up one of the stilts braced against the hull and then, for the first time, I'm on deck. It's a bright day and the sun glaring off the pristine white composite is blinding. It makes me feel even dizzier. With both hands I grasp the helm and glance out over the bow as if staring at open water, not Manhattan. I must look like a kid pulling at the wheel of a turned-off car, going "Vroom vroom" as if he were accomplishing something.

Belowdecks the heat is thick and punishing—moving through it is like pushing through a headwind—and it has a strangely lifeless odor. It's just plastic, chemical, unstained mahogany, textile. Nowhere is there a trace of anything biological. The odor is humanless, which makes it a little soulless, unreal even,

74 Kong's boat, I remind myself. *Kong's.*

as if the boat is waiting for someone to make it real by occupancy. Simply by being alive in it. This should be a comforting smell—it is so full of potential—but instead it just makes me lonelier. True, I'm here now, but I don't count. Not really. The boat doesn't belong to me.

I've paid for it, God knows, but it still isn't mine.

When I pry open my bag a new fragrance is introduced: pharmacy. That comforts me some. I upend the bottle over the table and a multicolored swarm of pills covers the white plastic. I swirl them around, admiring the kaleidoscope, then wash them all down with bourbon. After a long time, the cabin starts shifting. It becomes faint and umbral, a tunnel of darkness constricting around it. It keeps getting tighter and darker until I am floating in a neutral black plasma.

When I wake up it's a different world. Before I passed out the river hardly said anything. Its mouth was clogged with trash and staleness. It mumbled. But now it has voice. The cabin is also rich with the scent of fish, capers, spinach, sultanas. And the world is on funhouse tilt. It pitches, it rolls, it heels over. I try to stand but the floor is not where it has been located historically by long-standing agreement with my feet. I make a move on it, whiff entirely, and next thing I know I'm turtling on my back. The vertigo tries to pull me under again but I am revived by someone rubbing a wet, warm, abrasive towel on my face. When I open my eyes I see that I am on the receiving end of an elongated pink tongue, scrolling and unscrolling with abandon.

I blink at the puppy, bewildered. The puppy blinks at me, adulant. Then it urinates unashamedly.

I think: I didn't take that many hallucinogens, did I?

Normally I can will myself into the visions I want but this

time I cannot. After a few minutes of failed imaginings I conclude that I must ride this one out. Carefully, I tidy up the floor,
put the puppy under my arm like a piece of carry-on luggage,
and head up on deck.[75] The air as I push up the companion-
way is still hot but it isn't resistant. It lets me up. It practically
invites me up. It tastes as if it's been run through a filter of salt
and pure ozone. I let down the puppy and suck in a few deep
mouthfuls, washing my lungs in it. My eyes are so accustomed,
to looking finely—at tiny details in confined spaces and minimal light—that it takes them a moment to long-focus on the
scene around me. It takes an additional moment for them to
believe it.

To starboard: nothing but open water.

To port: nothing but open water.

Astern: nothing but open water.

Dead ahead: Charlie Izzo.

She is lying on her back, propped by several pillows,
very aware of her openness and challenge—odalisquey. She
is wearing a white bikini, ovoid sunglasses, and a knowing,
nascent smile, a gibbous slash of teeth and lips. At her hairline
is a pink, centipede-like scar that is beginning to heal. Scattered on the deck, like pieces of red-yellow shrapnel, are the
shredded skins of pomegranates. Lying next to her towel like a
beach book waiting to be read is the Nakamura sword.

"The boat's more fun when it's in the water, don't you
think?"

As if I didn't know I was aboard a boat until she said it, I

---

75 Even if it is an illusion-puppy, I can't leave it belowdecks. Hallucinations have their own hallucination ethics, and it's not nice to leave a puppy
cavorting in its own piss.

again cast about me. The sky overhead is an otherworldly blue, an impossible gentian. The waves are small white-tips, crisp jabs of water, and as the boat troughs through them it sends jolts of sea spray over my face. Again I breathe in salt air that has never been breathed in by anyone but me. It tastes fresh, like a second chance. It does not, however, do much to resolve the issue of whether this is real.

What else can you do with a fantasy? I play along.

"Did you steal it?"

"The boat?" she says as if scandalized at the suggestion. "No. I paid Kong top dollar." Then, sheepishly, she holds up the Naka-mura sword. "*This* I stole. But don't worry. I'm sending it back to Nakamura just as soon as I find a specialist who can remove the microchip without damaging the hair on the hilt."

"And then?"

"Then I'm going after the *Saqueador*," she says. Then, coyly drawing a circle on the deck with one fingernail, she says, "I thought you might want to come."

"Even if I wanted to, which I don't, why would I try to help you? I can't even fire a gun. I'm useless."

"Not true. We never would have made it out of Azar's if you hadn't used your"—she wriggles her fingers to indicate the magic of my hypersensory perception—"and you took out the guy with the gun, and took care of Jimmy the Hat...."

"Oh God," I say. "Don't remind me."

"I think we make a pretty good team."

"Is that what the puppy's about? You trying to butter me up? By giving me back something that was taken from me?"

Charlie smiles girlishly.

"It was a dirty trick," I say.

"Is it working?"

Perhaps sensing he is the topic of conversation, the puppy roisters alongside and frolics at my ankles as if he has been waiting his whole life for ankles this tasty.

"You don't have to decide now," she says. "We have a lot of time."

This is a proposition I have never considered. It's baffling but it is also strangely enticing. I can't protect anything as a pulse. That's clear. My pulsing days are over. Could my talent days be starting? Could I do the right thing by doing the wrong thing?

And can I trust Charlie?

"What took you so long to contact me?"

"You were being watched."

"You weren't busy getting the sword?"

"I got the sword the same day we got out of Azar's."

"You went back in?"

She nods.

"How did you avoid the cops? They tore that place apart."

"Air shaft."

"Air shaft?" I exclaim. "Those amateurs!"

"You're telling me."

For the first time, we laugh together on this subject. It feels great. It contains a powerful feeling of relief, as if I've been underwater for five minutes and finally broke the surface; each laugh feels like a lifesaving gasp of oxygen. When the heady glow of togetherness wears off, however, and we stop laughing, I am confronted with reality.

"I'll be a fugitive. I'll never be able to go back home."

"That's true," she says.

"We'll always be on the run."

"Also true," she says. "But not alone."

She shrugs in a way that affects her whole body. Her hips swivel, as if sending me a message in a pelvic foreign language, and the scar on her shoulder pinches into a barbed hieroglyph of significant meaning. This sparks a flashback of what my life was like before Charlie—the dark rooms, the solitude, the nev-erness. It also provokes an oracle-flash of what my life could be like if I had her. It seems almost too much to hope for. It seems not like wishfulness but greed.

Still, I think: what do I want?

And, as the Covet girl would say, what will I do to get it?

"You're wearing the ring," I note.

"Are you kidding? I've only taken it off once," she says, "to fix it."

Charlie springs to her feet and crosses the distance between us. With a dainty Victorian gesture she gives me a view by offering her hand. As billed, the ring is perfectly restored.

Suddenly the boat stalls and the jib luffs loudly—it sounds like applause—but then it goes tight with wind and the point of sail corrects itself. We lurch as the boat yaws, and for a moment it looks like Charlie's body is going to jostle into mine, but it doesn't. She catches the lifeline and then holds very still as if afraid she might spill some of herself if not han-dled carefully.

"Jesus," I say, "who's sailing this thing?"

"It's on auto-nav," Charlie says. Then, tentatively: "Want to go belowdecks?"

"I don't know," I say. "I'm confused. I'm not even sure if this is real. I took a lot of hallucinogens. I feel pretty shaky."

"You don't believe this is real?"

"I don't know what to believe."

Her skin, bronze and taut, gleams with suntan lotion. She smells of coconut, cream, sweat, swimwear, the dense living scent of her hair, pomegranates. Then, hugging her elbows, she pushes her body forward, giftlike.

Charlie makes me believe.

Acknowledgments

This book was made possible by contributions from Michael Davies, E. Beth Thomas, Harry Sawyers, Katie Hofstadter, Senseis Dan Webster and Susan Easton, Leena Sidhu, Patrick McCord, Bill Augustin, Miriam Baron, Chris Springfield, Frank Crane, Gary Hall and Anthony Attardi of Wright Square Café, Kim Wang, and, naturally, the Pinnikins.

Special commendation to the Great and Inimitable Boz.

Incalculable gratitude to Paula Wallace and my colleagues at SCAD.

Some sources that have helped the researching of this book include INTERPOL's database of stolen artworks, *The Return of Cultural Treasures* by Jeanette Greenfield, *The Rape of Europa* by Lynn H. Nicholas, *The Art Forger's Handbook* by Eric Hebborn, *The Expert Versus the Object* by Ronald Spencer, *Feminism and Art History* edited by Norma Broude and Mary D. Garrard, *Art Theft Forgery and Investigation: The Complete Field Manual* by Robert E. Spiel, Jr., *Rogues in the Gallery* by Hugh McLeave, *Museum of the Missing* by Simon Houpt, and nearly everything by Thomas Hoving, who gave a talk in Savannah recently that I—curse my hide—had to miss; I hope he will accept my gratitude here.

I am fortunate beyond words to say that the following people at Riverhead are mine: Pam Barricklow, Sheila Moody, Ben Gibson, Tom Haushalter, Sarah Bowlin, and the redoubtable Megan Lynch. Additional special thanks to Geoff Kloske.

And Esther Newberg, Josie Freedman, Kari Stuart: thank you a googolplex.

From  Helum Davies
331 w. Clearton St
Savannah, Gat 31401

TO

Ms Marie Arana
Washington Post
1150 15th St NW
Washington, DC
20071